VIRGINIA'S
Ghost

CAROLINE
KAISER

Editors: Irene Kavanagh
         http://www.editors.ca/profile/7624/irene-kavanagh
Arlene Prunkl
         http://penultimateword.com/
Cover design and page layout: Scarlett Rugers
         http://www.scarlettrugers.com/
Back cover photo: Louise Kiner
         http://dksister.daportfolio.com/

Library and Archives Canada Cataloguing in Publication

 Kaiser, Caroline, 1963-, author
      Virginia's ghost / Caroline Kaiser.

Issued in print and electronic formats.
         ISBN 978-0-9938137-0-2 (pbk.).
         ISBN 978-0-9938137-1-9 (mobi).
         ISBN 978-0-9938137-2-6 (epub)

      I. Title.

PS8621.A464V57 2014   C813'.6   C2014-904046-6
                                              C2014-905385-1

Caroline Kaiser on the Web:
https://www.facebook.com/carolinekaiserauthor
http://www.carolinekaisereditor.com/

VIRGINIA'S GHOST

CHAPTER 1

Few places are quieter than an auction house at night, especially when you're alone. You're surrounded only by the clutter of dusty old things once owned by people you'll never meet from eras you'll never know. Working with inanimate objects owned by dead people—it doesn't get much quieter than that. And as you might imagine, it's not an easy, comfortable silence. You might say it's the very definition of dead silence.

You'd never think one of those long-gone strangers might reach across time and space to break the silence. At least I never did.

But for most of the twenty years I worked at Gable & Co., the fine art and antiques auction house in Toronto, I didn't dwell on who might have owned the old things I handled. Mostly, I focused on what I needed to get done each day. I didn't have time to worry about much else; as the antique ceramics, glass, and silver specialist, I was always up to my bloodshot blue eyes cataloguing old stuff that had come in through estates and consignments, and I was just trying to keep my head above water.

My job sounded interesting enough: I described, measured, and estimated the value of these items, which on lucky days were comparable to the fine *objets d'art* seen in museums. But more often than not, I saw the most prosaic of decorative objects, dainty but worthless dust collectors you'd find in your grandmother's curio cabinet. The world has an endless supply of such trinkets, given as "family heirlooms" to the unappreciative by well-meaning parents and grandparents. Part of my job was to sift through the trash to find the treasures. Keeping up with this perpetual deluge of objects necessitated a lot of late nights.

Gable & Co. operated in a pre-WWI warehouse building on Queen Street East. The place was at its most unnerving when I was working late and needed to venture alone into the dark, damp basement—for that was where the kitchen was— to satisfy my caffeine craving. It wasn't just the silence that put me on edge; it was also hearing my own footsteps echoing dully on the concrete floor. Sometimes, if I was tired enough, I wasn't even sure they were mine, and a chill would shoot through me as I imagined someone coming up behind me. And then there were the piled-up mounds of furniture casting menacing shadows in the gloom; I wondered what lurked among them.

I was certain that spending too much time in the basement was a sure path to mental illness. Alexis Harrow, who'd once worked in the carpet and textiles department, was ample proof of that. Shortly after I started at Gable & Co., she told me, her black eyes wild with fright, that she'd heard voices emanating from the basement where she'd been working the night before. At the time, people dismissed her experiences as hallucinations precipitated by severe stress. We all knew Alexis was a self-flagellating workaholic, and if being such a person wasn't stressful in itself, I don't know what was. Everyone was convinced that the only voices she'd heard were the ones in her head; she'd been driving herself too hard, forcing herself to the breaking point. It took years to discover for myself that there might have been something to Alexis's claim.

My views began to change about five years ago. It was a blustery late-October night, the sort of night borrowed from wordy Victorian Gothic novels. The wind whistled through the crevices in the building while the rain pelted down madly on the windowpanes. It must have been nearly ten at night, and I'd been upstairs alone in the cataloguing room, a big space with cramped cubicles that provided an "office" for each of the specialists. Lucky me, my cubicle was a spacious corner one and the envy of my colleagues. Floor-to-ceiling bookcases lined the walls. A giant oak table sat in the centre of the room, its surface crammed with clocks, lamps, toys, dishes, vases, bowls, flatware, and other assorted decorative objects, while larger items were stowed beneath it. Half-empty coffee cups littered the table. The room, which had little ventilation, smelled like every dusty, musty old house I'd ever been in. That night, I was working on a massive collection of Royal Doulton figurines for the Christmas auction. Nearly two hundred little porcelain ladies were crowded onto the table, all with demure, pale faces. Most of them wore enormous plumed hats and poufy Victorian dresses, each with a surprisingly revealing décolletage.

I plucked another one randomly from the crowd. The figurine was greasy, as if she were coated with oil. She nearly got away from me, narrowly escaping a plummet to certain death on the concrete floor. I checked her for chips and cracks, inspecting her by eye and running a pin over her surface to detect any irregularities that would indicate repairs. I measured her and scribbled these words on an index card: *Chloe. HN3269. With beribboned blonde bouffant and pink and pale blue floral ball gown. Height 23 cm. (9 in.). Estimated selling price $60/90.*

Looking at the figurine, I suddenly felt hostile. "Oh, stop your simpering," I said. Now that the urge to speak to my tiny porcelain friends had overcome me, I knew it was time for a break. I felt the irresistible pull of chemical stimulation: a strong cup of coffee would be just the thing to get me through another hour or two.

The kitchen's inconvenient location meant I had to flick on the staircase light and creep down a set of creaky wooden stairs to get there. Hidden at the back of the cupboard was my Edvard Munch *The Scream* mug, which I always reserved for stressful bouts of overtime; it expressed my mood at such times perfectly. I kept a stash of my favourite blend, Moroccan Mystique, and my own coffee maker in the corner of the counter. I put the coffee on and listened to the reassuring gurgling and sputtering as it trickled into the carafe. Sitting down at the table, I leafed through the tabloids an unknown colleague had generously donated to the Gable & Co. kitchen "library." But the tawdry headlines failed to arouse me from my exhausted state; I needed coffee. What happened next, however, would revive my sagging senses far more than any amount of caffeine could.

I got up and stood near the kitchen door. Over the pitter-patter of a now gentle rain I heard a quiet little whimper, followed by silence. I froze. The whimper started again, growing slightly in volume. I couldn't tell where it came from, and I couldn't decide whether I needed to know. Confused, I just stood there, twisting this way and that and peering out into the darkness where those piled-up mounds of furniture loomed. A few seconds later, I bolted so quickly up the stairs that anyone watching would have seen a streaky blur, as if I were a cartoon character escaping the jaws of death.

Back in the cataloguing room, the crowd of Royal Doulton ladies quivered from the force of my footsteps as I flew past them, as if they too were trembling in terror. I grabbed my purse and dashed out the door. Cursing and shaking, I dropped my keys twice before I managed to lock up. I ran hard for the streetcar, catching it just as it pulled up to the stop. I sputtered my breathless thanks to the driver, who looked at me as if I'd lost my mind. But I didn't care what he thought. All that concerned me was putting as much space between Gable & Co. and me as possible. I sighed gratefully as the streetcar whisked me home through the dark autumn night.

CHAPTER 2

The next morning I arrived about twenty minutes late for work. Rushing through the front door, I collided with Mark DuBarry, the specialist in miscellany; he catalogued and appraised clocks and lighting, as well as all the weird things like taxidermy specimens that no one else would touch. Mark was a big man with a hearty laugh, and he sported a bushy moustache and wore horn-rimmed glasses. He was the only person who'd been at Gable & Co. even longer than I had.

"What's your hurry, missy?" he said, laughing. He was carrying his battered old briefcase, so I assumed he was going out on an appointment to appraise the contents of an outsized mansion in Forest Hill or Rosedale or some other posh Toronto neighbourhood.

"I'm just late, that's all." I felt irritable.

"So?" He smiled at me, his blue eyes dancing with mischief. "Hey, do you want to come on this appraisal? You don't have anything better to do, do you? There promises to be a stuffed monkey. Maybe even a shrunken head."

I couldn't help but laugh. "Now there's an offer I can hardly refuse. But I'm afraid I can't join you. The Doulton ladies await."

"Oh, damn the Doultons! I was hoping for some company. And I'm a little worried about being alone. The client sounded completely whacked over the phone, so I may not even get out of there alive." He grinned.

"Right." Not paying much attention to what Mark was saying, I made a split-second decision: I'd tell him about the whimpering I heard in the basement. I'd known him for nearly half my life, and he was my friend, after all, so he wouldn't laugh at me—at least not too hard.

"Mark, when I was downstairs last night, I heard a noise. Something was—um—whimpering."

"Really?" He looked amused. "Virginia Blythe, if I didn't know better, I'd say you were turning into another Alexis Harrow, God rest her soul. God help you. And God help *us*." His eyes softened. "You've been working too hard, my dear. As we both know, you have no life outside this place. I know I've said it before, but isn't it time to start moving on and … getting past certain things? Are you quite well?" Mark gently placed his palm on my forehead. "When was your last vacation, anyway?"

"I don't like taking vacations alone, so it must have been years ago. And I haven't been working any harder than anyone else." My tone was much more defensive than I'd intended, and it occurred to me that maybe Mark was right and I *was* turning into another Alexis Harrow. "And why did you say, 'God rest her soul,' for heaven's sake? She isn't dead."

Mark sighed dramatically. "Ah, but she might as well be. She's lost to us now, poor thing. When did she last come in to see us?" Then he lit up from some bright spark of inspiration, his expression disturbingly gleeful. "Hey, did you say *whimpering*? Do you suppose a stray dog wandered in and gave birth to puppies? There could be a litter in the basement. Shall I look into it for you?"

I inhaled through my teeth and sucked in my stomach. "No need to. I'm a big girl. I'll go down there and see for myself." I wondered if he could see my hands trembling.

"Of course you will," he said, chortling. He turned around to leave and looked back at me over his shoulder, his eyes brimming with good humour. "Oh, by the way, let me know if you're giving the puppies away. I want the pick of the litter."

"Ha ha, DuBarry—very funny." I was trying to sound stern, but the second Mark was out the door, I caught myself smiling.

Within an hour, everyone in the building seemed to know about the mysterious whimpering in the basement. Of course, it couldn't have been Mark who'd told them. I could only think it was Dora Snelling, the nosy, abrasive office manager whose desk was closest to the front door. I knew she liked nothing better than to eavesdrop on conversations in the front foyer, and it would be just like her to tell the world. Not surprisingly, my colleagues were keen to hear about the whimpering, and there was a lineup of people pumping me for information at my cubicle in the cataloguing room. Like Mark, most reacted with amused skepticism. There were, however, a few exceptions.

Taylor Hurst, my black-clad young assistant who sported exotic purple bangs, simply said, "Whoa, cool!" when I told her. Then she calmly went back to writing emails. Chloe O'Rourke, my best friend at work and the toy specialist, seemed to believe implicitly that there really was whimpering in the basement— that I wasn't either making it up to get attention or hearing things because I was crazy. Barely five feet tall and with a freckled face and a halo of frizzy dishwater-blonde hair, she looked at me with doe eyes when I told her about it.

"Well, of course you heard whimpering. Of course it was real." Chloe was so emphatic about this that I wanted to hug her. It was reassuring to know that at least one person didn't think I was going mad. Unlike Mark, however, she offered no theories about the source of the sound; it was as if it didn't even matter to her.

Over the next few days, no one heard any whimpering—or admitted to hearing it. While Mark continued to stick to his puppy theory—he was such a tease—those few people who hadn't already written me off as suffering from psychosis made other suggestions about the source of the sound. But none of these took into account that it was whimpering I'd heard, not squeaking. Old pipes were to blame, suggested Taylor. Dora horrified us all by insisting we had a rat infestation, though no one had seen a rat. But George Schlegel, the lanky middle-aged accountant who'd barely said two words to me since starting at Gable & Co. a year earlier, had a different idea.

One morning, he encountered me in the upstairs gallery where we held auctions. He nodded at me as I loaded up a tray with glassware, a subtle spark of excitement in his dark eyes. It unnerved me slightly; it wasn't like George to express emotion; I thought of him as Mr. Neutral. I hadn't said a word, but somehow he knew I was obsessing about the whimpering. "Maybe some poor homeless waif was crying outside the building, and her sobs were loud enough to penetrate the walls," he said, smoothing his neatly trimmed salt-and-pepper hair.

Doubtful this was the case, I looked at the floor and mumbled, "Sounds a bit Gothic. Um, I really don't think so."

When I glanced up, George looked a little disappointed that I'd rejected his suggestion. Without another word, he shrugged and left the gallery.

Whatever the reason for the peculiar sounds emanating from the basement, I felt uneasy about going down there again. Actually, much to Mark's amusement, I strenuously avoided it. He tried to goad me into venturing downstairs to get coffee in exchange for buying me lunch for a month. His offer was tempting enough that I very nearly took him up on it, but I opted to play it safe and instead walked to the nearest Tim Hortons coffee shop some eight blocks away. But one night, I realized I couldn't avoid the basement any longer.

With the Christmas auction cataloguing deadline just two days away, I stayed late to work on a collection of nineteenth-century American pressed glass. After three hours of looking up glass patterns in a book, I found myself staring in dazed fascination at a butter dish in the Westward Ho pattern. A single frosted glass Mohawk brave holding a tomahawk crouched on its lid; a frosted band depicting a running deer, a charging buffalo, and a log cabin decorated the sides of the lid. When I began seeing two Mohawk braves wavering before my eyes, I knew I was in big trouble.

I thought I'd faint from fatigue if I didn't have my caffeine fix immediately, preferably by injection. The espresso bean chocolate bar I'd been nibbling on to stave off my craving paled in comparison to a rich, aromatic cup of Moroccan Mystique, so I resigned myself to a quick trip to the basement. My plan was to sprint like lightning down the stairs, not allowing myself to slow down enough to hear anything suspicious. And I hoped that the sputtering of the coffee maker would drown out any disturbing sounds. Once I had my mug in hand, I'd move up the stairs as fast as I could without slopping coffee on myself.

According to plan, I flicked on the staircase light and charged down the staircase. I hadn't counted on slipping on the final step. My tights ripped, and I felt a stinging sensation as my bare flesh scraped across gritty concrete. I'd landed hard, and pain tore through my knee. Sprawled on the floor, I noticed that my skirt was hiked up around my waist and that my hair had worked itself free from its loose bun and tumbled messily to my shoulders. As I struggled to rearrange myself, I saw blood beading on the scrape.

At times like these, when I was frustrated, exhausted, or hurt, I just wanted to call Mom and Dad. Mom would have offered sensible advice about whatever was troubling me, though not necessarily much sympathy, particularly if she knew I'd done something stupid. Dad would have calmed me with kindness no matter what I'd done. But they'd both been gone for nearly a year now. They were driving home from the theatre one night—it had been their forty-fifth anniversary celebration—when a head-on collision with a drunk driver killed them. At times it still didn't seem real. Realizing all over again that I couldn't just pick up the phone and talk to them made me choke up in an instant, the grief surprisingly fresh. A tear splashed down my cheek.

Wiping my eyes, I said, "Get a grip, Virginia." Mom and Dad would have wanted me to. I hauled myself up, smoothed my skirt, picked some stray blonde hairs off my sweater, and limped toward the kitchen. Even though I was bleeding, I'd do what I had to do—in this case, getting that cup of coffee. The Blythes were a plucky lot, and I intended to carry on the family tradition. I dabbed at my scuffed and bloody knee with a damp cloth and then made the coffee; I poured the blessed liquid into my mug.

Sprinting up the stairs was a non-starter. I was wincing with each step and carrying a full-to-the-brim cup, so I could manage only a slow, agonizing hobble. I'd just begun the long trek upstairs, coffee mug precariously in hand, when I heard it. My heart seemed to drop into the pit of my stomach.

It wasn't a whimper this time.

CHAPTER 3

The sound was more like a wail—a high-pitched keening. There was no mistaking it: the noise was human, not canine, and I guessed it was also from a woman, one who was unquestionably inside the building. For one wild moment, I imagined it was Helen Clark, the administrative assistant who'd lost her husband to terminal illness just weeks earlier. Helen was a model of sphinx-like poise at the office, but I suspected that since she was obligated to maintain a calm, controlled demeanour all day in front of colleagues, she fell apart dramatically after working hours. But why would she choose the basement of Gable & Co. as a suitable place to release her grief? It made no sense, yet I found myself idiotically calling her name in the darkness.

The wailing ceased for the briefest moment, the duration of a heartbeat or two, and then erupted at a much greater volume. I sighed with resignation. There was no escaping it—I'd have to do something now. With my mug in hand, I inhaled and closed my eyes briefly, steeling myself for travelling farther into the black depths, for the sound seemed to be coming from the furniture storage area, way at the back of the basement next to the freight elevator. I found myself trembling. Little twitches—leaks of excessive nervous energy—danced through my muscles. Blood pumped through my temples alarmingly; the throbbing was more painful than any migraine I'd ever suffered. Was I about to have an aneurysm? Terror at that thought numbed me, and I stood there, rooted to the floor.

Finally, I managed to have a practical thought. The first thing to do was find a light switch. But even after working at Gable & Co. for so long, I still didn't know where most of the switches in the basement were. The only light sources were a few bare bulbs in the staircase, the kitchen, and the storage area. As the wailing continued, I tripped over the slender cabriole leg of a chair and stumbled into an upright piano, making a discordant crash as I slammed down one hand on the keyboard in my struggle to steady myself. Simultaneously, I slopped hot coffee down my dress. I cursed and shuddered as a pain shot through my leg.

The wailer became frantic at the mishap; her cries rose to a hysterical pitch.

"Sorry!" I called out. I managed to disengage myself from the troublesome piano, and the wailing subsided gradually. I could barely see a thing as I picked my way through the confusing labyrinth of dusty, rolled-up carpets and rickety furniture. I found a light switch on a pillar and flicked it on.

The bare bulb overhead twitched to life, offering only dim light. But I could make out a teetering tower of stacked dining chairs a few yards ahead, and I was sure I'd find the woman right behind it. When I leaned forward and peered behind the tower, I saw her, faintly visible in the shadows. I felt a sudden chill. I saw another light switch on a post and flipped it.

Squinting from the light, she sat alone on a midnight-blue velvet-upholstered art deco settee. She couldn't have been more than twenty. Although her delicate face was arresting in its beauty, it wasn't her face that made me gasp but her hair and the clothes she wore. She had raven-black straight hair cut to a chin-length bob, and she was wearing a sleeveless purple velvet drop-waist gown that shimmered with black beading. Her high-heeled shoes were black satin with a bow and a T-strap. Her slender white neck was graced by an elegant diamond and amethyst lavaliere set in platinum; it gleamed slightly with each subtle movement she made.

I must have been hallucinating, just as Alexis Harrow had when she'd put in too much overtime. Apparently, a refugee from an F. Scott Fitzgerald novel was hiding out in the basement of Gable & Co.

Tentatively, I moved aside some chairs and approached the girl. She looked down forlornly, her wailing having already ended. I sensed my presence had calmed her a little. Tears continued to flow freely down her face, dropping off her chin, and her thin lips trembled slightly. Having adjusted to the light, she looked up at me, a ferocious quality animating her brilliant green eyes. I felt completely out of place, as if I had no right to intrude on her grief, and I stood awkwardly, not knowing what to say or do to comfort her. But despite my embarrassment, I knew I couldn't just leave her. Not in her condition.

I cleared my throat and spoke hoarsely. "What's the matter? Will you be okay?"

She shook her head, her expression grim, and looked down at the floor as if to say, "It's hopeless."

"Isn't there anything I can do?"

She shook her head violently and thrust one hand up at me in a halting gesture. Her eyes brimmed with a fresh wave of tears, and she quivered as a sob burst forth from her.

Undeterred, I moved a little closer still, determined to do what I could to help her. I tried to tap her lightly on the shoulder, but before I could, she moved away from me like a cornered animal. "What's your name?" I said softly.

The girl looked up at me once more, her expression blank this time. Then her outline grew fuzzy, and like a slow dissolve in an old black-and-white movie, she began fading from view.

"Hey!" I shouted. Maybe if I could just grab onto her arm, I could make her stay. But when I reached out, my hand passed right through her. Feeling powerless to stop what was happening, I watched the shift, fascinated: one moment she was as solid and real as any person, and the next she was vague and insubstantial. A pale peach glow surrounded her entire body, blurring her outline even more. The colour deepened to an intense orange and then a crimson that flickered and crackled like flames for a few seconds before it completely faded away. The girl herself became little more than a transparent wisp, and the last I saw of her was a winding pale grey trail that hung in the air like cigarette smoke. She was gone.

I dropped my Munch coffee mug. The fragmented screamer stared up at me from the concrete floor. But I didn't bother to pick up the pieces. Gritting my teeth through my pain, I just ran.

CHAPTER 4

When I came in the next morning, Brian Gable III, the president of Gable & Co., was standing in the foyer, looking ready to stalk out the front door. A khaki trench coat smeared with an unidentifiable yellow stain was flung carelessly over his shoulder. He fixed me with his icy stare, condescension oozing from his pores. I hated how he could never bring himself to call me Virginia like everyone else did; after all these years, I was still Miss Blythe to him, and he insisted that I and nearly everyone else call him Mr. Gable. And I never for a moment bought his ludicrous story that he was distantly related to Clark Gable; there must have been thousands of Gables out there, and it was too much of a stretch to imagine that this slovenly, smelly one could possibly be related to golden-age Hollywood royalty. Rhett Butler he was not.

I fidgeted nervously. "Good morning, Mr. Gable."

"What's wrong with you?"

"Um—nothing." I suddenly realized I was blocking his exit.

Gable insinuated his way past me, and his meaty hand clutched the doorknob. He shifted his weight uncomfortably from one foot to the other and turned around to look at me. "Right. So let's talk about it later. Not now," he said in his surly way.

"Sh-sure. Looks like you're going somewhere. When you get back, then." Maybe by then I'd be able to come up with something useful to tell him.

He pushed the door open and was on his way.

I breathed freely again; he was in one of his better moods.

When Gable returned early that afternoon, I was happily absorbed in cataloguing more of the pressed glass collection. I was surprised to hear him bark out an announcement via the paging system that all staff were to assemble at three o'clock sharp in the upstairs gallery, the site of many an auction preview and sale over the years. What could this possibly be about?

Those who arrived at the meeting first got the choicest seating, arraying themselves on the plush chairs and settees we'd later be auctioning off. Some twenty staff members—specialists, front office types, accounting staff, catalogue production crew, and floor staff who moved furniture and unpacked boxes—sat in the gallery. I limped out, still favouring my knee, which was swollen and bruised from the previous night's fall. As a latecomer, I could only find a spindly dining chair to sit on, and as I sat down awkwardly, I prayed it wouldn't collapse and send me straight to the floor. As usual, Gable kept everyone waiting for a good ten minutes before he lumbered in at last, wielding a big box of a dozen Tim Hortons doughnuts in each hand and smiling.

He began his customary ritual of arranging the doughnuts on platters he'd scoffed from my department, positioning each treat with precision so that approximately half an inch separated it from its neighbour. I always half expected him to take out a measuring tape to check his accuracy. "Wouldn't want the chocolate and the maple to touch each other," he said, wrinkling his nose. The way he was acting, you would have thought the damn doughnuts were inbreeding. Afternoon fatigue was setting in, and I eyed the maple dip one in frustration. The rule was we couldn't eat them until after the meeting was over. It was just one of the many small ways in which Brian Gable III tortured his staff.

When he'd positioned each doughnut to perfection, he perched on the edge of a swivel chair and looked at me, his eyes tinged with weariness and impatience. "Right. Miss Blythe called a meeting. I'm not sure why." He gestured toward me with a dismissive wave, slumped back into his chair, and stared at me from beneath bushy brows.

"I did?" I said in a small voice. Hadn't we been going to have a private talk?

No, he couldn't be doing this to me. But considering how often I'd been at the mercy of his bullying, I shouldn't have been surprised. My heart began to pound furiously. Tiny beads of sweat accumulated on my forehead. I hated speaking in front of groups of people, whether they were strangers or not.

"Get on with it," said Gable.

I had no idea what I was supposed to say, so I talked about the one thing I couldn't get out of my head. "I-I've got something to tell you all."

Leaning even farther back in his chair, Gable folded his arms and sighed. I thought I detected mild amusement in his eyes, and I found myself wishing he'd fall backwards.

"I know some of you will think I've lost it at last, but there's s-someone in the basement who shouldn't be."

Everyone was just staring at me, gaping expectantly, waiting for me to explain properly what was going on. It was embarrassing to have so many pairs of eyes turned on me. Mark, who was sitting beside me, said, "More whimpering, Virginia?" He smiled, not as if he were making fun of me, but as an encouraging friend would.

It cheered me a little that someone who wasn't cranky and didn't intimidate me had spoken, enough that I began to relax. "No. Sobbing and wailing, to be exact."

Gable looked grimly at his watch. "Miss Blythe, please get to the point, will you? I'm sure we've all got better things to do."

"Like eat doughnuts, Brian?" said Taylor. Her soft voice somehow managed to sound sly yet innocent, if that was possible. She made no attempt to hide the fact that she was staring directly at Gable's pear-shaped bulk. In the two years she'd worked under me, I'd noticed her remarkable propensity for getting away with the type of pointed remarks the rest of us would be crucified for. Apparently, she even enjoyed the rare privilege of being permitted to call Gable by his first name. It could only be because she was young and cute in a gamine sort of way. Taylor flipped her purple bangs away from her face with a quick wave of the hand and smiled at Gable.

"Yes, like eat doughnuts." He glanced at her nervously, his normally pale complexion reddening. His eyes gleamed, and I could see the muscles of his mouth working furiously, trying to suppress some sort of expression—I couldn't tell if it was a smile or a frown. He swivelled his chair around in my direction and barked at me. "Miss Blythe, can't you just spit it out already?"

His brusque impatience and my concerns about looking like the company lunatic made me tremble violently, and my voice shot up nearly an octave. "Um, okay. Last night there was a woman down there. And you're not going to believe it, but she looked like a f-flapper. But she disappeared when I t-touched her."

An uncomfortable hush descended over the room as everyone exchanged glances. I was surprised to see that George was the first to look me in the eye, his expression kindly. This reassured me until Jared Schmuttermayer, the scrawny, unkempt little guy in charge of the floor staff, raised a skeptical eyebrow and let out a lengthy sigh. Then Dora threw back her head like some sort of bad actress on the stage and burst out laughing, the flesh of her double chin jiggling. Helen looked at her disapprovingly, her lips and eyes narrowing. She glanced over at me, obviously embarrassed for me.

"Dora! For heaven's sake—that's enough already!" Mark shot a hostile glance her way, and her laughter died away to a mere snicker or two. She glared at him.

"Do you suppose Dora even knows what a flapper *is*?" a voice with a posh English accent whispered behind me. I looked around to see Sally Lynch, the fine art specialist. She was blessed with an abundance of wavy auburn hair, a model's figure, and the most enviable cheekbones I'd ever seen. She was looking at me impishly and trying to stop herself from giggling. Seeing her friendly face, I recovered my equilibrium a little.

Chloe, who was sitting next to Mark, leaned over him and patted me on the forearm. Her grey eyes were round. "Are you talking about a *ghost*, Virginia?"

"That would seem to be obvious," said Gable.

I winced and inhaled sharply. "Um, I wasn't sure if I should use the *g*-word. I've never seen anything like that before. But there's something—or someone—down there. Do you really think it's a ghost?" Given how the flapper had faded into a wisp right before my eyes, I hadn't really thought she could be anything else, but I didn't necessarily want to broadcast my opinion.

Chloe looked pensive. "Oh yes, it definitely sounds like one to me. I've seen lots of them before." A few snickers erupted around us, mostly from Jared and the other floor staff. She looked over at them and smiled sweetly. "It's really not surprising she's here, you know—not when you consider all the old stuff we get in. The ghosts probably ride right in on the sofas."

"Along with the stray dogs," said Mark.

Everyone laughed except Gable, who rolled his eyes at the ceiling and inhaled deeply. "Okay, okay, fun's over." He glared at me and jerked his head toward his office. "You—Miss Blythe—I want a word with you. Now."

Knowing full well what was coming, I snatched the maple dip doughnut before anyone else could and trotted dutifully behind him. If I was going to be yelled at, at least I'd have the pleasure of eating my favourite type of doughnut first.

Inside Gable's dark, dingy office, I sat down in a boxy hunter-green leather club chair, the kind that was studded with gold nailheads. I peered at a bookcase in the corner displaying coffee-table books about antiques; their pristine condition suggested their primary function—to impress clients invited into the office. A mangy, dried-up ring-necked pheasant was mounted on the wall behind Gable, who sat behind his expansive mahogany desk. It was covered in tall, messy piles of paper that threatened to tumble to the floor at the slightest hint of a breeze. For all his ability to place doughnuts with astounding precision, he couldn't keep his desk orderly to save his life. I'd never been able to reconcile his sloppiness with the obsessive-compulsive doughnut ritual.

Gable's hands formed a steeple as he looked at me in a disconcertingly grave way. I couldn't bring myself to look back at him for more than a second or two. The thought flashed through my mind that he wasn't about to administer just another routine dressing-down; this was much more serious. For reasons I'd never understood, the man had always hated me, and perhaps he was finally going to fire me. Anxiety made sharp pains dart through the back of my head and into my eyes; I'd never endured the humiliation of being fired before. What would it be like? Would he mouth an idiotic cliché like "This hurts me more than it hurts you"? If he said any such thing, I could easily imagine leaping up, dislodging that awful pheasant from the wall, and hitting him with it. Stealing another glance at him, I broke off a piece of my doughnut and nibbled at it.

Gable said, "Look, if you're feeling burned out and you need a lieu day or something, just let me know. I'm kind of worried about you. I have been ever since you lost your parents. You just can't seem to pull yourself together. And these stories you make up ... we're *all* worried, Miss Blythe." In a clumsy attempt at reassurance, he leaned across the desk and pawed at my hand. Feeling a slight chill, I withdrew it as politely as I could.

I was mystified by this show of compassion. Did he really have a soft, squishy underbelly after all? Was it finally emerging after all these years? I knew I hadn't hallucinated the flapper in the basement, but perhaps I *was* hallucinating Gable's kindness. At best, I'd expected him to blast me for wasting company time and causing a stir. Instead, he was acting like a nice, normal person, which was uncharacteristic. The more

I thought about it, the more it began to disturb me, filling me with a deep cynicism about his motives. He was undoubtedly lulling me into a false sense of security, and it was only a matter of time before he pulled a knife on me right there in his office, with only the desiccated old pheasant with its sightless glass eyes to bear witness to the crime.

Somehow, I think I managed to sound confident. "Mr. Gable, I'm fine. Really. There's nothing wrong with me. It's true I'm still getting over the death of my parents, of course. It hasn't even been a year. But I'm not making up stories, and I'm not hallucinating. Yes, I'd like to take some lieu days but only because I've been working so hard on this deadline. I need to catch up on my sleep."

He looked doubtful. "Well, okay. Take whatever time you need. Give more work to Taylor if necessary. She can handle it. But you'd be smart to take my advice: whatever you do, don't ever talk about seeing ghosts at work again. It would definitely be in your best interests to keep quiet on the subject of this … this sudden paranormal obsession of yours."

"In my best interests? Paranormal obsession?" My voice was rising again. I raised an eyebrow and sat back in my chair, folding my arms.

Gable mumbled slightly. "Perhaps I need to be more direct. You wouldn't want certain people to think you're a lunatic, would you?"

There it was, that word *lunatic*. I should have expected it, and now that I'd heard it, strangely enough it made me feel reckless and bold. "Certain people. Oh, I see. You mean certain people like you?" I was so taken aback by my own audacity that I began to perspire.

He looked flustered, as if I'd thrown him off balance. The colour rose in his face, and he was breathing heavily. When he calmed down, his eyes seemed to shoot poison arrows at me. The old Gable was back. "Yes, that's precisely what I mean. For reasons that should be glaringly obvious, I'm certainly someone you should be concerned about." He paused. "Time to get back to work, Miss Blythe. I trust we won't ever need to speak of this matter again."

Before I could say another word, he got up from his chair and shooed me out the door with a big sweep of his hand, just as a towering stack of his papers toppled over and crashed to the floor.

CHAPTER 5

Much to my annoyance, Gable proved to be right—it really was in my best interests to stop talking about ghosts. Over the next couple of weeks, I couldn't help noticing that lively conversations often stopped abruptly when I entered a room, leaving an awkward silence; my co-workers would stiffen and exchange glances that excluded me. Sometimes, I could even clear a room just by walking into it. When these things happened, I could only assume I'd been the subject of the conversation. And people who'd previously been friendly— or at least polite—refused to meet my gaze or say a word as we passed each other. Jared was worse than all the rest put together. He looked at me with unconcealed hostility every time our paths crossed, his dark eyes burning. Even Taylor assumed a poker face and became more monosyllabic than usual during our already strained conversations. It felt like being in high school all over again, and I dearly wanted to see Mom and Dad so I could cry on their shoulders.

But I exaggerate a little; not everyone was being horrible. There were some—Mark, Chloe, Sally, and in a quiet, rather sweet way, George—who treated me like a normal human being. Mark teased me affectionately about having a new assistant downstairs and told Taylor she ought to worry about the competition. Chloe supported me in her grave and earnest way; she even told me she'd spoken up in my defence when Dora said I was becoming the company fruitcake. Sally acted as if she weren't even aware anything odd had happened and I was as sane as ever. George made friendly small talk about the weather and other innocuous subjects whenever we encountered one another, which was more than he'd done previously. And once, to my surprise, he complimented me on the teal-blue suit I often wore, saying stiffly that I looked "willowy and elegant" in it. I was grateful for the friendship of these colleagues, but as the days passed, I began to question what I'd really seen that night. I'd never really know unless I steeled myself and faced it head-on. Returning to the basement was the inevitable next step.

I decided I'd go down when I wasn't feeling too stressed out to begin with; I wanted to approach it with a clear head. And I decided not to do it on my lunch hour, which was when I was most likely to be alone in the building, as few staff ever took their lunch in the kitchen or elsewhere within Gable & Co. If something horrible happened—not that I could even imagine what that might be—I could scream for help and know that someone would hear me.

On the day I finally worked up enough nerve, a Monday afternoon in mid-November, I set out for the back of the basement. No one was down there, but I could hear creaking, scraping, groaning, and footsteps above my head as Jared and the boys moved furniture upstairs. I crept over to where the old settee was nestled in the gloom, and the flapper was already sitting on it as if she owned it. I made a mental note to find out which client had brought it in for auction, as maybe that would give me an inkling of who she was.

Why she hadn't wailed to get my attention this time, I didn't know, but her silence made me feel much less afraid. I expected to find the same weepy, hopeless girl, but she was calm and composed now, as if she'd somehow been anticipating my arrival and was waiting patiently for me. She sat primly on the velvet settee, her back straight, her hands clasped in her lap, and her ankles crossed tidily. When she noticed me, she looked up with a serene, steady gaze. She brushed her bangs away from her eyes. A small cloth-bound notebook sat beside her.

She smoothed the fabric of her purple velvet gown as if she was trying to make a good impression on me. It was the same gown I'd seen her in last time. Since I assumed she really was a ghost—and not an elaborate figment of my weary brain— I'd probably always see her in that same gown, as it seemed unlikely a ghost would change her clothes. Suddenly, I had a macabre thought: she was wearing it when she died. And how young she must have been when death took her. How on earth had it happened?

When I got within a few feet of her, she rose to her feet. I was struck by how tall and slender she was, and how her clothes draped loosely on her frame. She looked at me in an earnest, imploring way and held up the notebook. Without any fuss she passed it to me, and her hand fluttered in a little goodbye wave.

"Wait—don't go yet!" I said, reaching out to her. "Let's talk about this. Why are you doing this? Why are you giving me the book?"

A shimmering lilac haze surrounded her, and it glowed and pulsated softly around her form as she stood calmly looking at me. Within seconds, the colour deepened gradually to amethyst and then shifted to an ultramarine, nearly as dark as the bottom of the ocean. The flapper's outline blurred before she and her colourful aura faded away in a slow dissolve. As before, she left behind a small wispy trail that hung in the air.

"No!" I cried.

I was kicking myself for not having brought Mark, Chloe, or just about anyone else along to witness this strange spectacle. My credibility would have soared if only I'd had a reliable witness. Then it occurred to me: even if I'd brought Brian Gable III himself down to the basement, he probably wouldn't have seen the flapper. I'd heard before that some people were incapable of seeing or sensing spirits, and insensitive clod that he was, Gable couldn't help but be one of them. And though I wasn't sure how I knew it, I was certain this particular ghost had been intended just for me.

Intrigued, I sat down on the settee and examined the notebook. It looked utilitarian, like the sort of thing people used to do their bookkeeping in. The faded blue cloth cover was embedded with dust. The corners were bashed up and the spine was falling apart, threads dangling from it. On the inside cover, lettered in blue ink in sprawling calligraphic script, was *1928*, surrounded by artistic flourishes. At the bottom of the page, in more modest script, were the words *Constance Virginia Rose Pendleton* and *127 Elm Avenue, Toronto*. Hmm, there was my name. Well, it would have been a common enough one at the time. I flipped through the notebook. The pages were filled with tiny, neat script written in a delicate feminine hand. Whoever had written in the book was careful and attentive to detail, which pleased my perfectionistic nature. The writing also had a pronounced rightward slant and big lower loops, both of which suggested emotional expressiveness and depth.

I put the book down beside me when something fell out of it and fluttered to the floor. I bent down and picked up a sepia photograph of a couple standing. A beautiful young girl with a Louise Brooks-style shiny bob was leaning affectionately on the shoulder of a tall, lean, angular-faced young man with smooth dark hair. Both were formally dressed: she was resplendent in a pale, gauzy dress that sparkled with beads and was trimmed with a delicate fringe around the hem, and he wore a well-tailored white summer suit with a faint thin stripe throughout. They were standing in a sunroom full of immense potted ferns and elaborately scrolling wicker furniture. She smiled sweetly and openly, whereas his expression could only be described as inscrutable. Although there was a slight curl to his upper lip, it was impossible to tell whether he was amused, angry, or something else. His dark eyes, staring out through the soft-focus image, gave nothing away. But perhaps it was a quirk of the light and he was neither amused nor angry but merely content. I studied the girl's face, and I experienced a sharp jolt of recognition. Of course—my flapper! But who was the man? I expected to see a caption in the same neat script on the back of the photograph, but when I flipped it over I found nothing. The only thing to do now was open the book and begin reading.

January 1, 1928

Happy New Year! Last night was yet another New Year's Eve at Mildred's. She does have the most delicious parties, and with such smartly dressed people swanning around. It's just too marvellous! But it was a good thing her parents were off somewhere on the French Riviera for the holidays— they certainly wouldn't have approved of what went on in their house. It's no exaggeration to say they would have been properly horrified.

Naturally, we had a toast to 1928 right at midnight, but I'd been drinking well before then, I'm afraid. I must have had at least five or six glasses of champagne, one right after the other, before I staggered to my feet to make a toast. And everyone else seemed to be in a similar condition, if not worse. And why not? It was the first New Year's Eve everyone's been able to drink legally in this province since sometime during the Great War, so no wonder people got absolutely squiffy.

I vaguely remember some tall, handsome rogue kissing me after everyone shouted, "Happy New Year!" but who knows who he was; I know ever so many fellows who fit that description. It probably doesn't much matter anyway. Still, I must make a point of asking Mildred about this; he may have been one of her cousins. I'm afraid they do all look rather alike to me, especially after I've been drinking champagne. I'm convinced I must have had a wonderful time, though there's not much I remember specifically other than a few songs playing on the gramophone: "Ain't She Sweet" and "The Best Things in Life Are Free." Mostly I recall feeling giddy, warm, and flushed. Everyone—including the unidentified rogue—seemed to take on such a lovely, bright glow last night. How fitting for the festive season.

Unfortunately, I don't feel the least bit festive this afternoon. I've got a pounding headache, though I don't dare admit this to Mama. She'd rightfully think it's because of the drinking.

Naturally, she'd disapprove, as she was all in favour of that Prohibition nonsense and extremely riled up a few months ago when they got rid of the Ontario Temperance Act or whatever it was called. And God forbid anyone should think her darling daughter is a drunk. I just hope she didn't hear me stumble in the door last night. I stubbed my toe and let out a curse word that would have made her blush to the very roots of her hair. Heaven only knows what time it was, though I'd be surprised if it was much before four o'clock. At least the sun wasn't up yet.

Since it's the first day of the year, I thought I'd start off on the right foot and do something useful. This may come as a tremendous shock, but I've decided to make up a list of New Year's resolutions. I imagine this year's batch are all quite attainable—though they do look remarkably similar to last year's, so perhaps I'm wrong about someone like me being able to accomplish them. Still, it's not as though climbing to the summit of a mountain is on my list. Sensible Mildred told me it will help motivate me if I write my goals down, and I expect she's right. She's so often right about everything, which is something I appreciate but find terribly annoying, if that makes any sense.

Here they are, Constance Virginia Rose Pendleton's 1928 New Year's resolutions, not necessarily listed in order of importance:

Lose ten pounds so I can fit into those frightfully revealing new bathing costumes. I'll have to give up trifle, my favourite dessert.

Lose Bernice, my distressingly beautiful, smart, and popular friend, with whom I can't even hope to compete. I haven't resolved how I might accomplish this without offending her.

Lose virginity (this one's a secret, so don't dare tell Mama). I've had offers but am extremely selective.

I seem to have lots to lose, but I don't expect the effort to be terribly draining. Perhaps I should add another resolution: find some respectable but not hopelessly dull young man to marry me. This one sounds like scads of work, but I'll consider including it just to please Mama and Papa. At the moment, though, I'm not in the mood to please much of anyone but myself, thank you! And I desperately want this frightful headache to go away.

I closed the diary. How disappointing! Why was I wasting my time reading a lot of party-girl piffle? If this was all I'd find, it seemed pointless to persevere, and I had to get back to work anyway before Gable noticed my absence and sent out a search party. I returned to the cramped cataloguing room and placed the diary on my desk, next to a tall stack of Royal Crown Derby Imari pattern bone china dinner plates. These and an assortment of figurines, vases, bowls, jardinières, tea services, dinnerware, stemware, and flatware had claimed the entire surface of my desk, along with a wobbly stack of dusty, dog-eared reference books.

Mark was sitting at the cubicle beside mine, leaning dangerously far back in his swivel chair, the telephone wedged between his shoulder and his ear. He glanced at me and with his index finger made circular motions to his head, which could only mean he had a prospective client who was crazy on the phone. He wore the glazed expression of unspeakable weariness that only such calls inspired, the muscles of his face working as he tried to suppress a yawn. He held up an old postcard he'd found of an ocean liner and dangled it before me.

"Ah." Now I knew exactly what was going on. We'd saved the postcard especially to signal "I have something from the *Titanic*" calls.

"I doubt very much that your porcelain cup and saucer is really from the *Titanic*," said Mark to the caller. "Yes, I realize Uncle Horace says a relative brought it onto a lifeboat, but do you really think they were expecting to be served tea there? Family history about these things isn't always reliable, and… no, I'm not calling him a liar. Absolutely not. It's just that I'd have to see it … well, I can't give you a value otherwise … that's right, I need to look at it … no, I absolutely cannot tell you over the phone what it's worth. You'd have to make an appointment. Yes, really ... well, can't you take public transit? We're conveniently located at ... maybe a friend or neighbour could bring you in? No? What about a cab, then ... oh, I see. No, I definitely can't come to Montreal and get you myself. That's just out of the question. Your only choice is to send me a picture, then. Oh, you don't have a camera ..."

Cringing, he paused to hold the receiver at arm's length. Although I couldn't make out the words, I could hear a female voice in full rant rising to terrifying shrillness. The voice buzzed like an angry wasp, and poor Mark groaned as if he'd already been stung.

"For your own good, just hang up," I said.

But he appeared to be in the mood for punishment, for when he put the phone back to his ear, he made little attempt to cut the conversation short. "No, we can't come out to see you for just a cup and saucer, ma'am. Especially since you live in Montreal. No, we're not ... our office isn't in Montreal. You've called Toronto. Honestly, I don't have time to talk about this anymore, even if it *does* turn out to be from the *Titanic,* which I—" A very long pause ensued, during which the sweat that had started to bead on Mark's forehead trickled down. "Oh you *do*, do you? Hold on a moment, please."

He set the receiver down and sighed. "She wants to talk to the 'man in charge.'"

"Naturally, she assumes it's a man. Brian Gable III? Clark's great-nephew thrice removed, or something like that? If he's related to Clark Gable, then I'm Greta Garbo. Anyway, some might say he's in charge," I said.

"Okay, okay. But what should I *do*?" Mark's expression was pained.

"Whatever you do, don't put her through to Gable. Just tell the old dear there's no one in charge."

He sighed again.

"Well, it's true, isn't it?"

"Old dear?" said Chloe, frowning. She was standing at the big table that dominated the cataloguing room. She appeared to be wrestling with a gigantic Steiff mohair teddy bear that was nearly as big as she was, but she was only trying to measure it. "That's not a very nice thing to say, Virginia."

Dear Chloe—she was always so concerned about being nice. I'd stopped caring much about that after my parents died, as some days it seemed to take more effort than I was capable of. "I can think of a lot worse things I could have said about her. You heard her screeching, didn't you? She's not exactly being very nice herself." Turning to Mark, I said, "So what are you going to do about her?"

"I should hand her over to you. What am I even doing talking to her? *You're* the damn porcelain specialist."

But the caller had saved him the trouble of doing anything at all; she'd already hung up, probably assuming he'd abandoned her. Mark clapped his hands excitedly and grinned at me.

"We both know, of course, that she'll call back," I said softly. "They always do."

His grin faded; he knew I was right. I felt a little bad that I'd destroyed his fleeting moment of triumph over the old dear, but now that I'd done it I couldn't undo it, so there was nothing more to be said. Mark looked a bit worried, and I knew that for the rest of the day he'd avoid taking calls. I also knew that the next time he checked his voice mail, he'd find at least one rant of epic proportions from the crazy *Titanic* lady. He'd play the message for our amusement several times on speakerphone before he worked up the nerve to call her back.

"You're right. She'll be back to haunt me." Then he perked up. "Hey, speaking of haunting, how's your little flapper ghost? Seen anything of her lately?" Grinning, he looked over at my desk and pointed at the diary. "Hey, what's that?"

"Nothing."

Mark sprang to his feet, but I was quicker than he was. I snatched up the diary and held it tightly to my chest, where he was unable to pry it loose.

"I don't feel like sharing," I said. "Now buzz off!"

He darted toward me like a snake to a snake charmer. Ever the gentleman, he made broad swiping motions at me to see if he could dislodge the diary from my clutches without pawing my chest. I twisted every which way possible to stay out of his reach and finally ducked behind my chair and under my desk to safety. But he bent down, reaching toward me as I crawled into a corner. Chloe stood there watching our tussle, giggling as much as Mark was. Just then, gum-chomping Taylor sauntered into the room, dressed like a cat burglar in her standard uniform of slim black jeans and a turtleneck. She didn't even raise an eyebrow at the scene that greeted her.

"Hey guys, what's up?" she said. She plopped herself down in her chair at the cubicle next to Chloe's and turned around to watch Mark and me. "What're you doing under the desk?"

I got up from the floor and shouted at Mark, "I said I don't feel like sharing!"

"Okay, okay!" He threw up his hands in surrender and walked back to his chair, laughing, while I dusted cobwebs off myself.

"Whoa—must be something *super valuable*," said Taylor, looking at the diary and smiling. She could never smile in the relaxed, happy way a normal person did; it was as though smiling hurt her face, and sometimes her smile was so tight, it looked like a sneer. Her dark eyes mocked me, and I felt faintly ridiculous. I'd always suspected she snooped around my desk when I wasn't there, looking for things that might incriminate me (I wasn't sure to whom, but possibly to Gable). Now that she'd spotted the diary, I'd really have to watch what she was up to.

I put it in a locking filing cabinet for the rest of the afternoon, slipping the only key into my purse. At the end of the day, when everyone had left, I removed the diary and tucked it into my purse, determined to discover whatever secrets it would reveal.

CHAPTER 6

Later that blustery November evening, I sat at home in my tiny one-bedroom apartment, which occupied the top floor of a small house in Riverdale that had originally been built as a factory worker's cottage before WWI. I warmed myself with a hot cup of coffee, curled up in my plushest armchair, and covered myself in a red fleece blanket. All I needed to complete this picture of cozy domesticity—besides the obligatory dog and fireplace—was a husband.

Well, I'd had one of those once for about three miserable years, but now, fifteen years after I'd last seen him, I could barely recall what Aaron looked like. That he rarely crossed my mind anymore filled me with relief. When I thought about him at all, I just remembered his anger; he'd seethed with it endlessly. I couldn't remember what we'd fought about, only that nothing I'd ever said had been the right thing to say, no matter how tactfully I phrased it or gently I said it. When I'd finally found the guts to leave, I was overjoyed to be free of him.

But after all my years of solitude, I'd finally started to hunger for a deeper sense of connection, an intimacy well beyond what I experienced in the friendships I made with co-workers and the occasional neighbour. It had been alarmingly long since I'd had anything resembling a date, unless you counted last winter's walk in the park with my next-door neighbour, Ivan.

When he first moved in, Ivan told me he was a paleontologist at the Royal Ontario Museum, and after chatting with him briefly I thought he was pleasant and interesting enough to at least take a neighbourly walk with to Withrow Park. Bundled up against the February cold one Sunday afternoon, we strolled through the quiet streets and discussed my preference for coffee over tea, and his for tea over coffee. When he said he preferred cats to dogs, I realized we probably didn't have a hope of true compatibility, so I relaxed and treated the occasion as a nice afternoon out. We entered the park, which was deserted. I was watching big fluffy clumps of sugar snow fall softly from the grey sky when, wild-eyed and desperate, Ivan clutched my arm with a powerful grip. His intensity came out of nowhere; we'd been discussing the most innocuous of subjects, and he'd been politeness personified until then. He whispered hoarsely in my ear, guttural words I could only assume were Russian. I had no idea what he was saying, but I didn't want a translation. He planted a sloppy kiss on my lips, and I shuddered with revulsion.

Shouting at him to let me go, I wriggled free and dashed north to the main drag, Danforth Avenue, for safety. I observed bewilderment and sometimes alarm on the faces of the passersby who saw me panting and gasping my way to the nearest Starbucks. Shaking, I ordered an Americano, and when it came, I took quick, anxious gulps. I expected Ivan to walk through that door any minute, so I hid at the back behind a large group of boisterous students. But he didn't come. It took nearly an hour for my panic to subside, and for the numbness his grip had caused in my arm to dissipate. I was terrified of going home since it was inevitable I'd see him.

We never said a word to each other after that, but I was grateful when, five months later, he moved out of the house next door. I no longer had to experience flashbacks of that horrid winter walk every time I saw him or tolerate his greasy, predatory smile as he stood in his driveway sizing me up while ostensibly tinkering with his wreck of a car. What a creep!

Unfortunately, my brush with Ivan had seriously impaired, if not completely annihilated, my desire for a relationship, and months later I was only just coming around to the idea that developing a relationship with a man might be a good thing. Ivan was crazy enough to make me paranoid that there were others out there just like him, waiting to prey on unsuspecting, lonely women like me.

In an effort to avoid his kind, I was often content to drowse away my evenings alone with the classic movie channel, my head bobbing up and down as I shifted from sleep to wakefulness. Chloe, who was also single, would sometimes join me for the movies. She was particularly fond of anything syrupy, like the romantic tear-jerkers of the '40s and '50s. I'd serve her shortbread and cups of strong, steaming Earl Grey tea while we gossiped about co-workers or planned weekend brunches and shopping outings before we settled into the evening's movie. Although she knew little about the old films we watched together, she seemed to enjoy herself, and I was glad of her company. I couldn't speak for Chloe (who was reticent on many subjects, especially her love life), but I chased my romantic thrills vicariously, imagining I was a quivering, breathless Joan Fontaine in *Rebecca* succumbing to Laurence Olivier's fearsome magnetism. It was so much safer than pursuing a real love life, but I was beginning to get a little weary of my nightly routine.

Now, as I curled up with Constance Virginia Rose Pendleton's diary, I sensed I was about to enter another world of vicarious thrills—clumsily expressed in antiquated, teenaged prose, of course, but far more real than anything I'd see in those magical movies I adored. Maybe the realism would be a nice change. Excitedly, I opened the diary and began to read.

But I soon became disillusioned. Although it had already occurred to me that Constance was trying to tell me something by giving me her diary, whatever message she wanted to convey was lost on me, for the diary consisted primarily of gossipy descriptions of petty female rivalry played out at fancy Rosedale parties. And the drama—the thrills I'd been chasing—just didn't materialize. I slumped unhappily in my chair as I read. But when I got to April, I abruptly sat up. Almost overnight, Constance Pendleton's interest in her female friends was eclipsed by a compelling new obsession.

April 11, 1928

What a night! Who would have thought I'd ever meet someone as splendid and clever as Freddy? And to think he's actually Mildred's cousin! Honestly, I thought I'd met all fifty of them by now. Where the devil has she been hiding him all these years? I must have a word with her about her extraordinary thoughtlessness. But first, I need to jot down the riveting story of how Freddy and I met.

Mildred's twenty-first birthday party was last night, and I attended with Lydia. It was a lavish affair held in her family's ballroom, which is absolutely sumptuous. I've always adored the vaulted ceiling, carved wood panelling, crystal chandeliers, velvet-upholstered furniture, and Oriental carpets in that room. The one thing that's always been disconcerting about it, though, is having so many of Mildred's pinched-looking ancestors staring down at me from painted portraits; the Galloways seem such a disapproving lot.

Things were very dull at first, so Lydia and I contented ourselves with eavesdropping on nearby conversations and watching people. White-gloved waiters seemed to glide through the room, carrying silver salvers with glasses of champagne for the guests—the men natty in black tie, the women ravishing in bejewelled headbands and colourful silk gowns that sparkled with beading and sequins as they moved.

Suddenly, a handsome dark-haired stranger swept into the room. All the girls were agog, especially that perfectly dreadful Bernice, who grows more slatternly with each passing day. As if that little tramp doesn't have enough men lined up at her door! She ought to give other girls a chance now and then. She was giving the handsome stranger the once-over from the moment he arrived. But she certainly wasn't the only one—you could see heads swivelling around when he came in, and it was impossible not to stare, for he cut such a dashing figure. With his dark, brooding face, he was even more handsome than dear departed Rudolph Valentino himself. And quite tall, which suits me very well indeed.

Sipping the champagne a waiter had brought around, we both watched him as he navigated through clusters of people, smiling easily and shaking hands. We wondered who he was, of course. I was acquainted with most everyone in the room, but not him. Or had I met him at another of Mildred's swanky affairs and just couldn't remember? I suddenly had a dreadful thought.

"Lydia, do you suppose he's that fellow I told you about, the one I was drunkenly smooching on New Year's Eve? If so, how horribly embarrassing! Can you imagine? But maybe he won't remember. After all, he must have been squiffy as well. Everybody was. But what will I do if I'm introduced to him and he happens to bring it up?"

"It can't possibly be him." Lydia patted my arm reassuringly and smiled. "Even if it is, he wouldn't have the nerve to say anything."

"Oh, I just don't know!" I said, feeling giddy with fear.

"Hush, Constance. Oh no—he's looking at us!" Lydia looked pale. I hoped she wouldn't faint.

We'd been whispering and staring. Apparently, the newcomer couldn't help but notice two silly creatures looking at him, so he all but leaped over the furniture to come over and introduce himself. My heart practically jumped out of my chest when I saw him bounding toward us, and I suspect Lydia's did the same. It was terrifying and thrilling all at the same time, much like those amusement park rides at Hanlan's Point a few years ago.

Without the slightest hesitation, he walked up and said, "Good evening. I'm Freddy Alderdice, Mildred's cousin." His voice was deep and resonant, like an actor's. He thrust out his hand and shook mine firmly. He was so confident, so at ease. I could scarcely believe there could be such a man, let alone that he was standing right in front of me.

Lydia, who is always such a bashful little thing, immediately began giggling into her handkerchief and looking down at the floor. She's so hopeless in the presence of handsome males that she's barely able to string two words together. Her shyness can be endearing, but I do get weary of it too; I was forced to step in and introduce us both.

"Mr. Alderdice, I'm Constance Pendleton—or Connie for short. And this is my best friend, Lydia Wilton."

"Miss Wilton." He vigorously shook Lydia's hand and smiled pleasantly. Gaping, she looked up at him.

"Miss Pendleton." He shook my hand as well. "Well, I'm very pleased to meet you both." He took us in with a sweeping glance and then looked just at me, his dark eyes glowing like embers. "And how exceptionally lovely you look this evening." Then he looked at Lydia. "Both of you."

Such polished manners, such good breeding! He was so thoroughly unlike the tiresome lot of teasing rakes and roués I'd grown accustomed to at Mildred's parties. It made for a refreshing change. Lydia seemed so impressed by his appearance and manner that she couldn't stop blushing, poor thing. It was becoming most embarrassing.

"I didn't know Mildred had a cousin. Or rather, I didn't know she had a cousin like you. Good gracious, where has she been hiding you all these years?" I blurted out. The instant I said it, I felt the blood rush to my cheeks. I'd been a perfect dunce, much too effusive toward a fellow I'd only just met. "Oh, I *am* sorry!"

But Freddy was such a gentleman that he didn't bat an eye. As though I hadn't already made a complete idiot of myself, he smiled. "Didn't Mildred tell you? I've been studying abroad. The classics, mostly, as per Father's instructions. Dreary stuff, to be frank. I'm just not cut out for academic work, but I did manage to earn my degree. I'm rather glad to be back in Toronto."

"When did you return?"

"Oh, just a couple of months ago."

What a relief! He couldn't possibly have been the fellow I'd kissed on New Year's Eve, then. "Oh, thank goodness for that!"

He narrowed his eyes as if he hadn't quite heard me. "Miss Pendleton?"

"Oh, never mind!" My cheeks were still burning. I wondered how many other blunders I'd make before the evening was over.

Just then, I noticed that Lydia's attention had been captured by Mildred, who had edged her way into our circle. I'd noticed her watching us earlier, her eyes glittering with mischief. She looked radiant in a plum silk gown that complemented her chestnut hair and alabaster complexion.

"Dear Miss Galloway!" Freddy spoke with mock formality and took a deep bow. "Happy birthday, Mildred darling." He leaned over, clasped her hands warmly in his, and kissed her on each cheek.

"Thank you, Cousin Freddy," said Mildred. "It's lovely to see you, especially after such a long time. And I see you've already met two of my dearest friends." She winked at me, inclining her head slightly toward Freddy before turning smiling eyes on Lydia. "Lydia, dear, would you like another glass of champagne? And perhaps you'd enjoy seeing my latest watercolour. I've been experimenting, and it's different from the others I've shown you. I'd very much like your opinion."

Lydia exhaled and smiled. Mildred smoothly led her away, chatting merrily all the while. I was relieved that she'd rescued Lydia from her own awkwardness. I was also overjoyed to be free to give Freddy my full attention without feeling I was being rude to poor Lydia by neglecting her.

Maybe it was the effects of the champagne I was drinking, but Freddy's eyes seemed to sparkle—almost unnaturally so. I looked more closely at them; they were the most fascinating mixture of green and brown. I would have said they were plain old brown if I'd been far away from him, but the truth is, we were already standing scandalously close together. Mama would have been dismayed, even infuriated, by my conduct. And I could feel the other girls' eyes upon me, watching me with that delectable mixture of shock and envy, no doubt. But I wasn't looking at them—only at Freddy.

"So what will you do now that you're back in Toronto, Mr. … ?" Goodness, I'd already forgotten his surname.

"Frederick James William Alderdice, though *you* may call me Freddy," he said. His playful look and warm smile made me feel I'd been granted an exclusive privilege.

"I have a rather long name myself. I do wonder why it's necessary to have two middle names, don't you? It's so cumbersome. Are you ready for this? Constance Virginia Rose Pendleton!"

"What a superb name!" he said, and I couldn't help feeling he truly meant it. He smiled down on me. Did I mention he's extremely tall? Freddy is head and shoulders above me, even though I was wearing my darling red velvet T-strap shoes last night, which add nearly three inches to my height.

He paused briefly before saying, "Do you not go by Rose, then? Somehow you look more like a Rose than a Constance, though I can't for the life of me say why."

"Good gracious, no! I've always been Constance or Connie."

He smiled. "Very well, then, but would you mind awfully if I called you Rose now and then? As a sort of nickname, perhaps?" He was already intimating we'd be seeing one another again. Although I should have been floored by his presumptuousness, I was instead charmed by his smile.

"Well, I suppose that *might* be acceptable on extremely rare occasions. That is, if you take care to fill out all the proper permission forms first."

His smile faded, and he looked somewhat taken aback. But after a moment's pause, he laughed. "Oh, I do love a girl with a sense of humour!"

I felt a little flutter of excitement inside. "Now that you're back in Toronto, have you any idea what you'll do?" I asked again.

He paused for a moment as if to ponder the matter seriously, and then raised one eyebrow mischievously. "Perhaps join the circus?"

"Oh, you can't mean it!" I was laughing and starting to feel delightfully tipsy.

"Of course not, though wouldn't it be a lark? Quite frankly, it's complicated. Father wants me to join his law firm, of course, just so he can finally have the pleasure of calling it Alderdice & Alderdice, but perhaps my younger brother will follow in his footsteps and free me of that onerous responsibility. I confess I haven't the slightest interest in the law. Perhaps I shouldn't admit this to a respectable girl like you, but I have it in my head to be a jazz musician. I'm a pianist, and I've already played several gigs since I've been back in Canada. It would help, of course, if Father supported me at this early stage." He grimaced.

"So he's not the sort to lend a helping hand if he doesn't approve of your plan?"

"Sadly, that *is* the case."

"Oh, how dreadful!"

"Dreadful, indeed, but I'll find a way of making a go of it. I've already been playing piano in the movie theatres, but word has it there soon won't be much of that sort of work. Not with talking pictures becoming all the rage, especially in America since *The Jazz Singer*. And there are already signs the craze will spread to Toronto." He looked a bit grim. Then brightening, he said, "Miss Pendleton— Constance—perhaps we might find a quiet corner where we can chat properly, away from the hubbub of this noisy soirée?"

He spoke ever so politely. With no inkling that what we were about to do might be in questionable taste, I nodded and followed Freddy from the living room past raucous groups of people and through the narrow passageway that led to Mildred's conservatory. It was always such a splendid place, for it was full of immense exotic plants, most of which I didn't know the names of. Her father had them imported from the tropics. They had the most luxuriant foliage and colourful blooms; I'd only ever seen them in the daylight, the sun making their leaves glowing and translucent. But now it was dark, so Freddy and I had to pick our way through the conservatory, ferns delicately brushing our faces and our path lit by an enormous full moon suspended low in the sky. As if party guests were expected to use the room, someone had thoughtfully lit candles and set them on the end tables flanking the curving wicker settee in the far corner. But we were alone, and the conservatory was still and silent. Only faraway, faint peals of laughter, occasionally floating in from the party, interrupted the silence.

Freddy and I sat down next to each other on the settee. I drank in the night air, heavy with the perfume of lilies, and sighed. The combined effect of the fragrance and the champagne was making me sleepy. In the moonlight I watched him smoothly extract what looked like an engraved silver cigarette case from his pocket.

"Cigarette?"

"Oh no, I couldn't possibly!" Mostly, I was thinking about how Mama would react. It was shocking enough that I was alone in the conservatory with a gentleman I'd met a mere twenty minutes ago; to smoke as well would be beyond the pale, putting me in the same category as Bernice. Besides, although I'd tried smoking once or twice before, I couldn't say I liked it.

"Nervous?" Freddy spoke in the same offhand manner he'd used when offering me the cigarette.

"Oh no!" I said it too vehemently. I was suddenly conscious of jiggling my leg up and down, my heel clicking on the floor. It was an embarrassing old habit from my childhood, a holdover from the days when I was called upon to recite poetry before my classmates. I had to cross my legs to stop myself. I only hoped that Freddy hadn't noticed my foolishness.

He pulled out a lighter and deftly lit his cigarette. The flame momentarily cast a warm glow on an angular face that was all high cheekbones, prominent nose, and sharp jaw. He stole a glance at me, the creases around his eyes crinkling with amusement.

"Good heavens, Constance, there's nothing to be frightened of. We're just sitting here talking. Now tell me about Constance Virginia Rose Pendleton. I simply must know everything."

I liked the way he said my name, enunciating each syllable precisely, and I already dared to imagine he'd soon be saying it to me again and again. Quite overwhelmed, I was sure all intelligent thoughts had flown from my brain. He wanted to know everything? What could I possibly have to tell a sophisticated, worldly fellow like Freddy? "I-I scarcely know where to begin, Mr. Alderdice."

There followed an exasperated sigh. Although he'd had only a couple of puffs, Freddy stubbed out his cigarette, grinding it into a glittering crystal ashtray. He said slowly, "My dear girl, please *do* call me Freddy. I thought we'd already cleared that little matter up."

"Oh yes—how silly of me! Freddy it is, then."

"Much better! Now, I'd very much like to know what Constance—or Rose, since you did say I could call you that—does all day and what she's passionate about."

Under Freddy's stare, I shifted uncomfortably in my seat, as though I was being interviewed for an important position. Perhaps I was.

I drew in my breath before launching into a reply. "Well, truth be told, I don't do much of anything. Mama and Papa tell me I don't need to, though Papa has on occasion suggested I become a nurse. He's a pediatrician, you know. Maybe you've heard of Dr. Pendleton? I fear I'm a bit of a disappointment to him, as I'm terribly squeamish. On the other hand, I don't suppose he and Mama really expect very much of me, only that I get married and supply them with oodles of grandchildren. Until then, I might learn secretarial skills like typing and shorthand should I ever feel the need to make myself useful."

Even in the moonlight, I could see Freddy's face fall. "Hmm. You don't actually like that sort of thing, do you?"

Feeling the sting of his disdain, I said, "Well, I hardly even know, since I haven't done it before. But there's nothing so very wrong with studying it, is there? Especially when one has no particular talent for anything else?"

He shook his head emphatically. "Of course not. I just don't see *you* doing it. It's much too mundane for any girl with the impressive-sounding name of Constance Virginia Rose Pendleton. Secretarial work is for ordinary girls, and you're not without a 'particular talent,' I'm sure. Like many girls your age, you do yourself the disservice of underestimating yourself. You, my dear—you have the sensibility of an *artist*. I knew it at a glance. You ought to be a novelist or a painter."

I tried to stifle a burst of nervous laughter, but it escaped. "A painter? My goodness, absolutely not! Your cousin Mildred is twenty times the artist I'll ever be. She took all the art prizes in school, and her watercolours are exquisite, as you surely must know. But a novelist ... I confess it has some appeal."

"Yes?" Freddy lit another cigarette, and I caught the eager gleam in his eyes.

"Well, I'm always making up the most ridiculous stories, you know. Mama used to be rather perturbed about it when I was little. She worried so that I couldn't tell the difference between fantasy and reality, but Papa assured her I was a perfectly normal child, and being a doctor, his word carries considerable weight. And you know, I remember every word of every conversation I have, so I write them all down in my diary—the interesting ones, that is."

"Like this one, I hope. Well, there you have it, then—it's all set. A novelist you will be!" He made choosing a career sound absurdly easy, like selecting a dish from a restaurant menu. "I just knew you were a cut above ordinary girls."

"Really?" It was tremendously flattering. I felt the colour rising in my face, and I was grinning. I just hoped Freddy couldn't see in the dark how silly I must have looked.

"Oh yes, really. Constance … you are quite extraordinary." His voice grew soft and rich, like velvet. He was leaning toward me, and I was on tenterhooks wondering what he might do next. I jumped a little when he slyly took my hand in one of his and stroked it with the other. His feathery touch was deliciously unexpected, and I shuddered.

"Cold in here, isn't it?" I murmured.

"Well, we can easily solve that problem. Come a little closer." He drew me toward him, enfolding me in his arms, and I nestled into him. "Darling!" he whispered.

I was speechless, and I thought I'd pass out from excitement. Once my head stopped swimming, I peered up at Freddy's face and saw his eyes shining as they caught the light from the sputtering candle on the side table. His features were faintly illuminated by the moonlight. A slightly spicy aroma clung to his skin. Breathing deeply of his scent, I felt delirious. He began covering my face with greedy kisses, squeezing me ever more tightly. Any sensible girl would have wriggled free of him, called him a beast, and slapped him across the face, but I was anything but sensible. Instead, I breathlessly pressed my lips to his in the most intoxicating kiss of my life.

CHAPTER 7

That was the end of Constance's diary entry, and I looked ahead to the next one, which began with the subject of dancing. Maddeningly, she'd left me dangling from a precipice, and I felt nearly as breathless as she must have. Why had she stopped so abruptly? I imagined her mother walking into the room at the most inopportune time possible, just as she was writing about the kiss. She would have had no choice but to slam her diary shut, shove it in the nearest drawer or under the bed, and pretend she'd been busy doing something else. Or maybe that wasn't what had happened at all. Perhaps Constance, with all her worries about impropriety, had simply grown coy. But where she'd ended must have been just the beginning of her grand love affair, and what immediately followed that night had ranged from slightly risqué to explicitly naughty. I feared she'd disappoint me by never giving up the details of what had happened after the first kiss.

Though Constance's love life was already infinitely more interesting than mine, which continued to consist of fantasy affairs with handsome, long-dead movie stars who people twenty years younger than I was hadn't even heard of, I no longer had time to ponder her escapades. The very next day, I became consumed with preparing for the coming auction.

Gable & Co. was getting ready for a big four-evening blockbuster fall auction, and it was my job and Taylor's to set up the goods from our department that would be auctioned off on one of those nights. This meant hauling out antiques to the auction gallery and positioning them artistically in glass cases, where they'd be on display all weekend during a public preview. Crowds of clients would then traipse through and inspect the goods before deciding which items to bid on. Taylor and I would be subject to the usual probing questions about the authenticity, provenance, and condition of the pieces. Most people were respectful and nice, but a few complained noisily about cracks and repairs—almost as if they thought we'd damaged the pieces ourselves. We couldn't help it if the clients who'd consigned these tchotchkes for sale at auction had come from families who were inconsiderate enough to damage the family heirlooms—or who employed cleaning ladies who did. Still, it seemed hard to convince certain people that Taylor and I weren't somehow responsible for the imperfect condition of the goods. Although I liked a good many clients, the difficult ones were very wearisome, especially when I'd had to put up with them for so many years.

For this auction, we were featuring an important porcelain urn that was sure to attract considerable attention and, if we were lucky, considerable money. Although it was valued at $12,000 to $15,000, the interest was so great that I wouldn't have been surprised if the price skyrocketed to as much as $25,000. The Snodgrass Royal Crown Derby Floribunda pattern porcelain presentation urn had belonged to Toronto robber baron Morton P. Snodgrass (the *P* stood for Phineas). He'd acquired it on a trip to London in 1903 and presented it to his eldest son the following year. Standing nearly three feet tall, the classical-style urn with a 1903 date stamp featured two foliate handles lavishly decorated with gilding, and it was elevated on a square pedestal foot. Apart from its superb provenance, what made the piece so wildly desirable was its perfect condition and the hand-painted floral panel signed by one of Royal Crown Derby's foremost flower painters of the period, Lady Florence Twaddlebury. This panel showed a lush bouquet of densely clustered multicoloured roses, while the much smaller back panel, which lacked Lady Twaddlebury's distinctive touch, depicted a sprawling country estate. The latter had probably been painted by a skilled assistant. Beneath the roses was an elegant cursive inscription with these words: *Presented to James Morton Snodgrass, on the occasion of his marriage to Millicent Anne Hartwick, May 27, 1904.* During the preview Taylor and I would be fielding all kinds of questions about the piece, from the pertinent to the irrelevant, just as we'd already been doing. We'd also be giving our muscles a good workout as we hauled the enormous urn out from behind the counter to show people and then hauled it back again.

The day we started setting up for the preview was the anniversary of my parents' deaths. It was impossible not to think of the devastating phone call I'd received at work exactly a year ago, and to remember how Chloe had whisked me away to the hospital and stayed by my side for hours, offering comfort as I slowly began to absorb the news. At the time she had only been at Gable's for a few months, and my parents' deaths had brought our budding friendship into full flower. In the first few weeks after the tragedy, Mark brought me cakes and cookies he'd baked and Sally treated me to lunch at cheerful, bustling restaurants, but it was Chloe's limitless compassion—the frequent hugs and encouraging chats—that really saw me through that terrible time.

Now I was feeling both sad and weary. Trying to work up the energy and enthusiasm to get started, I drank back-to-back cups of coffee as Taylor and I started hunting in the cupboards just outside the cataloguing room for the items to be displayed. After three cups my sadness tipped into irritability, and my hands began trembling. Taylor was perched precariously on a spindly-looking ladder, leaning forward as she searched through dark cupboards. How could she possibly see anything with those long purple bangs flopping over her eyes? I stood below, drumming my fingers on cupboards as I waited for her to hand me something—anything at all—to take out to the auction gallery.

"Where's that Dresden-type thing? I haven't seen it for a while," she said.

"Hmm?" I bit my lip. We had so many items that could have been described as Dresden-type things, and it was all I could do to restrain myself from snapping at her.

"You know—that thing with the shepherd." Taylor wrinkled her nose when she said *thing*, her tone peevish. She waved her hands in the air in a vague, incomprehensible gesture and nearly lost her footing. I held the ladder steady.

"Well, that sure narrows it down. Which thing with the shepherd? We've got several."

She rolled her eyes like a sullen teenager. If I'd been a lesser person, I might have succumbed to the temptation to knock her off the ladder. It wouldn't have taken a very forceful swat, for she was petite and the ladder was rickety.

"Which thing with the shepherd?" I repeated, more loudly than before.

"You know—that big, ugly thing with the shepherd in the middle. He's sitting on a bench, and there's this lady beside him."

"Gee, could you possibly mean the shepherdess?"

Taylor groaned. "Yes, the freaking shepherdess! And there's a big, fat, nasty sheep sitting at their feet."

Her inadequate description was nonetheless sufficient to conjure up an image in my poor, overworked brain of the porcelain masterpiece. It was a massive Dresden figural group about two feet high, manufactured around 1950. A seated shepherd, holding a crook and dressed in a tricorn hat, jacket, waistcoat, and breeches was extending his hand and leering as he sidled up to a blonde shepherdess. Her voluminous gown exhibited a surprising amount of cleavage, but she blushed demurely behind a fan, which partially obscured her face. At the shepherd's feet, a plump white sheep drowsed contentedly among the flowers. The whole was hand-painted in nauseating pastel pinks, yellows, and blues accented with tiny gilded flowers. Typically for such a piece, the shepherd's arm had broken off and been sloppily glued back on. Trails of yellow glue oozed from the arm, and chunks of the hapless limb were missing. Yet still he leered, apparently delighted by the sight of the shepherdess's cleavage despite his injuries.

It was hard to imagine that anyone might want to buy such a thoroughly objectionable decorative object, but on the merits of size alone, we'd appraised it at $800 to $1,200. Ugly or not, it had to be found.

Taylor, who could usually be relied upon for her cool demeanour if not much else, was strangely distressed. "You didn't take it out of this cupboard, did you? Did you put it somewhere else?" she asked, her voice trembling. "Oh God, I knew something like this would happen." Would I witness the rare spectacle of Taylor's tears? The prospect of an emotional display was more than I could cope with.

"*I* didn't put it anywhere. And what do you mean you knew this would happen?" Not waiting for her to answer, I said, "Get down off that ladder, go get yourself a coffee, and I'll take a look." I knew I'd spoken sharply, but I was much too annoyed with her to regret my tone. Her tears wouldn't help us find the missing Dresden figural group, and she'd just have to pull herself together, for heaven's sake.

"Okay." Taylor wiped her eyes, hopped down from the ladder, and took herself off. I was glad to see the back of her, if only for a few minutes; in her absence I always felt much calmer. I got up on the ladder and scoured the cupboards for the figural monstrosity, but it was nowhere to be seen. Soon I became conscious of Brian Gable III's presence looming and his bad smell lingering nearby. I could see him from the corner of my eye, but I continued poking around in the cupboards as if he weren't there. Maybe he'd become bored with watching me and go away, I thought hopefully.

No such luck. "Is everything all right, Miss Blythe?" His tone was pleasantly casual, and I was surprised he'd initiated a conversation with me at all. Ever since our little chat during which he'd advised me not to talk about ghosts, he'd been avoiding me. When we passed each other in the hallways, he'd glance at me, his face smugness itself. As always, I was suspicious of any expression of friendliness from him.

I leaned into one last cupboard and strained to see if it would yield the elusive shepherd and friends. With exaggerated cheeriness, I said, "Just trying to find a little something, that's all!"

"Hmm?"

I took it my voice was muffled because I was talking into the cupboard, so I twisted around on the shaky ladder to look down at Gable. But I hardly saw him at all—just his boldly striped orange-and-white T-shirt, glowing like a neon sign and emphasizing his big belly. "I'm just looking for a piece of porcelain."

"You mean something's *missing*?" He let out a gasp, and his eyes popped. He had the most annoying flair for the dramatic.

"Not at all—it's simply misplaced." I tried to project confidence, but my voice wobbled slightly.

"You're not talking about that Snodgrass thing, are you?"

I was surprised he was even aware of the urn; he paid so little attention to what we sold at auction. "Oh no, that's down below in the cupboard right in front of you," I said, pointing. "I'm searching for something else. I'm sure it'll turn up." I attempted to smile reassuringly.

"Well, Miss Blythe, I trust you'll get on this right away and take care of it." He sounded so utterly pompous, and my irritation grew. His oily forehead was furrowed, his eyebrows linking like a pair of furry caterpillars wrestling.

Gable looked far more disapproving than the situation warranted. Little did he know that in my world, so-called missing pieces of porcelain were routine since items were moved around a lot; they had to be inventoried, catalogued, photographed, and labelled with lot numbers before they even made it out onto the gallery floor for the preview. Because they inevitably reappeared sooner or later, I'd grown blasé over the years when I couldn't find something at first. It just wasn't worth getting worked up about. Taylor had the same attitude, which made her distress over the Dresden figural group all the more puzzling.

"Of course I'll get on it. Right away." Just what did he suppose I was doing at the top of the ladder, anyway?

"Very good, then. Carry on." He treated me to a scowl as he headed in the same direction Taylor had. He was probably ill-tempered because he hadn't had a doughnut for at least two hours and was starting to go into sugar withdrawal.

A few minutes later, while I was still at the top of the ladder looking for the Dresden figural group, I heard the intercom crackle to life. Helen's voice sounded stiff and awkward. "Attention, all staff. At four thirty, we will be having a meeting. I repeat—all staff must attend a meeting in the upstairs gallery at four thirty sharp." It seemed that Brian Gable III was hungry and couldn't wait until dinner.

As it was nearly time for the meeting, I climbed down from the ladder and dragged myself out to the gallery. I sat on a gaudy red brocade settee with a tasselled fringe that looked as if it belonged in a turn-of-the-century New Orleans bordello. Already, Gable was in the gallery, arranging the Tim Hortons doughnuts on a pair of valuable circa 1810 Spode blue transferware platters decorated with a triumphal arch. As usual, he hadn't asked me if he could borrow them from my department—he'd simply made off with them when I wasn't at my desk to protect them from his thieving ways. Gable had no notion they might be worth more than two dollars, so he handled them carelessly, repeatedly knocking them together as he shuffled them around. I knew that a protest would get me nowhere, so I gritted my teeth and prayed they wouldn't be any the worse for wear after he'd finished with them.

Chloe sat down beside me on the settee. She was bug-eyed with curiosity, as if we were all about to hear some deliciously juicy rumour. For all her niceness, she liked gossip as much as the next person. "I wonder what this is about. It's nearly time to go home," she said.

I shrugged. "No idea." But I could guess what was coming, and I didn't want to think about it, let alone talk about it. My mind began to drift as everyone filed into the gallery, my thoughts turning to the disappointing choice of evening movies on TV.

Mark, who sat down on my other side, slowly exhaled as he watched Gable absorbed in doughnut arranging. "If I never have to see him do that again, it'll be too soon."

"No kidding," I whispered.

Taylor had settled down and was back to wearing her customary mask of inscrutability, her legs neatly crossed and her arms folded. Helen yawned and rubbed her forehead as if she had a tension headache. Dora stared open-mouthed at the ceiling. George, who looked pretty snappy in a slim-fitting dark suit, looked down at the floor and then up. Catching my eye, he gave me an uneasy smile, as if he somehow knew what was coming too. Sally smiled tightly, her eyes darting restlessly around the room. Jared and his crew of floor staff simply looked sweaty and bone-weary from hauling around furniture and display cases all day. They were probably glad to have the opportunity to sit down for a while. Given how late in the day it was, I was sure everyone just wanted to go home.

Brian Gable III, who held an apple fritter in one hand and a honey cruller in the other, gave no sign that the meeting was about to begin until he suddenly looked right at me and said, "Okay, everyone, there seems to be a problem." His booming voice jolted me into alertness, and I shifted uncomfortably on the settee.

"Problem?" I said, my voice quaking. All eyes were riveted on me.

Gable brought his fist down on the table, making the platters bounce and me cringe. "Yes, Miss Blythe. And perhaps you can tell us what that problem is."

Offended by his bluster, I became a little more confident. "I assure you, I haven't the faintest idea. As far as I'm concerned, there aren't any problems."

Gable paused to consider this, his eyes narrowing as he scratched at his chin. "Doughnuts!" he called out unexpectedly. That was our command to rise up and indulge; for reasons that weren't entirely clear, there would be no waiting today. He could probably already see I intended to be difficult, so perhaps he needed more time to concoct a plan to ensure my complete humiliation.

He'd whipped up enough tension that everyone in the room fell silent. His particularly brittle mood was obvious, so we quickly made our selections and sat down. I bit into my double chocolate doughnut, and Chloe and Mark glanced nervously at me.

Gable sighed wearily as he sat down on the dining chair next to the doughnuts and glared at me. Clearly, he hadn't approved of my response. I tried to suppress a smirk. Did he really expect me to take anything he had to say seriously when he was wearing that ridiculous striped shirt? He may as well have been standing before us in a clown suit wearing a bright red wig, a false nose, and floppy oversized shoes.

"Okay. Well ... contrary to what Miss Blythe says, there really *is* a problem. Valuable porcelain is going missing," he said.

I took a moment to screw up some more courage. "Correction. One piece of porcelain that's damaged and not terribly valuable, and which will undoubtedly turn up, has been misplaced."

My colleagues just stared at me. With jaw-dropping nerve, I'd done the unthinkable: I'd dared to contradict Brian Gable III. And I'd done so without hesitating, trailing off at the end, or shrinking like a wilted blossom. Confidence surged through me. It was liberating to have spoken my mind, but my triumph was short-lived. A moment later, I began to actually think. Consequences were certain to follow from my rash behaviour. If I got off lightly, Gable would go beyond ignoring me every day and become actively hostile, making my life a misery. At worst, I'd simply be dismissed. For all I knew, this might be my very last day at Gable & Co. The thought momentarily paralyzed me. I'd recently had a root canal, and while the procedure had lined my endodontist's pockets, it had all but emptied mine. I barely had enough left in the bank to cover my rent, let alone groceries. I began to sweat. Still, I wasn't about to wither pathetically in front of Brian Gable III.

"You're wrong, Miss Blythe. More than one piece of porcelain has been 'misplaced,' as you euphemistically call it." He crammed half the apple fritter in his mouth, and crumbs flew as he chewed. Chloe and Mark exchanged disgusted glances.

Forcing myself to speak, I said, "I'm only aware of the *misplaced* Dresden shepherd and shepherdess porcelain figural group."

The glint in his eye was decidedly threatening. "That statement only demonstrates how appallingly ignorant you are about what goes on in your own department." His words were muffled as his mouth battled with the fritter, chomping aggressively.

Any remaining paralysis I felt vanished in the face of his hostility. "There's no need to be insulting, Gable. And kindly replace those Spode platters to my department immediately after this meeting. I've had quite enough of your scoffing my ceramics every time you happen to feel like it and knocking them around during meetings. Do you have any idea what those platters are worth?" My heart started hammering away in my chest. I'd dropped the "Mr." Better yet, I'd ordered him around. God, it was exhilarating! He glowered darkly at me, no doubt contemplating my murder.

Everyone had been stunned into silence except Chloe, who emitted a small gasp. She said gently, "I'm sure the missing things will turn up, Mr. Gable. We've recovered missing items many times before, you know." It was just like her to try to smooth things over, and I was bolstered by the support. Feeling even more defiant, I smiled at Gable, who smiled icily in return.

"One would hope, Chloe, that the *five* porcelain items that have disappeared without a trace will be found. And if the director of the porcelain department is as on top of things as she evidently thinks she is, I must ask the following: Why has she not seen fit to notify anyone of the missing pieces?"

"Five?" I squealed as though someone had thrust a needle into me. "There can't be five pieces missing! Absolutely not! Who told you that?"

Gable said nothing; he reclined a little in his chair and stared at me as if he were some sort of self-satisfied, unblinking reptile—a Komodo dragon, perhaps.

A sharp intake of breath came from a few feet away from me. "It's not the Snodgrass Royal Crown Derby Floribunda pattern porcelain presentation urn that's gone missing, is it?" said Dora in an annoyingly high-pitched voice.

I was stunned—she'd nailed the title, right down to the last adjective. Who would have thought? "No, Dora, it's not."

"That's a relief," she said, smiling. I really didn't feel much better, but at least she was being nice for a change.

George then chimed in. "Perhaps the most productive approach to all this would be to circulate a statement describing

the five items. Then all staff could be on the lookout for them."
Everyone nodded, for he was being practical and sensible. And
his manner had a calming effect, which we all needed then.
Thank God for George. He flashed an encouraging smile at
me, his brown eyes lighting up. I couldn't help thinking there
was something more to that look than just encouragement.
Feeling a bit flustered, I quickly looked away. I couldn't afford
to let myself get distracted just then.

"Who told you there were five, Gable?" I said.

He looked uneasy, but he seemed to realize I'd developed
pitbull-like tenacity on this point. Reluctantly, he said, "Taylor."

Ah, of course. She'd run straight to Brian Gable III after
I told her to get down off the ladder. Or had he, seeing her
looking tearful and making a great show of feeling sorry for
her, pulled her aside and interrogated her? But why had she
told him that five pieces were missing when there was only
one? Although I'd always distrusted her, I didn't know she was
capable of being such a liar.

Taylor, who was sitting directly across from me, met
my gaze unflinchingly. It was difficult to imagine what she
was thinking behind those expressionless brown eyes. But I
intended to shake the truth out of her, even if doing so meant I
had to cross the room and grab her by the shoulders.

"Taylor, why would you lie like that? Why did you tell
Gable five pieces were missing?" My voice was stern, as if I
were reprimanding a small child.

She looked at me fearlessly and spoke in a quiet but firm voice. "Because it's true."

"Well, if there are—and I can't believe it—why the hell didn't you tell me? And what *are* the other four, anyway?"

Taylor looked from Gable to me before she shrugged. She began fidgeting with her bangs. That was no answer, of course. Mark was sitting right beside me, and he knew me well enough to have noticed that my frustration and rage were building to dangerous levels. "Don't," he said, placing a gentle hand on my forearm.

Gable shoved the second half of the apple fritter into his mouth and actually had the good grace to chew for a couple of minutes before he finally spoke. His voice dripped with contempt. "I can't believe you wouldn't even *know* that these five pieces were missing, Miss Blythe. Yet somehow Taylor knows, even though you're supposedly the one running the department. That in itself speaks volumes."

Mark's hand was still on my forearm, now gripping it tightly enough to stop me from getting up, marching over to Gable, and causing him serious bodily harm. Barely able to look at the man, I gulped down my anger so I could speak. "Do you have any idea how many objects I'm handling? Hundreds. Often we don't know something's misplaced until we're looking for it when we need to set up the preview. But these things always reappear—always."

Chloe poked me in the other arm and leaned in close to me, peering directly into my eyes. "We all know you're right— but don't make this worse for yourself," she whispered.

Now I was gulping down mounting hysteria. But Chloe was right, so I nodded weakly at her and tried to calm down. Much to my embarrassment, tears were forming, blurring my vision. I'd be damned before I let myself cry in front of everyone. But a tear finally ran down my cheek, and with that, Gable achieved what he wanted: my complete humiliation.

"Just take a deep breath, honey," said Chloe quietly.

Gable banged his fist down again, and the platters jumped once more. "Enough, everyone. Here's what's going to happen. Taylor, I want a list of the missing pieces with detailed descriptions on my desk before you leave tonight. Helen, I want the list typed up and circulated among the staff first thing tomorrow morning. And Miss Blythe, I hold you and you alone directly responsible for those missing pieces. I want them on my desk before the end of Friday. If they're not, you'll be dealt with accordingly." He cocked a menacing eyebrow at me.

It was already Tuesday afternoon.

CHAPTER 8

The next morning, I found a piece of fuchsia-coloured paper thrust through one of the palm fronds of a massive Victorian silverplate camel and palm tree epergne (or centrepiece) someone had deposited on my desk. Couldn't Taylor have just set the note on top of the piles of paper on my desk or put it on my chair? Both the epergne and the paper were illuminated by a shaft of sunlight that slanted in through the window. I gingerly removed the piece of paper. Fortunately, all the words were still intact. "MISING PIECES REPORT," the title screamed.

"More like missing *letter*," I said to the empty room. I read aloud the rest of what promised to be one of Taylor's literary masterpieces.

"'Dear Colleagues, Please keep an eye out for: 1) Massive Dresden-style sheppard and sheppardess figural group, two feet high. The sheppard has a broken arm that's been stuck back on, but its been repaired badly. She has a puffy dress on. There's also a fat sheep sleeping on the ground among lots of flowers. 2) A Poirot figurine, about eight inches high, wearing a black-and-white clown costume. 3) A parrot figurine with a long tail and green plumage, about a foot high. 4) A figurine of a lady in a powdered wig whose playing a harp, nine inches tall. 5) A Royal Doulton German sheppard figurine, six inches tall. If you find these, please notify Taylor at extension 666 (make that extension 366, actually).'"

The second I finished, Taylor strolled in, attired in her usual funereal garb. I guess I must have looked intimidating enough, for she shrank a bit when she saw me. Peeved by her stubborn refusal to learn how to spell properly and her strangely inappropriate irreverence, I waved the memo in her face. "You gave this to Helen to type, right?"

Looking at me blankly, Taylor nodded.

"I can't believe she'd leave in your errors! What's wrong with people in this place? *Sheppard* is the name of a major Toronto street you may have heard of, and the spelling of it isn't used when referring to those—either human or canine—who herd sheep. Don't even get me started on *Poirot*. And what's with this 'extension 666' nonsense? Don't you get how serious this situation is?"

Without looking at me, Taylor chomped on her gum and shrugged, which was more of a response than I'd expected, considering my angry tone. She sat down in front of her computer and turned it on.

Just then, Sally swept into the room, looking statuesque in a magnificent cherry-coloured suit and pumps to match. She patted me lightly on the shoulder. "I got that ridiculous, illiterate memo, and I just wanted you to know I'm keeping an eye out for the pieces." She then giggled. "Hey, can I ask what a Poirot figurine is? Not Hercule Poirot?"

I sighed and looked at the ceiling. "Taylor means the sad clown Pierrot, not the fictional Belgian detective."

"I thought it must have been something like that. Any theories about where the stuff might be?" She glanced suspiciously at Taylor, who was looking down, apparently engrossed in her own shoes.

"I haven't the foggiest. I just know that Gable will give me the sack if they don't turn up by the end of the week, since they have to be out for the preview before Saturday. He's in a sacking kind of mood, as he made abundantly clear yesterday."

"Perhaps that assistant of yours might make herself useful for a change and have a look around for you." She looked at Taylor with distaste, her upper lip slightly curled. But knowing Taylor, she wasn't about to turn around and give Sally the satisfaction of reacting to the insult.

What amazed me about Sally was how she always spoke as though Taylor weren't in the room. She didn't give a damn what she said. In turn, Taylor went about her business—she moved porcelain teapots and vases out of the way, shuffled papers, and became absorbed in replying to what I could only assume were personal emails, since she chuckled softly as she typed. Naturally, I imagined she was making disparaging remarks about me to her friends, or possibly to a colleague, though I couldn't see that she was particularly friendly with anyone at work.

"I think Taylor's busy catching up on important correspondence today." I tried to say this with a straight face but couldn't help smirking.

"Ha! Naturally. Well, I'll have a look around myself, then." Sally turned on her scarlet heel and strode out of the room.

"Wait—Sally!" I ran after her and caught up with her halfway down the hall. "Why don't we have lunch with Chloe today? I'm feeling unnerved and could really use the company. At the usual place?"

"Great idea. Come and get me when you're ready."

I returned to the cataloguing room and to Taylor, who was busy pretending I wasn't standing there looking over her shoulder as she typed. I took a deep breath. We were alone, so now was the time to get it over with. "Taylor, we need to talk."

Hunched over like an old woman, she swivelled around in her chair and looked up at me with those mysterious eyes of hers. She did look as if she'd had a sleepless night, but I could only speculate why, since she'd never revealed anything to me about her personal life and I'd never asked. Her complexion was sallow, and dark circles ringed her eyes. "Okay, well, say whatever you're gonna." She looked as if she'd just swallowed something bitter.

I sighed. I couldn't imagine this going well. "First of all, I apologize for snapping at you just now. But I found your memo impaled on the epergne, and I had to detach it very carefully before I could even read it. Not exactly impressive. I mean, was that really necessary? And I get so upset about your inability to spell. I know you think it's all nitpickery, but spelling correctly is important. You make sloppy errors, which Helen apparently doesn't even bother to correct, and you never look anything up. You haven't even taken the plastic wrap off that dictionary I bought you last Christmas. Why don't you at least ask me when you're not sure how to spell something?" I knew I sounded like the most persnickety schoolmarm ever, but it was hard to stop myself now that I'd started; I'd already gained so much momentum. "And—"

"I know." Her voice was a whine. She started fidgeting with her hair and swivelling back and forth in her chair.

"But more importantly, I'm *very* upset—livid, in fact—that you didn't bring the matter of the missing porcelain to me directly. There was no need to go to Gable first. We could have found the pieces without his ever knowing they were missing. Don't you agree? You used to notify just me when you couldn't find certain things. It was never a big deal, and we always found them. Why didn't you do it this time?"

Taylor nodded absently and turned her tired, worn face toward the ceiling. Clearly, I was boring her. As if to drive the point home, she yawned. Our talk had turned into a lecture, not the conversation it should have been. I felt it was all my fault, but I didn't know how to make it anything other than what it was.

"When did you notice them missing?"

"Yesterday." Although she replied, she was shutting me out even more, doodling on a pad of paper, scribbling stars and cubes as she continued to look up.

"And you went to Gable immediately?"

Taylor sighed as if I were hopelessly thick and finally turned to look at me. "No, I didn't *go* to Gable. He saw me looking upset after we'd been looking for the Dresden thing, and he cornered me. That's when he got it out of me. You know how he is—he digs and digs. And I was gonna tell you about the other four pieces."

"Just when were you planning to do it? The preview starts Saturday, and it's already Wednesday."

"I know, I know. It was hard enough telling you about the first one. I didn't even know how to tell you about the rest. You've been in such a crappy mood lately." To my astonishment, she looked as if she was going to cry. Her lower lip quivered, and the tears began to well up. What a strange bird she was; I couldn't for the life of me figure her out. Her tears just irritated me; she wasn't the one who had reason to cry.

"Maybe I'm stating the obvious, but there's a lot riding on finding these pieces, Taylor. My job, for example. In case you hadn't noticed, Gable's keen to boot me out of this place, and I don't know what I'll do if he does. I live alone. I don't have parents to help me out. You'll remember they died a year ago. The anniversary of their deaths was yesterday."

Taylor looked at me gloomily. "I'm so sorry ..."

"Even if they were still here, they wouldn't be able to support me. Besides, I'm middle-aged and quite capable of looking after myself—at least I have been until now. I'm also an only child. I have no one. And I don't need to tell you that getting another job in this field is next to impossible, given how small our industry is in Canada."

By now, the tears were rolling freely down Taylor's cheeks. She slumped forward on the desk and made muffled sobbing sounds into her sleeve. But I had more to say and felt powerless to stop the diatribe I was subjecting her to.

"I need you to do something," I said.

After a few moments, she managed to look up at me with bloodshot eyes and nod. She blubbered a few words through stifled sobs, but I couldn't make them out.

"What I need you to do is look for the goddamn porcelain with me. Today is *not* the day to chat about your wicked boss with your buddies on email. And it's not the day to circulate any more stupid memos like the one you stuck on the epergne. Today is the day we scour this building from top to bottom until we find the missing porcelain. Am I making myself clear? I need you to care about this, Taylor. For once, I need you to be on my side and working with me—not smirking at me behind my back. I won't tolerate your undermining me."

She nodded as the tears streamed down. "Okay." She snuffled and blew her nose. "I'm with you. I'll help. I really will." I'd never seen a pleading look in her eyes before, and I knew she was sincere. It was the first time I'd ever seen her so transparent and emotionally raw.

My tone immediately softened. "Thank you. Look, I'm sorry—I know I've been hard on you. But this has been a trying time for me as well. I have a lot at stake here."

Just when I thought she might be recovering, she shuddered and said, "But the porcelain's not here. I know it's not." She put her head down on the desk again, nestling it in the crook of her arm, and began shaking and sobbing.

I laid my hand on her shoulder, trying to soothe her. "Good grief, Taylor. What makes you say that?"

But she wouldn't stop crying.

CHAPTER 9

L unch was a casual affair a few blocks away at A Step Back in Time. The name, spelled out in elegant script on a neon sign, made the place sound more like an antiques shop than a mid-twentieth-century diner. The decor probably hadn't changed since the place opened in 1963. Near the window, three of us crammed into a tiny booth intended for two; Chloe and I squished together opposite Sally. We were at home with the dingy orange vinyl banquettes and the beige arborite tables. Rockabilly chugged along in the background as we looked over the laminated menus we'd pulled out from behind a big glass jar of sugar. In her beautifully tailored suit, which she was wearing for an appraisal she'd be doing later that afternoon, Sally seemed misplaced among all the construction workers and students. But in the jeans and hoodies Chloe and I wore for setting up the preview displays, we blended right in with the lunchtime crowd.

Frank, our burly, charmless waiter with a scraggly walrus moustache, swooped by our table to take our order, which was our usual greasy treat: three grilled cheese sandwiches with fries, and to wash it all down, strong coffee for Sally and me and weak, milky tea for Chloe.

I was quiet, exhausted from the morning's emotional confrontation with Taylor. Sally, however, was in a caustic mood.

"So what did the little wench have to say for herself? Did you have it out with her?" she asked.

It stung to hear Sally call her a wench. During the walk to the diner, while Sally and Chloe had been talking, I'd been thinking about Taylor; I was consumed with guilt about the harshness of my lecture and the tears I'd caused. I'd grown sympathetic toward her since she was obviously suffering from the loss of the porcelain too. But it was becoming increasingly clear that she wasn't upset just from being bawled out; there was more to it than that. And irritating as she was, I was her superior at Gable & Co., so I needed to try harder. I vowed to be nicer to her from now on and to try to create a better working relationship. Now I found myself sticking up for her. "She didn't take the stuff, Sally."

"What?" The single word was sharp and high pitched, as if I'd pinched her. She gaped at me.

"No. It wasn't Taylor. What possible motive would she have? Besides, she's way too upset, so I'm dead certain it wasn't her. You can't fake that sort of emotion—not unless you're an incredibly gifted actress, which I doubt she is. But she must know who did take it because this morning she insisted it was gone for good. She's too afraid to tell me how she knows, though. I'm surprised she hasn't drowned in that puddle she's created. She's been crying like there's no tomorrow, and I can't get a word out of her."

Chloe smiled beatifically. "Oh, what a relief!"

I was floored. Sally and I exchanged bewildered glances across the table. "What's a relief? Can you explain why you just said that?" I said, utterly failing to conceal my crankiness.

Chloe flushed slightly and hesitated before answering. "Oh … I just mean that maybe you guys won't be fighting anymore now that you know for sure she's not a thief. I mean, now you can work together to find the missing pieces. Harmony has been restored, right?" She looked at me with bright eyes and smiled reassuringly, but I felt anything but reassured. Mostly, I just felt an uncomfortable tension tightening like a rubber band across my forehead as a headache announced itself.

"Well, yes …" I was struggling to come around to Chloe's way of thinking. "Trust you to find a kernel of optimism in this nightmare. I guess that's why we're such good friends—you balance my negativity, and God knows I need all the help I can get. Still, the problem isn't exactly solved, is it? I've got to find a way of getting Taylor to tell me what she knows. And I've still got to find the goods or Gable will have my head."

"On a silver platter, no less," said Sally with a sly smile.

Chloe laughed. "How very appropriate, considering how many silver platters there are where we work," she said without a trace of sarcasm. Sally looked bemused.

"No kidding." I didn't find any of this very funny, and I smirked uncomfortably at the gallows humour.

A gloomy silence swept over our table. Because the throbbing in my head was growing stronger by the second, I felt desperate for a breath of cool, fresh November air. The urge was becoming so overpowering that I wanted to bolt from the restaurant. But just then, Frank plopped down before us appetizing plates of limp fries and oozing grilled cheese sandwiches, garnished with soggy dill pickles. Gradually, as we began to eat, the dark mood dissolved. And after I'd sipped some coffee, the throbbing in my head began to subside a little.

"Ketchup, anyone?" I waved the bottle enticingly at the others.

"Don't mind if I do," said Sally, snatching it from me. "So what happens now? What are you going to do?" She blanketed her french fries with a thick red layer.

"Damned if I know. Got any suggestions?"

"Are you sure you've looked everywhere?" said Chloe.

It was stating the obvious, which always made me irritable, but I tried to keep the sharp edge out of my voice. "Of course, Chloe. I've combed all the cupboards and display cases in the building."

"But have you checked unexpected places? For all you know, someone might have dumped the missing pieces behind boxes or under furniture. There are all sorts of nooks and crannies where they might be. What about the basement?"

She had a point. I hadn't yet descended to the bowels of the building because I didn't really feel up to the excitement of another ghostly encounter with Constance. With chasing down lost porcelain, my life was stressful enough as it was. And unless it was found, Gable would divest me of a position I held dear, and consequently I'd have to empty my savings account. I didn't need another supernatural experience with that flighty flibbertigibbet to push me completely over the edge.

"You're right, Chloe. I guess searching the basement will be next. I ... um ... haven't been down there much because of the ghost." I gulped some coffee listlessly and tried to smile.

Chloe nodded and looked at me in a knowing but kindly way. She patted my hand. "I thought you might be reluctant. I don't blame you. How's your ghost, anyway? You haven't said a word about her lately."

"Yes, what's going on with that?" said Sally, her eyes shining with curiosity.

I hesitated. "Well, Gable really spooked me, if you'll pardon the expression, into not talking about it."

"Oh, right. He thinks it'll make you look like a nutcase," said Sally.

"I don't like to admit it, but he's right. You've noticed how people have been making a point of ignoring me."

Sally looked as if she was about to say something, but her eyes shifted from mine as something caught her attention. Chloe and I both turned around to look.

Just then, Brian Gable III pushed the door open, bringing with him a cold gust of wind. A newspaper from a neighbouring table flew up through the air and scattered itself messily across the floor.

Sally looked at him and said under her breath, "Crikey, look who's here."

"Oh God," I said.

To shield her face, Chloe held up a bodice-ripping novel that a previous diner had abandoned at our table. She was trying to muffle a giggle. Sally and I bowed our heads toward what was left of our meals, as though the untidy crusts of bread and the ketchup-laden french fries could somehow rescue us from being forced to acknowledge or speak to Gable. But we needn't have worried. Oblivious to us, he lumbered past in his worn brown leather jacket and faded jeans. Out of the corner of my eye, I noticed the same ugly orange-and-white T-shirt he'd worn the day before, and I caught a whiff of the foul odour of sweat.

Gable landed heavily in a booth at the very back of the diner. His thin, wiry reddish-brown hair had been tossed about by the wind and was sticking out at all angles. A yellow maple leaf had threaded its way into his hair, springing up as if it were growing right out of his scalp. He looked uncharacteristically pale, and his hand trembled as he held up an empty tumbler left behind by the last customer and waved it wildly in Frank's direction. Chloe and I exchanged concerned glances, and Sally turned around and looked furtively at him, but he seemed not to see us and wanted only to get Frank's attention.

"I need some water here! For God's sake—could I get some service for a change? Water!" His speech was slurred.

"He's drunk!" I whispered.

All conversations came to an abrupt halt, and everyone in the place was now gawking at him. But with those glassy eyes, Gable wasn't looking back at anyone. For a moment I had the wild thought that he didn't even know where he was and was talking to invisible beings or to voices in his head. Maybe he was psychotic, not drunk. "Service, goddammit!" he said weakly, shaking his fist.

"Bloody hell, what's up with him?" said Sally. "I mean, he usually looks like a wreck—I'm used to that—but I've never seen him like this before, or not since the last Christmas party." Her lip curled slightly.

Chloe looked on with a kind of worried curiosity. "What'll we do?"

"Um, maybe we should go over there? Just to see if he's all right?" I said, and we all looked down at what remained of lunch.

But Frank, anxious to shut up a noisy, embarrassing customer, was making a beeline for Gable with a large tumbler of water in his hand. He set it down on the table. "What'll it be, buddy?"

"Double cheeseburger—with fries. Strawberry milkshake," said Gable.

"Good man. Be back in a jiffy." Frank smiled at Gable but then looked at us nervously, raising his eyebrows. The very second he turned his back, Gable slumped to the side and tumbled onto the floor like a rag doll. Several diners at neighbouring tables emitted a collective gasp.

While Sally prattled on about how disgusting it was that Gable was drunk in the middle of the day and Chloe nodded, a sense of alarm gripped me. In all the years I'd known Gable, I'd never seen him drunk at work (only at company parties). Sure, he'd been known to knock back a whisky before ascending the podium on auction night, but never was he inebriated. Something else was going on, though exactly what, I didn't know. I sprang to my feet but was otherwise paralyzed: it was as if the soles of my shoes were glued to the floor and I was unable to move toward the sprawling figure. Gable lay face-down, one arm thrown out in front of him as though he were reaching, his head resting in the crook of the other arm. One leg was straight while the other rested up against the booth, the knee bent. His dishevelled hair and the maple leaf covered most of his face. He mumbled incoherently, punctuating his speech with periodic moans.

I was sick of Sally's useless chatter, and we needed to do something fast. I realized I'd left my cellphone back at the office. "Call 911!" I finally shouted to the crowd.

A few feet away from me, a tiny woman wearing bright red lipstick squealed. About a dozen people dutifully pulled out their cell phones and began dialing. "Just one of you," shouted the woman.

They all put their phones back in their pockets except for one man with a loud baritone voice and a stern, take-charge demeanour. His voice floated above the din as he called in the emergency. "Yes, some sort of intoxication," he said. "Looks really bad."

A small cluster of people were standing around and murmuring, surrounding Gable and looking at him as though he were not so much a human being but a curious biological specimen that was under discussion. Several people did ask him if he was all right, but he simply continued mumbling. A nervous-looking waitress kneeled down to wipe Gable's forehead and talk soothingly to him, and a man covered him with his coat, tucking it around him.

A sad-eyed, towheaded little boy was peering out from behind a very tall woman. "Mummy, what happened to the man?" he said with the utmost gravity.

She draped her arm over his shoulder. "Well, I don't really know, honey. But he'll be just fine, I'm sure!" She spoke in that jocular way people adopt when they're frightened themselves but trying to be reassuring. Her eyes darted anxiously from Gable to her son and then to me. I shrugged helplessly.

Help was on its way, and not knowing how I could possibly make myself useful, I sat back down in our booth.

"Hmm, apparently no doctors in this crowd. Do you think he'll die?" asked Sally.

"Die?" A chill ripped right through me, leaving numbness in its wake.

"Let's face it—he's always been a heart attack waiting to happen."

Chloe looked like the screamer on my shattered mug: the fingers of both hands were splayed across her cheeks and her mouth formed an O shape. "Sally! That's a terrible thing to say.

Besides, he's just drunk." She looked at me and tugged at my sleeve, anxious to gain a supporter. "Don't you think that's a terrible thing to say at a time like this?"

All I could do was shrug and say, "I suppose."

Sally cocked her thumb at Gable's corpulent form. "This is a man who eats doughnuts three times a day and either cheeseburgers or hot dogs for breakfast and lunch. I wouldn't be surprised if he's reached the end of the fast-food highway, and you shouldn't be either, Chloe."

"It's hardly the time to talk about dying." Chloe was clenching her fists and quivering, while Sally merely looked at her, her eyes glinting with amusement.

I glanced over at Gable. Feeling slightly queasy at both the conversation and the sight of his limp, pale body, I quickly looked away. My head was now throbbing uncontrollably, as if I'd never had the coffee, and I started massaging my temples. "Sally, Chloe, please ..."

"What?" said Sally. She really didn't have a clue.

Before Chloe could continue being outraged, the tiny woman with the bright red lipstick briskly approached our table.

"Uh-oh. Here comes trouble. I guarantee it," said Sally.

We all stood up, and the woman was upon us immediately. She looked up at Sally, resentment flashing in her eyes. "Excuse me, ladies," she said, her voice booming. "My name's Alice, and I couldn't help but overhear you."

"Yes?" I said in a gruff, impatient way.

Alice was an odd duck. Her lipstick, frosted blue eye shadow, and beehive hairdo were too boldly theatrical for her delicate features, and her loose emerald-green satin dress with the ruffled collar overwhelmed her petite figure. She'd doused herself with a warm, musky fragrance that was already constricting my airways. She was standing too close to me for comfort, and I'm sure she would have squeezed herself into our booth the moment we made the slightest overture of friendliness.

Alice reached out to Chloe, grabbing her arm with a clawlike hand and looking at each of us in turn, her eyes popping. "Do I understand this correctly? You actually *know* that man? I thought almost certainly he was a homeless person."

Chloe spoke quietly and looked down at the floor. "He's the owner of a major auction house, Gable's. Maybe you're familiar with it—it's just down the street. His name is Brian Gable III, and he's our boss." She looked uneasily at Alice's hand, which still clutched her arm. I could tell she wanted to shake the woman off but was too polite to do so.

"Really? You must be joking! But he looks like an alcoholic wreck! So what do you think happened to him?" Alice's eyes sparkled too much for my liking.

"God only knows. He seemed all right this morning when I came into work," said Sally. "Well, as all right as he ever is, if you know what I mean."

Our nosy new friend seized on Sally's remark with alacrity. "I can't say I do. Just what do you mean by that, I wonder?"

She withdrew her hand from Chloe's arm and stepped back, crossing her arms and narrowing her eyes at Sally.

"It's complicated." Sally waved dismissively. "You wouldn't understand."

Alice looked at her and harrumphed. "You never know. I just might." Then she looked at all three of us, her eyes moving from one face to another. "Well, I must say you ladies are taking this remarkably well. You're all so calm. I'd be having a panic attack if it were *my* boss lying there on the floor, quite possibly dead."

"Can't you hear him mumbling? He's not dead," I said, crossing my arms in front of me. I just wanted this impossible woman to get herself and her perfume as far away from me as possible.

"Not yet, anyway," she said.

No one reacted. Seeming to sense that no delectable tidbits of information were coming her way, Alice looked a tad disappointed and wandered off to join the cluster of gawkers gathered around Gable, who remained sprawled on the floor.

A cloud of Alice's perfume hung in the air. Sally started coughing, and her eyes teared up. "Christ, that was enough to give me an asthma attack. Thanks a lot, Alice. Well, I better get out of here before I choke to death. And I should really get back to the office, grab my stuff, and hit the road. I promised Grace Crumbworthy I'd be there at two for the appraisal."

Chloe put her hands on her hips. "But what about Gable? Don't you care what happens to him?" she said, her voice rising.

"What about him? Standing around like the rest of these people isn't going to do him any good. Frankly, I don't really care to do much of anything anyway. Besides, Miss Crumbworthy's waiting." She shrugged and fumbled through her purse for her wallet.

I could see the colour rising in Chloe's face, and she was clenching her fists again. Gasping slightly to get her breath, she said, "Sally, I can't believe your callousness. He really *could* be dying, for all you know!"

"Ha! We should all be so lucky."

I sighed and looked at the ceiling. I could tell by the defiant spark in Sally's eyes that she wasn't finished—not by a long shot.

"Come off it, Chloe," she said. "Don't be such a hypocrite. It's not as though you'd miss the old sod any more than the rest of us would. What's he ever done for you, anyway? I mean, apart from making you feel useless and insignificant. What's he ever done for any of us?"

But Sally was wasting her breath, for Chloe's attention had been lured away by the thrilling sight of muscular paramedics bursting into the diner. They went straight to Gable and began checking his vital signs. A few seconds later, some firemen and the police arrived.

"Anyone know this guy?" asked one of the paramedics, turning around to scan the crowd. He was a tall man with high Slavic cheekbones and light blue eyes.

"He's my boss!" called Chloe, who waved frantically. I was astonished to see her elbowing people aside in her rush to speak with him. She chattered on and on, gesturing dramatically as she filled him in on the details of what we'd witnessed. It was all so unlike her, and I wondered what had come over her. Sally looked at me knowingly and winked; Chloe was doing just fine and didn't need our help, and Gable would be taken care of. Two policemen then came in and began loudly asking questions, and the din became unbearable. Anxious to escape the pandemonium swirling around us, we tossed a few dollars on the table, waved at Frank, eased into our coats, and slipped away into the crowded street.

CHAPTER 10

George needed to know what had happened, since I assumed he must have been in charge in Gable's absence; I wasn't sure who else would be. I knocked tentatively at his office door. Was it the disturbing scene I'd just witnessed that was making my pulse quicken or something else? I couldn't really tell.

When George first opened the door, he peered down at me, grinning broadly, but then his face fell. "What is it? What's happened?"

I stood by the door and related the whole story of Gable's collapse as calmly as I could.

As the news sank in, George looked grave. "When we find out which hospital he's been taken to, I'll go visit and see what I can find out."

"Okay." I turned to leave.

"Oh, Virginia …" he said softly.

My heart lurched. I glanced back at him, trying not to seem too eager.

He paused as if hunting for the right words. "Thank you for telling me all this."

That was it? He'd said so little, but I was sure he wanted to say something more. Seeing his dark brown eyes searching my face, I felt as flustered as I had when he'd smiled so brightly at me during the disastrous staff meeting. "Um—no problem. I mean, you're welcome. I should get back to work."

Staring at me, he nodded and lingered at the door before quietly closing it. I dashed away, wondering what exactly was going through his head. For an entire year he'd mostly ignored me and I'd done likewise to him, and now this? Not that I minded those looks of his. Oh no, not in the least. It was flattering to be noticed for a change. But more than that, George possessed a certain quality I was drawn to that my muddled brain was struggling to define in words. Although I barely knew the man, I felt a powerful pull toward him. That he was tall and slender and wore well-tailored suits and unusual but tasteful ties was an attractive bonus. But maybe it was time to stop analyzing the situation and simply start enjoying the attention. I smiled to myself as I set up the auction preview. But as the afternoon wore on, I began to go about my task listlessly, for the whole episode with Brian Gable III had both numbed me and sapped my strength, and coffee wasn't much help. I let Taylor haul out all the items while I dusted the porcelain, cleaned the glass, polished the silver, attached tags with lot numbers to the pieces, and placed them in display cases. Fussing over the arrangement of the pieces kept me from thinking too much.

Chloe wandered into the upstairs gallery about three hours after Sally and I got back from lunch. She looked worn as she explained that she told the paramedics and policemen everything she'd seen and then rode with Gable in the ambulance to ER, talking to him the whole while—not that he responded with anything apart from moaning. Then she waited with him, answering the admitting clerk's questions. I told her George wanted to know where Gable had been admitted. As she went off to tell him, I couldn't help but smile at how helpful she'd been. I needed to be more like her.

That evening, I stayed at home, feeling at loose ends. It was hard to settle down to anything in particular, but I needed to distract myself. During the day I'd managed to keep the disturbing images at bay, but now they kept popping into my head: Taylor's shaking and sobbing and worse, Gable's inert, flabby body. I wanted so badly to tell Mom and Dad about the awful things I'd witnessed; they would have given me coffee and cookies and soothed my troubled soul. Knowing I couldn't speak to them, I felt very alone and desperate to escape into another world, but the classic movie channel offerings failed to entice me.

There on my kitchen table, among all the glossy coffee-table books about antiques, was Constance's battered diary. Since reading her last entry about the delirious kiss in the conservatory, I'd felt resentful toward her and had been snubbing her—though it seemed ludicrous to snub a ghost. For the last couple of days, I hadn't read a word she'd written. Who was she to think she could leave me hanging about the kiss?

But why was I getting so angry? Perhaps it was because she made such a big production of her comings and goings, wailing piteously in the dark and dazzling me with light shows before she went on her way. It was all so ridiculous. But I had to assume I'd eventually glean something of value from Constance's accounts of her love life. Why else would she have given me the book in the first place? It must have contained something beyond sheer entertainment, vicarious thrills, and frustratingly incomplete diary entries. I resigned myself: I had to continue reading. With a cup of coffee in hand, I settled into my cozy plaid sofa, blew some dust off the diary, and opened it to where I'd left off.

April 27, 1928

Good gracious (as Mama would say)! I've spent every single night for the past two weeks out dancing with Freddy. Foxtrot, Charleston, Black Bottom—I've danced them all, plus a few I'd never even heard of before. Freddy's a superb dancer and he's been teaching me. We fall all over ourselves laughing every time I flub a step, which happens absurdly often. He's also been introducing me to all sorts of lovely artistic people and making me stay out until the wee hours of the morning. Not that it's such a dreadful hardship—I really don't mind a bit! Mama, however, is simply beside herself; she seems to vibrate with rage at the very mention of Freddy's name. Every morning over tea and crumpets, she complains that I ought to stop running with "the wrong crowd," as she calls Freddy's musician friends. As you can imagine, I groan every time she trots out that tired old phrase. And this morning she called Freddy "louche"! Can you imagine? Naturally, I was insulted and told her so. I also said she was being much too theatrical about the whole thing, but she gave me a warning look and said, "You'll come to serious harm if you insist on being wayward, Constance Virginia Rose Pendleton."

Of course, she'd feel very differently if she were to meet darling Freddy. But she won't consent to this. Mysteriously, Papa also resists. It's as if they think they already know everything they need to about the poor fellow. If she only gave him half a chance, Mama would be as besotted with him as I am, utterly incapable of resisting his charms. He has that effect on women, you see—even ancient, hopelessly stuffy ones like Mama. But because she's never even met him, I'm stuck with the job of trying to explain why she musn't be alarmed by any of those nasty rumours she's no doubt already heard. I've told her a thousand times: the Alderdices are a very respectable family, and Freddy does them proud. Has there ever been a time when he hasn't displayed the most impeccable manners? (That night of billing and cooing in the conservatory would count as an exception, but Mama needn't know about that.)

Perhaps she objects to the fact that Freddy has no profession, or at least not in the conventional sense that older people like her mean. Young men are all expected to be doctors, lawyers, accountants, or bankers these days—it's all so terribly dull! If Freddy were something of that sort, no doubt Mama would be thrilled to make his acquaintance and would automatically grant him her seal of approval. But a musician—and a jazz pianist who's been to New Orleans at that—well, she takes a dim view of that and simply has no time for it, no matter how respectable the Alderdice family is. As far as she's concerned, the jazz world is the devil's playground, and Freddy and his ilk are going straight to hell. He's not even a quarter as bad as she makes him out to be. And she just doesn't understand that he's not like regular people—he's an artist. He could never go to an office job every day, and why should he? It's so stifling and unimaginative, and it would be utterly soul destroying for him.

But never mind—Freddy and I are doing just fine without Mama's approval, thank you very much. Before I met him, I never even knew I could be so deliriously happy. Being with Freddy is just like having that dizzy feeling you get when a glass of champagne starts making your head spin—except it's a thousand times better! Colours seem brighter, music more melodic, and people much more pleasant and agreeable than usual. The world takes on the most delightful sheen, a richness beyond my wildest imaginings. But what would I do if this beautiful waking dream ever came to an end? Of course, I musn't even *consider* that possibility. Life without Freddy just doesn't bear thinking about.

If I could, I'd spend every moment with him. This isn't possible of course, and I must face reality, as Mama and Papa are quick to remind me. Now they're saying that since I'm not planning to marry well, I ought to do something practical, and if I'm not interested in becoming a teacher or a nurse, I should take some course of study to secure my future as a secretary. How the thought of spending my days taking dictation from some cigar-smoking stuffed shirt in a musty office thrills me to the core. Never!

Clearly, the only solution is for Freddy to make a name for himself as a jazz musician. Once he does— and I have all the confidence in the world he will—

both of our lives will change dramatically. He's on the cusp of greatness as I write, and I'm about to share in his good fortune. He said as much to me last night, and it's been just over two weeks since we met. I can scarcely bear the excitement of it all! Here's exactly what happened.

We were at another one of Bernice Croft-Pilkington's parties, the third she's invited us to in the past couple of weeks. I admit we've already become most reluctant to attend these affairs; they're excruciatingly dull and full of dreadful old snobs. But like it or not, I seem to have acquired a patina of glamour for Bernice ever since I've been seen in Freddy's company, so she's taken to calling me her "dearest friend" and insisting we come. I also suspect she invites us so she can ogle Freddy all night. Not that I blame the little floozie! But surely she could leave him to me and direct her sultry gaze at other equally charming young men. She's had little enough difficulty finding them before. I'm told there's no need for her to search at all: Mildred says a steady stream of avid volunteers are practically lining up at her front door. I have to wonder what precisely she's dishing out; it must be something extraordinary.

Ah, but I'm being cruel. Once you get past her relentless promiscuity, Bernice is actually quite an amiable person. She greeted Freddy and me very sweetly last night, smiling and embracing us both simultaneously, as if we were her oldest friends instead of merely her latest acquisitions. And before the butler had even taken my opera cape, she'd offered us champagne. Judging from her polite manner and the friendly twinkle in her eye, you wouldn't have known there'd ever been any animosity between us. It was as if that awful business at school—the time she copied my answers from my test paper and got caught—had never happened. Still, I do find it difficult to trust her after all that, which is why I've kept my distance from her until recently. And I suspect her sweetness is but a thin veneer. I'm not even sure what it might be covering—perhaps nothing of much substance. I must ask Freddy what he thinks.

After handing me a glass of champagne, Bernice said, "My, you're looking well!" I wasn't sure if she was directing the compliment to me or to Freddy, since her clear blue eyes flitted back and forth— most uneasily, I might add—between us. I couldn't help but notice she was wearing a silk dress of the most luscious coral shade, complemented by a sky-blue sash and a long string of beads of the same colour. Her silk shoes with their precious little bows had been dyed coral to match her dress. I have to admit, Bernice has exquisite taste.

"What a perfectly darling dress! Quite the thing with your blonde curls too." I stopped myself right then and there; she hardly needed more people gushing over her.

"Thank you, my dear!" she said. Her curls bounced with her excitement. "I had the dress specially made for the season." Well, of course she had, and no doubt it came from Paris. Her eyes were fixed on Freddy, who was vigorously brushing off his suit. "Really, Freddy, you're not in the least bit dusty, you know."

"I regret that I'm somewhat compulsive about keeping myself free of lint, Miss Croft-Pilkington," he replied, without returning her gaze. Then he looked at me. "Come along, Constance. Let's sit by the fire and warm ourselves. It's still rather inclement for April, and though you don't complain, I can see you're thoroughly chilled. If you'll excuse us?" He gave Bernice a tight smile. In return, she offered him a little pout of disappointment.

When we were some distance away, I leaned toward Freddy and whispered, "Really, Freddy, you ought to be a little nicer to Bernice."

He glowered at me. "That beastly old creature?"

I couldn't help but laugh out loud. "*Old?* Why she's the same age I am!"

"Surely not! Haven't you noticed the crow's feet? That's what comes of all her fast living."

"Freddy!" I said in a hushed voice.

Steering me by the elbow, he ushered me past various groups of people absorbed in animated conversation and toward the fireplace. I said, "And you know, of course, I'm not the least bit chilled."

"Yes, I realize that, my darling, but I couldn't stand there another moment listening to you chattering away with boring Bernice."

"Chattering away? Why, I scarcely had time to say hello!" I said, laughing.

"Bernice Croft-Pilkington. How did she manage to get such a ridiculous name? You know, I can't possibly imagine what all those poor saps see in her, and I dare not speculate how she manages to reel them in. But enough about her. I'd much rather be alone with you, as we have important matters to discuss."

I felt the most delicious little thrill run through me. We sat down on Bernice's straight-backed settee, upholstered in dingy ecru velvet. Her furniture was not just terribly out of date but uncomfortable as well. The settee lacked proper cushions to soften the insult of its hardness and may as well have been a wrought iron park bench. Only being able to snuggle into Freddy made sitting there bearable.

"Have you forgotten we're at a party, Freddy? It's quite impossible to be alone."

"That's what you think. Have you considered the possibility that Bernice, like Mildred, might have a pleasant conservatory or other secluded room where we could pass an hour or two unobserved?" The slight smile that had been playing mischievously about his thin lips widened into the most devilish grin.

"You brute! You're absolutely shocking!" I whispered. I shoved Freddy away, barely managing to hold back a smile.

He grinned at me playfully, and as thoughts of our passionate embrace in Mildred's conservatory flooded my fevered brain, I become light-headed with emotion. But unlike a swooning Victorian heroine, I was able to recover my equilibrium quickly, which was fortunate indeed since we now had company.

Lydia, who was wearing an unremarkable striped beige and dove-grey dress and a conservative string of pearls, sat down in one of the two armchairs that matched the horrid settee. With her drab, ill-fitting frock and light brown hair, she blended right in with the furniture. The only colourful thing about her was her eyes, which were a lively shade of green. A drunken fellow was slumped over and snoring loudly in the matching chair, a top hat perched precariously on his head.

"Hello, Lydia!" I said much too enthusiastically. I'd felt so guilty about her lately. Since I'd been seeing Freddy, my friendship with her had fallen by the wayside. In all honesty, I'd been neglecting her terribly. Whereas I used to telephone her daily, we hadn't spoken a word now for several days. The one time she called me, I'd been far too busy with Freddy to have any sort of real conversation with her. From the forlorn way she was looking at me, I could tell she was probably saddened by my recent behaviour. But now I was prepared to turn myself inside out to rectify the situation.

"How have you been, Constance? I haven't seen much of you lately." She said it mildly, as though the last thing she wished to do was offend. However, her point wasn't lost on me.

"I'm afraid I've been awfully scarce, and I do apologize for that. As you're aware, there's been a new development." I nodded at the new development beside me, who smiled tightly at Lydia and repeated his performance of brushing off his suit.

"Ah yes, of course." She looked at me knowingly and offered a sly wink.

"Lydia, you really must come to tea next Saturday. I have so much to tell you, and Mama and Papa would be absolutely bereft if you couldn't make it. You know how they dote on you so."

Lydia's face perked up, her eyes sparkling, and she nodded. "Oh yes, I'd love to come. I'd be delighted!"

Just when I was starting to feel better about the poor girl, Freddy swiftly delivered an elbow to my ribs and flashed me a warning smile. "Have you forgotten, darling? We have a prior engagement this Saturday." He looked at me uneasily, silently prompting me; he couldn't invent a plausible excuse quickly enough, so it fell to me to find one.

I wanted to elbow him right back. And I couldn't bring myself to look at Lydia, so I just stared at the Persian carpet. I felt my face flush slightly and become moist with perspiration. After a moment's hesitation, I said, "Why yes, of course! Good heavens, I'd forgotten. Freddy and I have been invited to my nephew John's birthday party next Saturday." I glanced furtively at her.

"Nephew?" Lydia's little face was pinched.

"John is my eldest brother William's boy. He's turning ten on Saturday, and William and his wife Laura are throwing a party for him." That much was true, though why I expected Lydia would believe I'd attend a children's birthday party when I could be enjoying more sophisticated pleasures was anyone's guess.

"I'd forgotten you even had a nephew, or perhaps I didn't know in the first place—I scarcely know which. Well, that *is* disappointing. I've been looking forward to having tea with you and your family again. It's been so very long."

"Well, we can't very well not attend John's party, I suppose." I was trying not to sound defensive but doing a poor job of it.

"That's right, darling," said Freddy, taking my hand and smiling at me.

Lydia looked crestfallen. I was certain she knew I was lying to her and couldn't fathom how I could be so cruel. She looked back at me, her expression like that of a wounded bird. Without another word, she got up from her chair, cast me another hurt glance, and walked off. I thought I noticed her lower lip trembling.

"Lydia, wait!" But she didn't turn back, and suddenly I was flooded with guilt. Blinking away the tears that rushed to my eyes, I turned to Freddy.

"Let her go. She must know things have changed now that I'm around." Disturbingly, his voice was dismissive.

"Of course she does. But that's hardly the point. I just lied to her!" I squirmed helplessly in the settee, looking from Freddy to Lydia and back again. She'd already moved to a distant corner of Bernice's immense living room, and her back was to us as she greeted a cluster of acquaintances. She then disappeared from view.

"Ah, it's just a little white lie, dearest. It's harmless enough. I suspect she'd do the same if she were in your position—not that it's liable to ever happen. She's such an earnest little milquetoast, isn't she? But I'm sure she'll get over it before you know it, and the two of you will be great friends again." He smiled at me and edged his arm cautiously around my shoulder; he seemed very conscious that others might be watching. Under Freddy's comforting influence, I was already finding it easier to calm down about Lydia.

"I'll make it up to her somehow," I said, my voice quavering. With my handkerchief, I dried a tear that had splashed onto my cheek.

"Don't look so very serious. Of course you will—just not on Saturday. Saturday is our day, Constance, and you know I want to spend every moment of it with you. But before we do, I have something important to say to you." His voice had grown husky, suggesting a degree of passion I hadn't yet glimpsed. It was thrilling to contemplate.

I said, "As you were wondering earlier … do you suppose Bernice really has a conservatory? Oh, I do hate to ask her, as she'll know precisely what it's about. You know what an incorrigible gossip she is."

"Absolutely right, darling—no secret is safe with that woman. Or so I've been told. Perhaps we'll have a wander on our own." Smiling, he got up abruptly and took me by the hand. It was easy enough to explore the massive house without being drawn into conversation with other guests. Apart from Lydia and Mildred—who was down with a nasty cold and couldn't attend the party—we really didn't know any of Bernice's friends. And they were clustered together in tight circles that formed impenetrable barriers to newcomers. Those few who happened to notice us gave us appraising glances and occasionally smiled or nodded as we passed. Our outsider status gave us the freedom to be alone, and for once I was relieved to be nearly friendless.

Freddy and I found a small room at the end of a long hallway. I pushed on the door and it gave way, creaking a little. Peering in, I saw that the room was illuminated only by a frightfully old-fashioned kerosene parlour lamp, the kind with a milk glass shade painted with flowers. While our eyes adjusted to the dark, we stumbled around, and I giggled when I tripped and caught Freddy around the waist. It took me some time to realize we were in the library. To get a better look at the room, Freddy picked up the lamp and carried it with him. The walls were lined with books from floor to ceiling— entire sets of leather-bound encyclopedias and musty old Victorian novels by long-forgotten authors. He seemed to have little interest in the books, passing over them quickly. What intrigued him more were the paintings that hung on the walls. He held the lamp up close to them; they were bold, modern landscapes executed with vigorous brushstrokes, the paint laid on thickly. Each was contained within a low-relief carved wooden frame. Below the largest of them sat an overstuffed, comfortable-looking settee, which in the dim light appeared deep red.

"Ah, finally a soft place to settle," I said with a sigh.

Freddy set the lamp down on the table beside us. We sat down, and he immediately flung his arms around me and kissed me passionately on the lips. I felt one of his hands exploring the small of my back. He pulled back from me a little and stared at me. The golden lamplight softened the contours of his face. "Now for that something I have to tell you," he said in a low voice.

"I'm all ears, Freddy." I was already light-headed from the kiss and thought I'd faint if I had to wait much longer for his news.

He clasped my hands warmly in his. "Father doesn't know this yet, but I've just been hired by Luigi Romanelli and his King Edward Hotel Orchestra."

"Luigi Romanelli? Not the King of Jazz?"

Certain I should be overjoyed for him, I withdrew my hands from his, clapped them, and tried to smile.

"Now darling, don't look so uncertain. Do you have any idea what this means to me? I'll be playing every night with the most renowned jazz orchestra in the country. Now that they've just started broadcasting the performances on the radio, we're destined to become even more famous. And just think—I'll even be touring Europe!"

It was that last bit that made my heart sink, but Freddy, caught up in the full force his enthusiasm, plowed ahead like a speeding locomotive. "This is exactly the sort of break I've needed. Never did I imagine Mr. Romanelli would hire me, but he loved my audition. And here I thought I'd be a complete unknown to my dying day! Aren't you just thrilled, dearest?"

"That's wonderful," I said softly. But I wasn't convinced it was, at least not as far as our blossoming romance was concerned. "Won't you be away rather a lot?" I couldn't help it; tears began welling up in my eyes.

Freddy clasped my hands again and stared intently at me with dark, moist eyes. "Yes, I suppose, and I won't have much choice about that. But Mr. Romanelli also spends a good part of the time at the King Edward—he has to, or the crowds would stop coming. The place relies on him to keep packing them in. But the point is ... you can be part of this too, you know. If you decide you're up to the task, you and I can *really* be together—if you know what I mean, dear girl."

I had no doubt what he meant. I nestled into Freddy's chest, and he embraced me. "Of course I'm up to the task. But tell me, is this a dream? Do you really mean it? I don't know what to say. Everything's happening so fast. We've only just met, and ..." I spoke in soft tones, my voice scarcely above a whisper. If I dared let myself speak at a normal volume, my voice would certainly crack and the floodgates of emotion would open; I'd completely lose what little composure I still possessed. As it was, I felt breathless, and the room seemed to be rapidly spinning out of control as I fell into a swoon. The champagne I'd drunk wasn't to blame.

"Of course I mean it. I've never been so serious in my life," said Freddy, squeezing me tightly.

Wrapped in each other's arms, we sat together quietly, and I allowed myself to envision a dazzling future unfolding before me. I'd be the wife of a prominent musician in the country's top jazz orchestra, and together we'd tour London, Paris, Berlin, and more, savouring the delights each city had to offer. My ordinary life was falling away, and I was stepping into an intoxicating dream that promised a whirlwind of enthralling adventures.

Suddenly, a sniffling sound intruded upon my reverie, bringing me back to earth. "What was that?" I said.

Freddy looked as puzzled as I felt. I looked across the room but at first didn't see anything. Then a slight movement caught my eye: a small figure huddled under a blanket shifted uncomfortably in an armchair. Slowly, the features of a pale oval face, lit by the glow of the kerosene lamp, began to emerge from the darkness. How was it we hadn't noticed her before?

"Lydia?" I said.

CHAPTER 11

I went to bed feeling cranky; once again Constance had stopped short of telling me the whole story. Her wailing and light shows were bad enough, but I was beginning to think this habit of leaving things hanging in her stories was much worse. I was sure something dramatic must have happened after she and Freddy discovered Lydia sniffling in the library and eavesdropping on their conversation. Perhaps Constance, already feeling guilty about abandoning her friend, had tried to soothe her, much to Freddy's consternation, for he clearly despised Lydia. Maybe he'd become enraged at the girl, yelling at her to get out. He and Constance might have had their first quarrel. But she wasn't filling in the blanks. I'd looked ahead and noticed that the next entry began with some sort of joke about being kidnapped, which just made me close the diary in frustration.

When I got up the next morning, I didn't think much more about Constance. I was filled with a sense of foreboding, as George had told me before he left work yesterday that he was on his way to visit Gable in the hospital and would give us an update first thing in the morning. When I arrived at work, everyone was shuffling into the upper gallery. Our serious moods would have benefited from sugar consumption, but in Gable's absence, there wasn't a doughnut to be had; no one had stepped in to fill the role of Tim Hortons specialist. We sat huddled together on sofas, talking in subdued tones, staring morosely at the floor, and sipping coffee, awaiting what could only be bad news.

George, who was long, lean, and pale, loomed over us in a black suit, his expression suitably sombre. Without any preamble, he said, "I've got something terrible to tell you all."

Chloe, who sat beside me, braced herself and inhaled sharply. Although she'd witnessed the handsome paramedic and his colleague loading the incoherent Brian Gable III into the ambulance yesterday and had accompanied him to the hospital, she probably didn't know any more than the rest of us did about his current condition.

George looked a bit tense, his eyes darting around from one person to the next, his weight shifting from one leg to the other. "It's unfortunate to have to discuss this with you all, but yesterday around lunchtime, a tragic incident occurred at that greasy spoon down the street. Correct me if I'm wrong, but I think it's called A Step Backwards. However, I don't really know for sure since I haven't gone in except in moments of extreme weakness. Whatever it's called, it's the retro diner where they serve all those fantastically gooey grilled cheese sandwiches and other bad-for-you delights with soggy fries."

"A Step Back in Time," shouted Dora. "That's what it's called." Although she stopped short of grinning, she did look pleased with herself.

George seemed to realize he'd been babbling; he stopped shifting about, straightened himself up, and with a calmer air, got down to business. "Yes, Dora. But more to the point, yesterday shortly after noon, Brian Gable III, displaying signs of probable intoxication, somehow staggered out of this building, collapsed, and ended up face-down and mumbling gibberish on the floor of the diner. Our three witnesses, Virginia, Chloe, and Sally, assumed he'd been drinking to excess—not unreasonable given his behaviour in the diner. All three had the misfortune of witnessing the whole disaster. And I understand that at least one other staff member—namely you, Dora—did see Gable stumble out of here around noon yesterday."

George looked at each of us in turn and then paused awkwardly. I was astonished by his burst of loquaciousness. Until this meeting, he'd practised such severe economy of language that I was beginning to despair of ever getting to really know him. I could only imagine that anxiety had now somehow made his inhibitions drop away. George's enigmatic aura finally began to dissolve, and I watched him in fascination, waiting to see what he'd say next. Other people, however, seemed impatient or bored. Mark, who sat beside Chloe, sighed loudly and irritably. Sally jiggled her leg up and down, tapping her heel sharply on the floor. Jared stared into space, his mind apparently a million miles away. Taylor examined her nails.

"So after he collapsed, the paramedics came and—"

Sally suddenly stood up. "George, we already know what happened. No one's talked of anything else since yesterday afternoon. I thought you knew that. So is he dead or not?"

George looked at her sourly.

Mark said, "I'm sorry. We just want to know whether Gable's alive or dead. The suspense is killing us. And we have to get to work. There's a preview coming up this weekend, and it's already Thursday."

"Oh, I see ... well, the answer's yes."

"Yes what?" said Sally. The longer George delayed the news, the crankier she became.

He sighed wearily. "Yes, Sally, he's alive."

Chloe said loudly, "Thank God!"

Despite Gable's shoddy treatment of me, I'd never wished him dead, but I somehow felt much less enthusiastic about his being alive than Chloe did. Judging from the dark look that Sally directed at me, she shared my sentiments.

"So what are the doctors saying?" asked Helen in a calm voice. "Is he going to be all right? You'd think so if he was just drunk."

"Well, this is the thing," said George. "He's not out of the woods yet. Actually, it's the opposite. He seems to be getting much worse."

"Worse?" Chloe emitted a dramatic gasp and covered her mouth with her fingertips. I wasn't sure why she was all that surprised, since when she'd last seen Gable, he'd been in rough shape. Sally raised an eyebrow at her.

Taylor, who until now had seemed detached and uninterested in the proceedings, suddenly looked scared. "Is he gonna die?" she asked in a small, shaky voice. Her words were punctuated with a sniffle.

"Nobody really knows. What the doctors have confirmed is that he's getting worse, and I managed to wheedle it out of one of them that the symptoms are consistent with poisoning."

At first I felt a jolting sensation in my stomach, and then a blanket of numbness settled softly over me, cushioning me from my emotions. My legs suddenly felt weak, as if they wouldn't support my weight if I stood up.

Dora's eyes were large and round. "Poison! Really?"

"Yes, really. He wouldn't tell me exactly what type of poison was used, though," said George. "I suppose they're working on that."

We all absorbed the news in different ways. Tears coursed down Chloe's face as she kept saying, "Oh my God, I don't believe it." Taylor, her lip trembling, wiped her eyes as she sobbed. Helen went pale and stared into space numbly. Jared continued to look unspeakably bored. Mark looked down at the floor and held his head in his hands. Dora created a huge fuss by hyperventilating and weeping hysterically; this was undoubtedly more about drawing attention to herself than feeling actual distress. Sally coolly watched one colleague after another, her eyes flitting from face to face. I could see the wheels turning in her brain as she assessed the reaction of each person.

As the din grew louder, George became irritable. He held up his hands to shush us. "Everyone, keep it down! Especially *you*, Dora. Now as you can imagine, a police investigation will be carried out here. Be prepared to be interviewed by the police, particularly if you were in the office yesterday morning. The doctor wasn't sure, but he guessed the poison was administered shortly before lunchtime. As Gable spent most of yesterday morning holed up in his office, it's already been cordoned off, and officers will be combing it for evidence. You can be sure they'll also explore the rest of the premises."

George cleared his throat and then looked at me. "Virginia, Chloe, and Sally, expect to be grilled thoroughly by the police since you witnessed Gable's collapse." He then looked at everyone else. "Oh, and if clients ask any of you about Gable, you're to say he's off sick—until I tell you to say otherwise. Apart from all this, we'll still be having the preview this weekend and the auctions next week. I know it'll be difficult for everyone, but we must carry on as if nothing strange were happening. As far as we and the public are concerned, it's business as usual."

George's last remark was our signal to get back to work, but an oppressive silence had fallen over our group. Everyone sat heavily in their seats, reluctant to stir themselves. Unasked questions hung in the air like oppressive smog. George seemed to know we weren't done yet and stood there looking expectantly at one person after another, probably wondering who would be the first to speak.

"I have a question," said Sally. "You said the poison was administered, which implies attempted murder. But do you think there's any chance Gable tried to off himself?"

"Sally!" It was Chloe again. She seemed to consider suicide more shocking than murder, but to me they were equally horrifying.

"Just wondering," said Sally. "I mean, poison certainly wouldn't be my method of choice if I were going to kill myself, but you never know. And from what I've heard, it's not typical for a man to use it."

George looked uncertain and bit his lower lip. "It's possible that a suicide attempt is within the—er—realm of possibility. But I don't want any ridiculous rumours started, so best not to discuss it. Is that clear?" He cast a sidelong look at Sally. "Back to work everyone, please." The sharp edge of irritation coloured his voice, and his face looked tired and strained.

I got up to leave, but George had other plans.

"Virginia, may I see you for a moment?"

His words cut through the numbness a little. I nodded and followed him into his office, which I'd never really bothered to look at before. It was bright and airy and as stark and spare in appearance as George himself. His office was refreshingly free of the usual auction house clutter—dusty, sometimes filthy objects, either whole or broken, crammed tightly together, and mountains of old reference books and dog-eared paperwork—

that consumed most of our desks. He opted for a minimalist approach: a laptop, calculator, notebook, phone, and two trays of neatly piled paperwork. I looked around, marvelling at this oasis of tidiness. A small framed photo of a dog, a springer spaniel, caught my eye.

"Great dog."

"Yes, Cissie was a wonderful dog." He smiled, but I caught a hint of sadness in his dark eyes.

"Her name was Cissie? Seriously? That's a Royal Doulton figurine."

He looked slightly embarrassed, and an awkward silence followed before he said, "My ex-wife gave her that name." He gestured to the chair beside his desk, and we both sat down. "But let's get down to business. I should have announced to the staff that, in the absence of Brian Gable III, I'm in charge."

"Yes, I figured that from the meeting, as I'm sure everyone else did."

"It's best to make it official, though. Anyway, I called you in here today because I wanted to tell you that, of all the people in this place, I trust you the most. I have absolute faith in your honesty and discretion."

"Really?" I didn't know this. But until very recently I hadn't spent much time wondering what George thought of me. I'd just seen him as the solitary accountant who didn't pay much attention to me and quietly went about his business. But all that was changing, and now I was intrigued. "Go on," I said.

"I'll take your honesty first. I know you truly have no idea where the missing porcelain is."

"I figured that was pretty obvious. I mean, isn't it clear I'm as surprised as everyone else that it's disappeared?"

"Of course you're surprised, but some people here think it's all an act."

"What?"

George looked at me with a knowing glance and nodded. "Ah, I figured you didn't know."

"That I'm regarded with suspicion? I know a lot of people don't like me very much, but I didn't know they thought I was acting. Seriously, I had no idea. All I know is I'm in hot water if those pieces don't turn up, so I'm trying my damndest to locate them. I've even got Taylor on the case." I felt my blood pressure rise just thinking of the missing porcelain.

George looked at me reassuringly and smiled. "Relax. First of all, the people who think you've been putting on an act aren't exactly models of credibility. Ditsy Dora, for example. Or that shifty Jared character who moves furniture. I think Dora got him going, as I doubt he even has enough imagination to start a rumour. I overheard him on his smoking break yesterday telling his pals you knew where the porcelain was. I nearly grabbed him by the scruff of the neck and heaved him into that Dumpster next to the loading dock. Instead, I just gave him a severe talking to about spreading lies. It was almost like I was his father, and I guess I'm old enough to be. He was probably laughing his head off the second it was all over. Anyway, I know the pieces will turn up. As you so rightly pointed out to Gable, they always turn up."

"And they do. But Gable was acting like I'd lose my job if I didn't find them by the end of the week."

George leaned forward and looked me straight in the eye. "Virginia, please ... whether Gable lives or dies—and he'll probably die—you're not going to lose your job. This place would be a mess without you. Everyone knows that. Gable just likes to play the big bad wolf. It makes him feel important. Think nothing of it." He waved his hand in a dismissive way.

For the first time since Gable had mentioned the missing porcelain at the meeting, I started to breathe more easily, and my shoulders, which had been hovering up around my ears for days, finally began to come down.

"You mentioned having faith in my discretion. How exactly does that figure into things?"

"I know you're discreet. You came straight to me about Gable's collapse and told me in a calm, objective way what happened. You didn't embellish the facts, and more importantly, you didn't babble on and on about the incident in front of clients."

"Who did that?"

"Both Chloe and Sally. They were talking up a storm in the auction gallery, and that gossipy old Mr. Alabaster was wandering around smiling to himself. I'm sure he heard every word."

"Mr. Alabaster?" I said. "Which one's he?"

"I call him that because he's so pale. I don't know his real name. The one who wears an eye patch and a panama hat. The guy with the slick smile who's always full of one-liners."

"Oh, him," I said with distaste. I remembered his wearying attempts to flirt with me at previews.

George laughed, but then his mood turned serious. "Virginia, there was a reason I announced Gable's collapse at the meeting. Of course everyone knew about it already, but I wanted to see if anyone would act suspiciously. And I want you to keep an eye on everyone and report back to me if you see any unusual behaviour. Yes, the police will be here investigating, but let's conduct a covert investigation of our own." His eyes were shining with glee, and he actually began rubbing his hands together and smiling. It was the most excitement I'd ever seen him show. "It'll be fun. Besides, I've always wanted to be a sleuth."

I felt one of my eyebrows lift. "You have?" I imagined George wearing a deerstalker and smoking a pipe, and I burst out laughing.

"What? What's so funny?" He was smiling, and I could have sworn I saw traces of pink in those pale cheeks.

"I just imagined you playing Sherlock Holmes, deerstalker and all."

"Well, I do look a bit like Basil Rathbone, don't you think?" he said, grinning. He wasn't far wrong. Instead of answering, all I seemed capable of doing was giggling. I was ridiculously pleased he'd even heard of Basil Rathbone, my favourite actor to portray Holmes. I was even more pleased he was giving me one of those intense looks again, and my heart skipped a beat.

Once I startled to settle down, George became serious and said, "So what have we got so far? A lot of missing porcelain—"

"Wait a second. Let's back up a bit. I just thought about what Sally said. Are you sure Gable didn't try to kill himself?"

"Him?" he said, his voice shooting up an octave. "Here's a man the whole staff despises—without exception—and whose entire *raison d'être* is tormenting everyone. I've never seen anyone get such pleasure from making other people miserable."

"Well, when you put it that way, it seems far more likely someone tried to kill him."

George nodded sagely. "Exactly. But going back to what we've got, there's a lot of missing porcelain making one department look inept and a useless company president who, after issuing a not-exactly-veiled threat to fire the head of the porcelain department, somehow manages to get himself poisoned. What does that say to you?"

"Well, if I didn't know any better, I'd say it makes me look homicidal—surely not a good thing."

"But you and I know better. You're not homicidal. Guess again."

I took a moment to think about who might appear guilty. "You suspect Taylor?"

George nodded again.

"Ah, but she didn't steal the porcelain or hide it somewhere, and for reasons I can't understand, she thinks it's gone for good. And she's just as freaked out about it going missing as I am—more so, if yesterday's three-hour crying marathon is any indication."

George looked startled. "Oh, I didn't know she was that upset about it. But I didn't really think she did anything with the porcelain. She knows her head will roll too if the missing items don't turn up. Gable doesn't respect her, and she damn well knows it. Everyone around here knows she's got precious little talent or motivation. I mean, would you have hired her?"

"No." I remembered how Gable had hired her on the sly a couple of years ago. He'd abruptly presented her—a young slacker with no relevant experience—as my new assistant. I still had no idea how he'd found her in the first place, as no one had ever explained. At least her work had improved since then.

"He only hired her for her looks," said George. "She probably knows it too. All the pretty decorative things around here aren't enough to satisfy him."

I snorted derisively. "So what are you saying?"

"Terrified she'd lose her job too, she tried to kill him."

I thought about that for a moment and said, "I don't know, George. Is it smart to kill the guy who signs your paycheque?"

"But Gable doesn't own the company, remember? Errol Thrasher does."

"Oh, of course. I keep forgetting about him." It wasn't surprising, given how little we saw of the man.

"And I have signing authority, of course. Gable just likes signing the paycheques so he can easily keep tabs on how much people are making. Wouldn't you agree Taylor's the most obvious suspect?"

"But it's not as if he threatened to give her the sack. I'm the one who—"

Before I could finish, I heard the floorboards creak behind me. Swivelling around in my chair, I saw the most obvious suspect standing in the dark corridor and peering through the door, which was slightly ajar. Though her face betrayed nothing, I wondered how long she'd been listening outside.

CHAPTER 12

George got up to open the door wide. When Taylor came into the light, I saw that her face was puffy and red, and tears coursed down her cheeks. She wiped her nose on her sleeve. "I just happened to pick up the phone. It was the hospital—he's dead." She spoke raggedly through her tears. "Brian Gable—is—dead."

We knew the news was likely to come, so we weren't exactly shocked. No, mostly what I felt was worried, and it was obvious when George and I exchanged glances that he was worried too. Maybe Gable would be the only victim, but maybe not. Would the killer strike again, and if so, who would he target? I looked at Taylor, who looked gutted by the man's collapse and subsequent death. In spite of how annoying she'd been at times, I found it impossible to feel anything but sympathetic toward her now that she'd disintegrated into such a helpless state.

I was tempted to step forward and hug her, but much to my surprise she lurched forward and launched herself heavily into George's arms. She barely came up to his shoulder. She was a weeping, heaving mess, and George stiffened slightly as he held her. It was obvious he'd never much liked Taylor, but then again, few of us ever had. Most of the time she was aloof and enigmatic, and her popularity with her colleagues had suffered as a result. It was difficult to like someone you couldn't understand. Now she was becoming increasingly unpredictable and emotionally unstable. She was a natural suspect, and it wasn't surprising that George had raised the possibility she'd murdered Gable. But we'd judged her too severely. Seeing how badly she was taking things, I couldn't imagine how she could possibly be the culprit.

As if he was reading my thoughts, George began to soften a little toward her. He relaxed into a hug and spoke in gentle, fatherly tones. "I know this is devastating for you, Taylor. But you must pull yourself together. It's of no help to the police investigation—or to our work— if we're all falling apart under the strain, is it?" He patted her on the back and then began gingerly peeling her off him.

Attempting to calm herself, Taylor gulped and nodded. "Yes, you're right. I'll try my best." She looked from George to me.

I smiled at her encouragingly. "Taylor, why not take the rest of the day off? Even though the preview's coming up, we're in good shape for it, and I'm not quite as worried about the missing porcelain now. There's not too much that's pressing today—or nothing I can't handle. If something urgent does come up, I can always call on Chloe or Mark. And I'm sure you could use some time to yourself right now." Mindful of how hard I'd been on her earlier, I spoke in a calm but upbeat way.

"Yeah. Of course. Awesome. I'll do that." She snuffled, wiped her tears with a tissue, and then stumbled out of George's office, nearly crashing into a chair on her way out.

When I turned to look at George, he was dabbing with a handkerchief at the wet spots Taylor's tears had left. Grinning, he said, "I think my new suit's officially been broken in."

"Indeed. On another note, what the hell happens now?"

"Hmm?" He was preoccupied with the tear stains.

"Gable's dead. I know you said you were in charge earlier, but does this mean you're officially now the president? Or does our mostly absent owner now have to step up and fill that position?"

George let out a guffaw. "You mean 'Ol Thrasher? I haven't seen him in months. Can you imagine him interrupting his glamorous life to preside over us common working stiffs?"

Errol Thrasher, whose first name I'd permanently abbreviated to "'Ol," much to the amusement of Mark and Sally, was supposedly Gable's right-hand man, though he spent at least ten months of the year doing vitally important work: lounging in the sun and honing his womanizing skills at his Tuscan villa. There were staff members who'd never even met him and sincerely believed he was fictitious. Thrasher did take an interest in the business, which meant he'd call to chew someone's ear off when his auction catalogues didn't arrive on time, and that he'd bid extravagantly on all sorts of oversized dust collectors he neither needed nor wanted. His gargantuan Forest Hill mansion was reputedly packed to the rafters with extravagantly useless items like giant plaster statues of Greek gods and gilded cupids. In his mind, big was better, so oversized was best of all.

"I suppose someone really ought to call him," I said. I fervently hoped George wouldn't insist I do it. The thought of listening to 'Ol Thrasher rant about the inconvenience of having to return to Toronto all because Gable had had the temerity to get himself murdered was far from appealing. It was actually more than I could stand, and I felt nauseated at the prospect. I wondered if I was getting pale.

George must have suspected I was feeling ill, for he said, "No, I wasn't proposing that you do it. I'm happy to. I'll tell him he doesn't need to fly here from Italy—that I'll take care of things."

I sighed with relief.

"Though there's always the chance he'll show up at our doorstep simply because he doesn't like me telling him what to do. You know what an arrogant know-it-all he is." George rubbed his chin and looked pensive.

"And who knows?" I said. "Maybe he'll even have fantasies about single-handedly rescuing Gable & Co. from certain doom. God knows his presence in our darkest hour will make a critical difference to us all."

"Do I sense some sarcasm?" George laughed, displaying

very nice, even white teeth. Why hadn't I ever really noticed them before? His warm brown eyes were shining as he looked at me. I giggled, and my face suddenly felt very warm. A marvellous little thrill zipped through me. I felt as if I were fourteen again, and in the best possible way.

"Um, I really should get back to work, I think. Unless there's something else." I tried to stop smiling.

"No, Virginia, that's all for the moment. Don't worry about 'Ol Thrasher. I'll handle him." He was still smiling too.

Thinking of how thrilling it was that George seemed to share my sense of humour, I closed the door softly behind me and spotted Mark walking through the auction gallery. He was cursing loudly as he hauled around a marble mantel clock adorned with a disproportionately large gilt-metal statue of a Spanish cavalier painted with red-and-black highlights. As we arrived back at the cataloguing room, he said, "You look a bit flushed, Virginia. Are you feeling all right?" The corners of his mouth were twitching, as if he was trying to suppress a grin.

"Gable's dead."

"Well, I figured as much. What an awful business. Taylor's been crying a puddle—or perhaps it was a lake—and she couldn't even tell me what was wrong. But you don't exactly have to be a genius to figure it out." He paused. "Hey, you still haven't explained why your face is red."

"No reason. Mind your own business."

Mark grinned slyly. "One day the truth will come out. Until then, all I can do is start rumours."

"Good line. I must remember that one." I swatted him playfully on the arm, and the Spanish cavalier became dislodged from the clock and clattered noisily to the floor.

"Sorry, Mark."

But he wasn't angry at me; instead he vented at the clock. "What a piece of junk this thing is! And did you notice the damn cavalier's cross-eyed? Strabismus—he suffers from strabismus. I've never seen anything like it. It's absurd." Mark bent down to scoop up the recumbent cavalier and came up instead with a ragged scrap of paper. He squinted as he tried to read it.

"What's that?" I asked.

"I don't know—I'd need to find my reading glasses first. They're here somewhere. But I think maybe this is for you. It was closer to your desk than mine." He tossed it on my desk and sat on the floor to attend to the fallen cavalier, swearing colourfully while attempting to attach it to the clock.

I started reading the handwritten note.

Dearest Virginia,

So you think you're safe now that Gable's dead, eh? No need to find that missing porcelain after all, right? No one's gonna care, since there all too distracted by poor old Gable's departure to the great beyond.

Think again, honey lamb. You won't last very long if you don't come up with the goods by tomorrow.

You really think George is gonna tolerate the sloppy way your running your department? Better snap to it before your hourglass runs out, Dorothy. If you don't, who can tell what might happen? Maybe the wicked witch will get you after all.

The note struck me as more of a puerile prank than a genuine threat, so I wasn't about to let it intimidate me. Strangely, rather than being hastily scrawled, it was a masterpiece of calligraphic curlicues, so embellished with feminine curves and loops that the words were difficult to decipher. I wondered why the writer had paid so much attention to the script itself and so little to the quality of paper; it was written on flimsy, crumpled foolscap. I searched my brain. Did anyone at Gable & Co. write like that? And why were *they're* and *you're* spelled wrong? As far as I knew, no one in the company but Taylor was in the habit of making these sorts of homophone errors, but this couldn't have been her writing.

I thrust the note at Mark, even though he was still fumbling with the clock. Seeming to sense my anxiety, he hurriedly set the piece of junk on his desk, found his reading glasses, put them on, and snatched the note from my hand. "What the hell?"

"Do you know anyone who has handwriting like this, Mark?"

"Lord no! Do you? And who says 'honey lamb'? For heaven's sake, what century are we living in? And what's with the *Wizard of Oz* references?"

"To answer your first question, no, I can't think of anyone who uses such outdated terms of endearment." But I didn't need anyone to tell me that such a pumped-up, exhibitionistic script reflected a writer with narcissistic personality disorder. I hadn't read books on handwriting analysis for nothing.

But he didn't share my impression of the writing. "Whoever wrote this must have really worked on it. It's a cunning disguise, don't you think? I mean, who in blazes writes like that normally?"

"Oh, you'd be surprised. The foremost narcissists of our time all write like that."

Mark looked puzzled. "How do you know that?"

"I've studied it." I grabbed the note from him and marched back to George's office. Perhaps he'd have an idea who'd written it. Whether he knew or not, he'd still need to know I'd received it.

The preview set-up was in full swing as I walked through the gallery; some of the boys were heaving the furniture around, others were polishing it, while others still were perched high on ladders, hanging paintings or lighting fixtures. Jared was pausing to assess whether a painting was crooked or not, and when he saw me, he gave me a tight, smarmy smile. I ignored it, preferring to marvel, as I'd done so often over the years, at the wonderful transformation that took place for each preview. In a few short hours, we went from having a room full of furniture scattered willy-nilly across the gallery to artistic and elegant room settings. The only thing that was different this time around was that a couple of police officers were silently wandering around the room. One stopped to poke at a stuffed beaver as though he'd never seen such a creature before. The other pulled open all the small drawers in a drop front writing desk; I hoped he was being just as thorough in his investigation of Gable's death. Both officers kept glancing toward George's office, so I could only think they were killing time while waiting to talk to him.

The door to his office was open just a sliver when I arrived. I could see him standing behind his desk, his arms folded under his chest. His eyes downcast, he looked deep in thought. The blinds had been drawn, so the room was illuminated only by a banker's lamp with a green glass shade, and I could see the outline of someone sitting opposite him. Unexpectedly, the door creaked open a little more to reveal Taylor. George's eyes immediately flitted to my face, and Taylor turned around to look at me, a wan smile brightening her ragged features and tear-stained face somewhat.

"Oh. I thought you'd gone home, Taylor."

"I was just … gonna." She fidgeted.

"I'll come back later, George. I have something important to show you. Will fifteen minutes or so be all right?"

He glanced uneasily at Taylor, who nodded, and then to me. "That'll be fine, Virginia. See you soon."

Taylor reached over to push the door behind me, slamming it shut. I didn't know why her presence in George's office made me so uncomfortable. She wasn't a bad person. I knew she hadn't written the note, nor did I suspect her anymore of having anything to do with either the missing porcelain or Gable's murder. She was deeply distraught by the recent turn of events, which was inconsistent with having committed theft or murder. I'm sure she was incapable of harming an ant. No, my unease had more to do with George's expression. Why had he looked so guilty? And of what?

Determined not to let myself slide into rampant paranoia, I pushed away all thoughts that he might somehow be doing something he shouldn't. Though I still knew little about him, he'd invited me to help him investigate the turbulent events that had rocked Gable & Co. Plainly, he trusted me; I had to trust him.

Breathing more easily, I popped downstairs to make myself a cup of Moroccan Mystique. The slurping and fizzing of the coffee machine nearly drowned out a sound I'd become all too familiar with. Nonetheless, after the trying day I'd been having, it came as an unpleasant shock to discover that Constance was back. The pitiful snuffling I heard at first rapidly snowballed into full-blown keening. This was my ghost's uniquely noisy way of demanding attention, and avoiding her wasn't an option.

"Constance?" I called out. I hardly expected her to answer, since it seemed she could make all manner of sounds—deafening wailing especially—except speech. I picked my way through the basement in the faint glow of the lightbulb to find her reclining on the same settee I'd seen her on before. This time, her arms flailed dramatically above her head, and her body rocked from side to side. Her ear-splitting wails were punctuated with pathetic little moans. She looked at me as I approached, and even though the light was dim, I caught the glint in her eye. It was as if she was imploring me to do something, but I was so disturbed by her hysterical performance, I didn't know what.

When I got within a few feet of her, she jumped to her feet. Her arms flew up and down so fast they became a blur. Then she seemed to be pointing at her feet, but it was dark enough that I couldn't really be sure. I was kicking myself for not having turned on another light. My coffee in one hand, I groped around for a light switch.

I soon grew exasperated with both myself and Constance. "What? What is it you're trying to tell me? For God's sake, Constance—I just don't understand you!"

I wanted to shake her, to tell her to get a grip on herself and stop with the nutty histrionics. They were of no use to me, and I couldn't see how they were helping her. Finally, I found the light switch and flicked it on, just in time to see Constance's pale visage, shot through with a look of alarm. Her body froze; her face was in profile, and one sinewy arm was suspended rigidly in midair, the fingers straining as if she were trying to clutch something. Her outline glowed and pulsated a fiery red that gradually turned bright white and started flickering madly like a strobe light in a disco. Nearly blinded by the glare, I watched as the light finally exploded like a firecracker, accompanied by a ferociously loud popping noise. Then all that remained was Constance, still frozen in alarm. Slowly she faded, becoming as sheer as gossamer and leaving behind that same faint trace of herself she always left.

I felt as if I'd just been assaulted, and the stirrings of a migraine were beginning in my temple. What a relief she was gone again. I sighed with exhaustion, turned around abruptly, and ran smack into Mark. Our collision caused hot coffee to slop all over my hand, and I let out a sharp cry, nearly dropping my cup.

"Jesus, Mark, I didn't see you there," I said. "You scared me half to death." Frenetically, I shook the drops of Moroccan Mystique from my hand.

"Sorry. Did it ever occur to you that maybe you shouldn't be coming downstairs alone, what with a murderer in our midst?"

"I had other things on my mind."

He wagged his finger at me. "You should be more careful. I noticed you heading down, so I thought I'd better follow. I also wanted to find out what George had to say about that snarky note. Does he know who wrote it?"

"Well, we haven't had a chance to discuss it yet, since last I looked Taylor was in his office with him."

Mark's eyebrows arched. "Hmm, so what do you suppose *that's* about?"

I held up my hand in a halting gesture. "I can't even begin to imagine, but I don't want to assume anything nefarious is going on. I just know I've been far too suspicious of Taylor lately, and without just cause. I admit I've never much liked her, but maybe if I just gave her a chance and trusted her more, we'd be getting along much better."

Mark scowled. "That's mighty charitable of you, but I still don't trust the little minx." He paused. "Hey, why'd you come down here, anyway? The siren song of caffeine? Or something else?"

"I just needed some coffee, which, in case you hadn't noticed yet, just scalded my hand when you bumped into me. Thanks, DuBarry."

"Don't mention it!" he said.

"And I guess my ghost must have thought we were due for another meeting. Didn't you hear that godawful uproar as you were coming down the stairs? Between her wailing and my shouting at her, it was really quite something. If I'd been smart, I would have sold tickets."

Mark's brow wrinkled as he looked at me. He seemed genuinely puzzled.

"Oh, come on," I said. "Are you trying to tell me you didn't hear any of that just now?"

"Nothing."

"Well, perhaps we were finished by the time you got close enough."

"Yes, that must be it!" said Mark, grinning. But judging from the vague, dreamy look in his eyes, I wasn't sure if he was responding to what I'd just said or to some insight of his own.

I glared at him. "What? Okay, stop trying to humour me. No, I'm not insane, so please don't look at me like that."

"No, that's not what I was thinking." He shook his head.

"Well, you're one of the few, then. Practically everyone else in this place has been looking at me like I'm cuckoo."

"That's not really true, you know. Chloe and Sally and I don't think you've lost your mind. At least not yet." Mark looked pensive. "Consider something for a moment, Virginia. No one else has ever seen or heard your ghost."

"In a lot of circles, that would make me delusional. Years ago, I would have been carted away to a sanatorium, and you would have had to visit me there and cheer me up with regular gifts of chocolate."

He laughed. "True to all that, but you're as sane as I am."

I planted my hands on my hips and cocked my head toward him, smirking.

"All right, you can stop with the skeptical look," he said. "You're right—saying you're as sane as I am isn't exactly saying much, is it? Well, you're as sane as George is, then."

I nodded. "That's much better. George is probably the sanest among us."

Suddenly, Mark started to look excited. His complexion glowed, and his eyes glimmered in the dim light. "What I've been thinking is, you're the only one to see Constance because she has a message just for you. She's been sent to impart wisdom you need at this particular time in your life."

I considered this for a moment. "Well said. I really hate to rain on your parade, but I'd already considered that possibility. I could definitely use some wisdom, now that Gable's dead, the porcelain's still missing, and Taylor seems to be falling apart, but aside from telling me she's a consummate drama queen, what's Constance trying to say? You should have witnessed today's insane exhibition of moaning, groaning, and flailing. What am I supposed to make of all that?"

"Somehow, you've got to decode it," said Mark.

"Too bad there isn't a book called *What Your Ghost Is Really Trying to Tell You*. It would be a bestseller for those of us driven mad by bothersome spirits."

We both laughed, but our laughter ceased abruptly when we heard a crash. I jumped and shuddered. "What the hell was that?" I said.

The noise was coming from a corner just a few feet away. I couldn't see what was happening because of all the furniture piled up in front of us, but soon I realized I'd heard the sound before. Hundreds of pieces of glass were tinkling and quivering, for someone had collided with a chandelier. I heard scuffling sounds, as if someone was struggling to become disentangled from it. A woman cursed softly under her breath.

"Who's down here?" Mark's voice boomed. "I didn't know anyone else was here."

As I edged toward the corner, Chloe's startled eyes met mine, and she slipped away into the shadows.

CHAPTER 13

What did it all mean? First, Taylor had been having what appeared to be an intense heart-to-heart chat with George in his office. As much as I'd tried to cast all my doubts about Taylor to the winds, the suspicion that she was somehow guilty of something bubbled up to the surface again and niggled at me. At the very least, her tears yesterday told me she was keeping something about the missing porcelain a secret. I didn't know exactly what her story was, but maybe George could help. I'd need to ask him to be straight with me about why she'd snuck back into his office long after I thought she'd gone home.

Then there was the upsetting sight of Chloe running away from Mark and me. We followed her upstairs and found her at her desk, blood streaming from a gash in her cheek. She was dabbing at it with a wad of tissues, which wasn't nearly enough to stanch the flow.

"Chloe, what happened?" I asked. "Mark, run and get Sally. She's got the first-aid kit."

When Mark was gone, Chloe said, "I was looking for something in the basement."

"What?"

"Oh, I don't know! Teddy bears or something. Wouldn't that seem logical? Does it really matter?" Her voice was raw with emotion, as if she'd truly come undone. She'd never spoken to me in that tone before, but under the circumstances, it was probably to be expected, so I just let it go. She dabbed some more at the angry gash. Blood pooled on her jawline and dripped to the floor.

At first I could only think she must have walked into the chandelier in the dark, and that the edge of one of its gilt-metal branches had been much sharper than you'd expect it to be. But given the extent of her injuries, it was unlikely they were caused by such a collision. At the moment of impact, a suspended chandelier would have swayed and moved away from her, so any cuts she sustained, even from a sharp branch, wouldn't have been deeper than superficial scratches.

Sally arrived to clean up and bandage the cut. She examined the zigzag in Chloe's face and said, "Good God! Don't you think you should go to the hospital? There's a lot of blood, and the cut's very deep. You don't want to get infected."

Chloe shook her head in exasperation. "Absolutely not! Just put some bandages on it and be done with it. It'll be fine, I'm sure."

When Sally was finished, Chloe wandered around the office, sighing and complaining about how the cut would leave scars. She was looking for crumbs of sympathy wherever she could find them, and it was hard to fault her for that; the cut was godawful. But exhausted by recent events, I couldn't seem to summon up the energy to do more than give her a couple of my chocolate chip cookies. Not long ago she'd been my lifeline, so I couldn't help but feel a bit guilty about my failure to show more compassion.

I was too tired to haul more things out to the gallery for the preview, and it could wait for tomorrow. Instead, I just kept my head down and catalogued a collection of twenty pickle cruets for the rest of the day. Each one consisted of an enamelled cranberry glass jar ensconced in an elaborate silverplate frame, complete with a dainty pair of matching silverplate tongs that would have been used by discerning Victorians to grasp tiny gherkins and remove them from the jar. Describing and measuring pickle cruets was a surprisingly calming activity after all the recent workplace traumas, not the least of which was the latest episode of being tormented by Constance. I quickly became absorbed in my task, and as I fell into a rhythm and hit my stride, I was comforted; it felt as if I were in the midst of a normal workday instead of immersed in a ghastly nightmare.

The tranquility was soon interrupted by Chloe, who was meandering around the cataloguing room carrying an Armand Marseille bisque head baby doll in her arms. She stopped at my desk and propped the doll on her hip. Gesturing toward the cruets, she said, "Can I work on these too?"

"Um, I thought you had other things to do. There are only about forty dolls and teddy bears on your desk. And why are you wandering around with that doll?" I spoke more sharply than I'd intended to, but I was becoming impatient. I just wanted to work quietly and without so many interruptions, even though I knew that was impossible at the best of times.

She eyed me coolly. "I just thought I might be able to help, that's all. As for the doll …" She shrugged.

"Why are you even the slightest bit concerned about helping me? You've got your own work to do, and frankly, if I were you, I'd be more worried about that cut than anything else right now. No one's going to mind if you leave for the day."

Chloe grimaced as she held her hand up to her cheek. "You had to remind me, didn't you?"

Immediately, I felt guilty. "Sorry," I said. "You know I didn't mean to upset you."

She nodded and smiled weakly before turning around, setting the doll on her desk, and sitting down.

Meanwhile, I heard Mark pick up the phone. "Hi, Helen. Miss Who? Aberfoyle? She has what?" There was a long pause. "The queen's raincoat?" He thought about this for a moment. "Well, I haven't got much time, but send her back here."

"Hmm, I'll bet she has a real treasure on her hands," I said.

Chloe and I swivelled around in our chairs, looked at each other, and burst out laughing.

Mark was trying to ignore us, but from the deep sigh he released I knew he was thinking the same thing. A few seconds later, Alice from the diner strolled in, and I knew that the possibility of getting any useful work done had just vanished. She was wearing some sort of poufy pleated orange satin dress with a ragged hem. This and her black tights made her resemble a pumpkin on sticks. Her cheap perfume wafted toward me, and I tried not to breathe.

"Hi everyone!" she said, waving and smiling. "Oh, good, some familiar faces!" She looked first at me and then at Chloe. "My goodness, whatever could have happened to your face?"

Chloe fixed her with a baleful stare, the likes of which I'd never seen before. She was certainly full of surprises lately.

"Sorry, dear. It's really none of my business, is it?" said Alice in a stage whisper. She let out a silly, high-pitched giggle.

Chloe nodded slowly and turned away. I pretended to work but was watching Mark and Alice from the corner of my eye.

"Miss Aberfoyle," said Mark, extending his hand and smiling tightly. "It's so nice to meet you. What do you have to show me?"

"Call me Alice, if you please." She extracted a rumpled, torn, and dirty beige trench coat from a plastic bag and laid it out on the table. As she did so, a cloud of dust ascended from the coat. Even though it was a few feet away from me, I began coughing loudly. To make matters worse, a musty smell was emanating from the coat and mingling with her perfume.

Mark caught my eye and cocked an eyebrow at me, and I tried to stop coughing, but it was difficult after being assaulted by dust and noxious odours. He handled the coat gingerly as Alice watched his every move. Assuming his expert appraiser face, he said, "It's made by Aquascutum. See the label? And the coat has the company's signature club check lining. It's an old firm dating back to the Victorian era, and they make very high-end things. But what makes you think your raincoat belonged to Queen Elizabeth?"

She looked at him as if he were hopelessly ignorant. "Ahem. Did you actually *read* the label? I'm beginning to wonder if you have any idea what you're talking about."

I watched as Mark's mouth opened and closed several times in rapid succession, as if he were a fish gasping, while Alice smiled at him in her smarmy way. Recovering himself, he finally said, "Okay, okay, so the label says, 'By Appointment To Her Majesty The Queen,' right? All that really means is that Aquascutum, the company that made the raincoat, is a supplier of goods to the royal family. It's called a Royal Warrant label. You'll also find it on various brands—I can't remember which ones—of things like toiletries, tea, jam, crackers, cookies, and chocolate."

There was a pause before Alice quietly said, "Oh."

"Where did you get this, by the way?"

"Goodwill, of course. That's where I get lots of my things. But this one is special." Alice picked up the trench coat and held it against herself. She then sashayed around the room, stopping to pose and pout every few seconds as if she were a runway model.

I was straining to keep a straight face, and I could hear Chloe snickering.

Alice stood back from Mark and looked him up and down. "So you don't think Queen Elizabeth wore it? You're sure? There's absolutely no chance you're mistaken?"

"No, Miss Aberfoyle—Alice—your raincoat doesn't belong to Queen Elizabeth. Really it doesn't. Trust me on this," said Mark in a weary tone. "I'm sure her Aquascutum raincoat, if she has one, is safely stowed in her closet at Buckingham Palace. And if she did give it away, I somehow doubt you'd find it here at Goodwill. Now if you don't mind—"

Alice put the coat down again. Her mouth was set in a determined line. "But what's it worth? As a royal heirloom, I mean?"

Mark sighed. "But I can't tell you what it's worth as a 'royal heirloom' because it's absolutely, positively no such thing. It's just a dirty, ripped-up old Aquascutum raincoat someone abandoned to a thrift store. It's not worth a cent more than you paid for it. I really must get back to work, so I think we're finished here. Goodbye." He turned around and walked to his desk.

Alice stuffed the coat into the bag, raising more dust clouds, and I began hacking away again. Everyone turned to look at her. Her beady little eyes glared defiantly at each of us in turn as she planted her hands on her hips and said, "Well! I don't believe you! And won't you be surprised when I take this to the *Antiques Roadshow* and prove you wrong!" With a flourish, she wrapped a black scarf around her neck and left. We heard the angry click of her heels disappearing down the hallway.

"Good luck!" yelled Mark after her, which made Chloe squeal with delight. Red-faced, he began gasping with laughter, his whole body shaking. When he was finally able to speak again, he said, "Where do these people come from?"

"A better question might be 'How many more of them must I endure?'" I said. "Alice was at the diner when Gable collapsed. She wanted us to give her all the dirt on him. And *someone*"—I looked over at Chloe, who was trying to compose herself—"told her where we work."

With a wide-eyed look, she shrugged and collapsed into giggles.

"Oh God, just you watch—that crazy dame will come in to show me every piece of crappy thrift-store junk she ever finds from now on," said Mark. "Just so she can have the pleasure of arguing with me!"

"Come on—you enjoyed that as much as the rest of us. Admit it." Chloe smiled and looked at me for support.

"Yes, quit your whining," I said.

"Knock it off, O'Rourke. You too, Blythe." Mark stuck his tongue out, and we all laughed.

Everyone settled back down into work. The quiet of the room gave me time to think, and all at once it occurred to me: I'd completely forgotten to speak with George about the nasty note—and to find out what Taylor had been talking about with him. I was certain he'd tell me. It was the end of the day, but I still had hopes he hadn't left yet. I dashed out of the cataloguing room. But when I got to his office, the door was already locked, so he must have gone home. Whatever I could glean from him would have to wait.

CHAPTER 14

When I arrived home that night, I was determined, clenched fists and all, to escape the hellish happenings in my life through mindless television, but I couldn't resist the call of Constance's diary. If Mark was right and she really was trying to tell me something significant, maybe it would eventually come to light in the diary. Perhaps her moaning, groaning, and flailing was simply meant to tell me I should get on with reading it. But if that was all she was worried about, why had she looked so frantic? What was I missing?

I brushed some more dust off the diary and flipped it open. When I'd looked ahead before, I hadn't noticed that Constance had written the next entry in June. A few weeks had elapsed since the last entry—a bit surprising considering the regular entries she'd made during the first four months of the year. Perhaps she'd been so breathlessly caught up in her whirlwind romance that she was too distracted to write. I couldn't blame her if that was true.

June 15, 1928

Anyone reading this diary (and I'm certain somebody will, even if it's years from now) must wonder where I've disappeared to for the past few weeks. Was Constance Pendleton kidnapped in the spring of 1928 and returned to her family only after her father paid a hefty ransom? Sorry to disappoint you, dear reader, but nothing so dramatic occurred. Well, I shouldn't say that because something devastating really *has* occurred, and I've been thrown for a loop. I've written precious little in the past couple of months because Freddy has kept me so busy, but I'm now turning to this diary to drown my sorrows—to the extent that I even can. At least it's cheaper and less destructive than drinking.

I've been crying all morning, and when I look in the mirror I see a tear-stained wreck of a girl with a puffy red face. Of course, Freddy's to blame, but I doubt he sees it that way. I expect he'll stay well away from me until he has a notion of what a colossal fool he's been. He's spoiled everything! I fervently hope he'll come to this realization soon, but I have no confidence he will. For now, it's probably just as well he's not around since I look such a fright. My appearance would only deter him from having anything to do with me. I really must get myself sorted out. Once I manage to collect myself, we'll need to discuss our future—if we even have one anymore.

Yesterday began like any other day; I never imagined it would end as it did. Freddy was just getting back on his feet after a bout of influenza, and he was having a rare day off from playing with the orchestra. We were all set to dine at the King Edward—luncheon in the Oak Room. It's not nearly as grand as, say, the Crystal Ball Room, with all those sumptuous chandeliers and that breathtaking view of the city from the eighteenth floor, but I do so love the Oak Room's gracious elegance.

Freddy was in a chipper mood as we arrived and was even humming that jaunty tune, "I'm Looking Over a Four-Leaf Clover." The maitre d' led us to our usual table, one tucked away in a corner at the very back of the restaurant, far away from the bustle of patrons coming and going through those grand oak doors at the front. A few other diners, mostly couples huddled together in murmured conversation, sat nearby, their faces glowing amber from the candles on the tables. Several jolly gatherings, including a group of businessmen who occasionally burst into laughter as they smoked cigars, were clustered near the front of the room. A slight haze of smoke lingered even where we sat. The room was softly lit by crystal wall sconces, and huge potted palms provided some measure of privacy. Our table was made cheerful by yellow chrysanthemums and a crisp white tablecloth.

Freddy delicately took my pale blue silk wrap from my shoulders and folded it neatly over the wicker armchair he pulled out for me. Sitting down opposite me, he smiled. He still looked a little peaky from his illness, but his face was glowing nonetheless. "So, darling, what will you be having?"

By now, I'd memorized the menu. "The roast beef with Yorkshire pudding and mashed potatoes. Followed by the lemon sorbet for dessert, I expect. That does seem rather a lot for midday, though, doesn't it?"

"Perhaps, but they are your favourites, and you're not to be denied. And the luncheon portion is lighter than the dinner one."

"You're right—I'd forgotten."

Freddy smiled again and looked across the room. Squinting, he grew serious and looked down at the menu, studying it intently.

"Good gracious, Freddy, you really ought to know the menu off by heart!" I said with a laugh. "How many times have we been here? Fifteen, if I've kept count properly. Not to mention that you're here playing in the orchestra all the time, and surely they must feed you."

"Yes, darling, they do," he said, without looking up.

An exotic floral scent tinged with spice wafted toward me. It seemed to me I'd smelled it before, but I couldn't say where or when—only that it was familiar. I suddenly became aware of a presence behind me. I looked over my shoulder and saw a willowy young woman standing behind me, looking at Freddy with startled blue eyes. She had curly auburn hair worn in a stylish bob, fine features, and the palest skin I'd ever seen. It was very nearly translucent and lightly sprinkled with freckles. She was wearing a mint-coloured silk dress with dainty navy-blue ruffles at the neckline and the hem. Freddy didn't look up.

"May I help you?" I said.

She glanced from me to Freddy and then back again, her expression shifting from puzzled to hurt. At last, he looked up at her.

"Elsie." His voice was thin and flat. And then he smiled—the strained smile I'd seen whenever we were approached by someone he didn't much like. "How nice to see you here." He gestured toward me. "This"—his voice faltered—"is Constance Pendleton. Constance, meet Elsie Trafford."

Elsie held out a limp, slender white hand for me to shake, which I did awkwardly. But her eyes were fixed on Freddy. "And who might Constance be?" She spoke with an English accent, her voice small and wispy as if she were speaking from a faraway place.

"Constance is my—um—fiancée. Or I should say soon-to-be fiancée." He looked over at me, his expression grim. "We're not yet officially engaged, but we soon will be."

Elsie turned sad eyes on me and blinked. "Fiancée. Oh, I see."

Freddy looked even paler than he had before. "Elsie, how have you been?"

"You know how I've been, Freddy. When was it we last met? But I think I ought to be going now. I really had no idea," she said in a monotone. "Congratulations, Miss … Pendleton." Elsie looked at me only briefly before she fixed her gaze on the floor. She lingered at the table, her words hanging in the air. Her lip quivered, seemingly from something left unspoken. After taking a quick look at Freddy, she turned around. I watched her delicate form glide off and get swallowed up by the shadows at the front of the restaurant, and I had to wonder if this ethereal girl had been quite real.

When I recovered sufficiently, I said, "Freddy, who was that *peculiar* woman?"

"Just a friend of mine," he was quick to say.

"Friend? But you've said nothing about her the whole time I've known you. Why is that? Why do I not know about this friend?" The anxiety, which had started in my chest when I first saw Elsie, now crept up into my throat.

"Relax, darling. It's nothing," said Freddy. He smiled tightly and took my hand, but I shook it off violently.

My voice was unbecomingly shrill, like that of a bad actress in hysterics. "Relax? You're serious? A woman I've never even heard of—and a strikingly beautiful one at that—approaches you and seems devastated you've got a fiancée, and you expect me to relax? Freddy, what the devil is this all about?"

Other diners swivelled their heads around to look at us, holding their cutlery in midair as conversation died on their lips. Some looked at me as though I was a pitiable creature. Others looked sorry for Freddy.

He glanced around at them anxiously before turning to me and raising an index finger to his lips. "Sweetheart, I can explain everything if you'll just keep your voice down. I'm well known here, so please—I beg of you—*do not* embarrass me."

I calmed myself by taking a few deep breaths, and then I waited for him to speak. "Well?"

His eyes darted around as he spoke. "Elsie and I used to be something of an … item, I suppose you could say. But it was some time ago, when I was studying abroad. The last thing I expected was to see her here in Toronto."

I was trying to keep my voice down but failing miserably. "Really? Some time ago? She hinted it was recent. And if it really was so long ago, why are you acting so guilty?"

He looked hurt. "Guilty? I'm just astonished to see her, that's all. And I'm embarrassed you're making such a dreadful fuss about all this. Everyone's watching us. Trust me—I haven't done anything to feel guilty about. Elsie and I had long since called it quits by the time I met you. And it wasn't much of a romance to begin with, frankly." He reached out for my hand across the table, but I slowly withdrew it and shrunk back into my chair.

"Why do I find this so hard to believe?"

Freddy's entire body seemed to stiffen as his hurt turned to anger. "That's your problem. Now if you don't mind, I think I'll be going. You'll either accompany me and we can discuss this quietly— if you think you can manage it—or we'll go our separate ways and speak when you're capable of being rational again." He pounded his fist on the table, making the cutlery jump. "There's nothing I loathe more than a hysterical woman!"

Tears were welling up in my eyes, making my vision blurry. I tried to speak, but nothing came out.

Freddy stood up suddenly and loomed over me. "Well, what are you going to do? Decide!"

I sat there on the verge of tears, unable to get up, unable to say anything—just completely at a loss.

Spinning around to leave, he accidentally knocked the vase of chrysanthemums over. He left without another word, marching briskly toward the door. I sat for some minutes in silence, sniffling and dabbing at my eyes, trying to regain my composure. The water dripped from the vase and slowly stained the carpet dark. I hardly knew what had happened— only that things wouldn't ever be the same.

Our usual waiter came to the table. "Will Madam still be ordering this afternoon?" He looked doubtful. He set the vase right and rearranged the flowers.

"I'm afraid not. I'm very sorry, but I really must be leaving now."

"We will see you again, I hope?" His expression was kindly.

I nodded, threw my wrap around my shoulders, and hurried to the door. On the way out, I noticed Elsie in the centre of a jovial group, but with her downcast eyes and hunched posture she seemed a world apart from the rest. Our eyes met briefly, but I read neither envy nor hatred in hers—only the shock of having cherished illusions ripped away. We had much in common: she looked stricken, I felt the same, and it was all because of Freddy.

I clapped the diary shut. Wow, no wonder Constance always looked so distressed nearly every time I saw her. Freddy's true nature had been revealed in a shocking way, and she'd been forced to the realization that she was in love with an unrepentant cad. Yes, she'd often annoyed me with her frantic ploys to get my attention, but I felt an immediate surge of sympathy for her. She was smart, beautiful, and utterly devoted to Freddy. He couldn't have asked for anything more, and with the way he'd behaved, he deserved far less. If only I could have reached back through time and convinced him of what a catch she really was.

CHAPTER 15

First thing the next morning, I encountered Chloe in the staff washroom. Even the dingy lighting, which cast long, dark shadows, and the careful application of concealer couldn't mask the angry red gash that zigzagged from her cheekbone to just above her jaw. I had to wonder why she'd taken the bandage off.

"Chloe, you never really said what happened yesterday. I apologize if I seemed a bit distracted or cranky. I'm afraid I was preoccupied with another ghostly encounter I had with Constance, poor thing."

"Constance? You gave her a name?" She was looking in the mirror, examining the gash. I thought I detected amusement in her eyes.

"No. That's what her name is."

Chloe levelled a skeptical gaze at me.

"I'll tell you more about it later. First I want to hear what happened to you."

"Well, I guess I was having an encounter of my own yesterday, but with an aggressive chandelier," she said. She looked a bit sad, but then her mood abruptly changed, and she let out a chuckle. "I'm such an idiot for smashing into it!"

"If you say so," I said, shrugging. "But it could happen to anyone." We left the washroom and strolled down the hall toward the cataloguing room. "Ours is a surprisingly dangerous business. I'll never forget the time Toby Hightower somehow managed to stab himself with a Georgian silver meat skewer."

A spark animated Chloe's face. "Toby Hightower? Who's he?"

We reached the cataloguing room and stood outside the closed door. "Oh, that was well before your time. Toby was the silver specialist about ten years ago."

"So what happened?"

"Well, get this. According to Toby, the thing flew off the shelf and just embedded itself in his arm when he was sitting at his desk working. Can you imagine?"

"Wow." Chloe gaped at me. "Then what?"

Talking about the incident still made me feel a tad queasy even after all these years, but I continued. "After it happened, he was found wandering around the auction gallery in a zombie-like trance, and that godawful skewer—it wasn't even a nice example—was still stuck in his forearm. The whole thing was ghastly. He was dribbling blood all over the Persian carpets, which annoyed Gable no end because of the cleaning bills. I don't think Toby stayed at Gable's more than a week after that.

He just didn't show up one day, and we never saw him again. Poor guy."

Chloe was staring at me, her eyes wide. "It just flew into his arm? Really?"

"Well, no one bought the story," I said. "I mean, meat skewers don't just fly off the shelves by themselves and impale people, do they? Some suspected it was a truly inept suicide attempt, as if Toby really hadn't thought it through at all."

Chloe was standing much closer to me now and watching my face intently. "Suicide? Didn't anyone think it might have been assault?"

"Well, Toby was clinically depressed. He told me so himself. He'd been to psychotherapist after psychotherapist and tried medication after medication, but nothing really worked. But he was a model employee—incredibly nice and helpful to staff and clients alike—and everyone liked him. Sometimes he didn't make it to work, which ticked Gable off. If you can believe it, we all managed to persuade him to be more tolerant of Toby's condition. I'd be surprised if Toby had an enemy in the world. I'm sure no one attacked him. What motive could they possibly have had?"

Chloe seemed to be turning all this over in her mind, and she looked skeptical.

"Seriously," I said. "Ask Mark if you don't believe the story. He'll remember Toby. The whole thing was pretty hard to forget."

She looked pensive. "Oh, I believe the story. It's not that. And I agree it's not likely anyone attacked him. I'm just thinking that maybe he was later 'successful,' as they say, in a suicide attempt, which was why you never saw him again."

Chloe's eyes glimmered. For one usually so easily horrified, she was certainly behaving like a ghoul. I couldn't imagine what had come over her. All those late nights spent cataloguing innocent little teddies and dollies couldn't possibly have brought on such dark thoughts. Perhaps she was simply reacting to the strain of recent events—the missing porcelain and Gable's unsolved murder. It was making all of us behave strangely. And now this unfortunate collision with the chandelier had pushed her to the edge. I'd have to watch that she didn't go over it. Perhaps I'd recommend to George that she take a few days off once the auction was over.

I said, "Can we get off this ghoulish topic now? I refuse to believe that Toby Hightower was a victim of violence, self-inflicted or otherwise. It was a freak accident. He's probably happily settled in the suburbs now with a wife, five children, and a job as a bank manager. On a related topic, how did you manage to get such a horrible gash from walking into a chandelier? I'm still struggling to understand this. It's not like you were speeding."

I saw Chloe's entire body tense. She turned around, and I found myself following her down the hallway. She was walking briskly, her fists balled up, toward the auction gallery. Two police officers who were there to conduct interviews eyed her with interest as she walked past them, and one whispered something to the other. Finally, when I'd gained on her and was a mere two or three steps from her, she whirled around and let me have it.

"Isn't it bad enough I have to walk around looking like Scarface? Do you have to keep drawing attention to it?"

I immediately felt a sharp pang of guilt. I'd been horribly insensitive. "Gosh, Chloe, I'm awfully sorry. I really don't know what I was thinking, harping on the accident again. It must be the strain of everything that's happened lately around here. It's getting to me. Not that that's really an excuse or anything. I really am such a fool," I said, babbling helplessly.

But she calmed down as quickly as she'd flared up. "It's okay. Really." The expression in her eyes was soft again, as if she'd already forgiven me. Her rapid mood changes disturbed me; she was really becoming peculiar.

"Sorry."

"No, really. It's fine. Honest." Now an edge of impatience shaded her voice.

We walked to the cataloguing room and our cubicles in silence. When we arrived, Mark was panting; he hugged an enormous painted plaster blackamoor to his chest as he struggled to take it out to the gallery. It was one of a pair.

"A new friend, Mark?" I said.

He gave me a sour look. "A worthy addition to any space—especially if you happen to live in a funhouse." The blackamoor, which grinned with glee at the sight of his exertions, was getting the better of him. "I'm way too old for this kind of workout," he said breathlessly.

"Maybe I can help you with that?" said Chloe.

"Thank you."

He set the blackamoor on its feet, and she grabbed the feet while he took the head. Off they went down the hallway with their cargo, Mark grunting and cursing the whole way.

Meanwhile, Taylor was leaning back in her chair, her feet up on the desk while she talked on the phone. Her pose always made me gnash my teeth, as I knew how easy it was to fall backwards and topple onto some innocent specimen of porcelain or glass that someone had been careless enough to set on the floor, smashing it beyond repair or even recognition. I'd done it once or twice myself over the years, and she'd done it a few times as well. Between the two of us, we were lucky we hadn't done more damage.

"Taylor!" I said. "Feet on the floor!"

Her whole body shook convulsively, and her feet dropped to the floor with a thud. She turned around, cast an embarrassed glance at me, and mouthed the word *sorry*. I was glad to see her being contrite instead of openly defiant for a change. We were definitely making progress. She ended her conversation quickly and hung up the phone.

Turning to look at me, she said, "I know, I know. I'm a klutz."

"Think nothing of it. I am too. You've seen me tumble to the floor before." I smiled as I waved her concerns away. "At the risk of sounding like a broken record, I thought I'd suggest we take one last shot at finding the stolen porcelain, since it should be out for the preview tomorrow."

"Stolen?"

"Um—missing? I don't really know what to call it anymore. I have this idea you think it was stolen, which is why you were crying so much."

She looked as if she wanted to say something more but went silent. "Okay, I'll help you look."

I absentmindedly looked at my desk. It was usually chock full of stuff waiting to be catalogued and you could hardly even see the surface of it, but I noticed a bit of empty space on one of the trays of Birks silver flatware I'd received recently. I was sure something was missing from it, but I couldn't put my finger on what it was.

"Taylor, do you remember what else was on this tray?"

She got up to inspect the contents. "Can't say I do," she said with a shrug.

"Was there a skewer in this set?" That possibility was uppermost in my mind because of the conversation I'd just had with Chloe. "Or a carving knife?"

"I dunno. Let's check the inventory list to see what's supposed to be there. It's not urgent, is it? I mean, the stuff's not even being auctioned off till January."

But I had no time to answer, for just then the door flew open and George burst into the room in a state of nervous excitement. His words tumbled out in a rush. "I found it! The missing porcelain. And you'll never guess where it is!"

CHAPTER 16

George charged down the flight of stairs so fast, I thought he'd become airborne, and I followed breathlessly behind him to the back of the basement. Behind the unstable tower of stacked-up chairs and the velvet settee where Constance had writhed hysterically were the five pieces of missing porcelain sitting on the concrete floor. Parts of them were obscured by the clutter, but it was definitely them. The large figural group with the leering shepherd and his shepherdess on a broad platform base was standing upright, its back to us. Scattered around it were the other four pieces: the green parrot lying stiffly on its side, Pierrot looking as if he were sidling up to the shepherdess in an unseemly way, the German shepherd on its back with its legs in the air, and the lady harpist facing the sheep in the figural group as if playing a tune for it.

Before I knew what had hit me, George caught me in his arms and was hugging me so tightly, I thought I'd suffocate. "Oh, isn't it wonderful they've been found!" he said.

Was he delirious? Staggered by his rush of emotion, I finally remembered to breathe and began to extricate myself from his embrace, which I had to admit was warm and exciting. When we were apart, I looked up at him, speechless.

He stepped back into the shadows, but I could see his eyes shining. He smiled a little, but I wasn't sure how to read it. Was he embarrassed? Excited? I wondered if he felt half as giddy as I did.

"Now probably isn't the time to say this, Virginia, but ..." He paused for a long time, looking down, pacing, scratching the back of his head, squinting, and scrunching up his face.

He seemed to be looking for precisely the right words, so I waited.

"Can I take you out for dinner next weekend, after this whole blockbuster auction business is over with?" He stepped out of the shadows again, and his face was fraught with worry. Did he really think I'd say no?

I was floating somewhere high in the stratosphere. Feeling warm and flushed, I said, "Yes, of course you can. I'd be ... delighted."

His face relaxed, and he released a loud sigh. "Good! I knew it all along."

"That I'd say yes?"

He nodded. "But I was still worried you'd say no."

"I wanted you to ask me."

We spent a couple of moments grinning at each other

foolishly. Then George straightened his rumpled suit and began behaving like the stand-in company president he'd become.

"What do you suppose the porcelain's doing down here?" he said.

"I really haven't the foggiest. It seems odd that someone would dump it here, don't you think? It's not even really all that hidden, is it?"

I'd just been down to this part of the basement to witness Constance's dramatic exhibition—how was it possible I'd managed to miss the porcelain when it was right before my eyes? Her bizarre theatrics must have distracted me. The memory of her pointing at something flashed into my head, and I simultaneously experienced a sinking sensation. *Ah, that was it!* It made perfect sense now. She'd been trying to show me where the porcelain was, and I was too obtuse to get it. Her frustration with me had made her wild with hysteria, and I couldn't blame her. Poor Constance!

"George, I feel like such an idiot. The ghost was trying to show me where the porcelain was, but I didn't get it. I just got angry at her." My vocal cords were taut, reflecting the strain of the last few days. I narrated the latest ghostly encounter for him.

"Well, never mind that. You've got the pieces back now. That's what matters, isn't it?" He smiled reassuringly.

I felt the tension ease in my shoulders. "Now I won't get the sack," I said, forgetting momentarily that Brian Gable III was dead.

George squinted at me curiously.

"I know, I know, he can't hurt me now. I can't believe I actually forgot for a second."

I wanted to inspect the pieces, but the only one I could reach easily was the German shepherd. The minuscule chip on its paw wouldn't significantly affect its value at auction, but I wondered if the other pieces had sustained any damage.

"I'll have Taylor take a better look at everything and report to me on the condition," I said. "Say, what made you think to look here?"

George looked a bit puzzled. "The thing is, I didn't think to look here. I was getting some coffee in the kitchen when I heard someone coughing. I walked toward where I thought the sound was coming from, but whoever it was had moved off. Not a soul was around. Then I glimpsed something glossy and white behind the furniture. It never occurred to me the porcelain would be here. I can understand it getting shuffled around upstairs, but why would someone bother to take it to the *basement*? I mean, that takes concerted effort."

"I can't help but feel relieved, George, but at the same time, we've got to find out who did this. You're right—it's no accident it's here. Oh, I meant to show you that threatening note I got. And there was something I wanted to ask you about."

"Note? From who? Should we give it to the police?" His forehead wrinkled with concern.

"I guess so. It's upstairs. I—" I heard soft footsteps behind us.

"So you found it, huh? Wow, at last this whole thing's over," said Taylor. She drew the back of her hand across her forehead, sighed, and allowed herself a slight smile.

"Well, not exactly," said George. "Naturally, we still have to find out who did this. It's a deliberate act designed to make Virginia look incompetent, and the culprit needs to be exposed."

Taylor shifted her weight from side to side and eyed us uneasily, her gaze moving from me to George and then back to me again. Pointing to herself, she said, "You don't think *I* did it?"

"No, Taylor. I know how upset you've been," I said. "And why would you do something that could potentially reflect badly on you too? It makes no sense. You're a member of this department too. Though sometimes, I almost forgot you were."

She looked a bit sheepish and shrugged. "I'll admit I haven't exactly been the greatest assistant the world's ever known. But I'll get better."

"And I know I haven't been the greatest boss. I'd love it if our relationship from now on became more cooperative and less … adversarial. Wouldn't you?"

There had always been an awkward distance between us, and I dearly wanted to bridge the gap. I was tempted to take a step forward and hug Taylor, but she wasn't the hugging kind. She stood there stiffly, her arms folded across her chest. She looked down. "Yeah. Well, I better get going and finish setting up the preview." She pointed to the porcelain on the floor. "Guess I should take these with me?"

"Yes, but don't take them upstairs. Jared took the photos on Wednesday, so these would have been missed. They need to be shot, so take them over to his studio."

The "studio" was a cluttered cubbyhole in the corner of the basement. There, Jared would photograph every item in the auction, and we'd project a slide of each one behind the auctioneer as it was being sold. That afternoon, he was scheduled to photograph any items that had come in at the last minute or that we'd somehow overlooked. We'd found the porcelain just in time.

Taylor reached behind the furniture and pulled out the four porcelain figurines. She scooped them up in her arms in the cavalier fashion she and I had developed after years of handling delicate objects. "I'll be back for the big one," she said, nodding toward the gaudy 1950s behemoth on the floor.

"Ask Jared to take that one in. It'll be easier."

She nodded and was on her way.

After Taylor left, George said, "Well, I'd better call a meeting to let everyone know we've found the porcelain."

"Oh, you can bet Taylor spread the word right after you burst into the cataloguing room, so there's probably no need."

He nodded. "I realize that, but I want to study everyone's reaction to the news."

"That's clever." I smiled and watched the corners of George's mouth twitch into an awkward smile. He looked faintly flushed.

"I'd like your—er—observations as well." He touched my forearm lightly.

I took his hand in both of mine. His expression went blank; I'd stunned him with the gesture. My heart was thudding so violently, it seemed about to burst free of my chest. On the one hand, I wanted to tell myself to get a grip on myself, that this was somehow dangerous, but on the other, I couldn't remember when anyone had last made me tingle with excitement from the top of my head to the tips of my toes, and I was enjoying the sensation. "Of course. We're a team, aren't we?" I whispered, leaning toward him.

He looked pensive and serious. Squeezing my hand, he said, "Yes, I believe we are, Virginia."

I followed George up the stairs, and he cornered Helen on the landing and asked her to announce a meeting in the gallery. Everyone arrayed themselves over the furniture, which had been invitingly placed in room settings. George and I sat on a stiff Victorian settee that made crunching noises when we sat down, making me wonder what it could possibly be stuffed with. Its fussy scrolling foliate design was so unlike the plain one my ghost seemed to favour; she had good taste. Next to us was a richly patterned tiger maple side table adorned with an art nouveau bronze sculpture of a sinuous nude with a flirtatious smile. From across the room, Sally kept looking at me, nodding toward George, winking, and smiling. He did his best to ignore her, while I struggled to make my face reflect a sort of puzzled innocence.

Everyone chattered away noisily. It was partly the excitement that usually came the Friday before a preview; the air would practically vibrate with energy once we were ready at last to present our treasure trove to the public. But the excitement seemed to be fuelled by something else as well: some sense of order had been restored because at least the lost goods had been found. And just as I suspected, everyone already knew it, for no one talked of anything else. Yes, a killer was still loose among us and some recovered porcelain was a flimsy thing to hang our hopes on, but it was better than nothing.

Above the din, George cleared his throat loudly, but no one but me seemed to notice.

"For God's sake, aren't there any doughnuts?" said Sally, her eyes sparkling. Silence fell over the group. Chloe looked horrified, while Mark tried to disguise his mirth by covering his mouth with his hand.

George looked mildly irritated and said, "Er—no, Sally. If you have no objections, that's not a tradition I wish to continue. Our waistlines and longevity will benefit greatly, I'm sure. And Tim Hortons won't suffer any great loss in revenue."

Sally and a few others chuckled, and everyone looked at George expectantly. Squinting and furrowing his brow, he got straight to the point, speaking in that crisp, no-nonsense way I had grown to admire. I couldn't take my eyes off him, and I hoped I didn't look like some sort of simpering, lovesick idiot. At this stage, I really didn't want anyone to know about our fledgling romance, if that's what it really was.

"Although you all seem to know this already, I just wanted to confirm that the missing porcelain's been recovered. Purely by chance, I found it in the basement behind the art deco settee and the big stack of chairs. Make no mistake, this whole episode has been extremely stressful for Virginia and Taylor. If you have any suspicions about who hid the porcelain, come forward immediately. And if *you* put it there, also come forward immediately—and good luck trying to justify your actions. If I find out you were responsible and didn't come forward, you'll be immediately dismissed."

No one said a word. George really meant business, and everyone knew it. I wanted to burst into ecstatic applause. This was the kind of authoritative leadership Gable & Co. had needed all along, not the insulting buffoonery of Brian Gable III. But remembering I was supposed to be watching other people, not mooning over George, I looked around the room. My joy turned to disappointment, for a perfect calm prevailed. No one squirmed, broke a sweat, or so much as even fidgeted. Such maddening inscrutability was intolerable; I'd been sure someone would give himself or herself away, if not openly confess. Fury was rising in my gorge, and I had a feeling I was about to say something I'd profoundly regret. Mark, who was sitting on the chair next to me, instinctively sensed my anger and placed a hand on my shoulder, which failed to calm me.

I stood up, quivering as I began to speak, my voice breaking. "This is addressed to whatever moron thought it would be fun to hide the porcelain in the basement. Because of you, I feared losing my job. Because of you, Taylor and I have been snapping at each other like dogs. And don't forget—you upset her too, not just me. We've both had our share of sleepless nights. Having to chase after lost items isn't our idea of fun, not by a long shot, and if you think it's fun, then—"

"Then *what*?" said Jared, snorting. "Cut the drama." He leaned back in his chair and yawned, stretching his arms over his head.

I gaped at George, not knowing what to say.

"Oh shut up, Jared!" said Sally. Her words resounded like a slap, and I heard Dora giggle.

George looked secretly pleased. "Go on," he whispered to me. "I'll deal with that little creep later."

"What I meant to say, before Jared so rudely interrupted me, was that whoever did this is some kind of a sadist. Whoever you are, don't make Taylor and me hate you more by being cowardly enough not to come forward." A small tear snaked down my cheek. I never could get furious without shedding a tear or two.

I was greeted by silence; once again, quiet Virginia had spoken up in a meeting, and no one knew quite what to do about it. Conditioned by years of cowering before Gable, I found myself worried about George's reaction, even though I knew full well my fears were irrational.

"Well said, Virginia!" He was grinning at me.

Relieved by George's reaction, I wiped away the tear and managed a smile.

Abruptly, a voice piped up. "Well? Isn't anyone gonna take responsibility?" Taylor's face was crimson, and her normally soft voice was hoarse with venom. She shot a murderous look at Chloe, and George looked at me, raising an eyebrow. All I could do was shrug.

Chloe leaped to her feet and was quaking with rage. The red gash that zigzagged across her cheek seemed to throb, becoming even redder. "It was Sally! She's the one you should be furious with, Taylor." She dashed out of the meeting, but not before Sally had released a lively whoop of laughter.

What on earth had just happened? I was stunned into silence and looked helplessly at George.

"Chloe! Wait!" he yelled. He got up and bolted after her. I jumped up from the settee and followed, but she'd already fled the building, slamming the front door behind her so hard, it shuddered violently. We stood outside on the sidewalk, looking from left to right on Queen Street, scanning each person who passed by in the bright autumn sunshine, but there was no sign of Chloe anywhere.

George looked at me earnestly. "We were right behind her. How'd she manage to get away?"

Standing there trembling, I had no answer. Just like my ghost, Chloe had somehow vanished before my eyes.

CHAPTER 17

Two grim-looking police officers were heading toward George and me as we stood on the sidewalk. They nodded as they passed us and stopped to light up cigarettes in front of Gable & Co. They'd been out of the building and had missed all the fireworks. But since they had a murder to investigate, I didn't suppose they'd have much interest in a few pieces of missing porcelain, so I wasn't about to say anything about what had just happened.

George gave them a little wave and then looked at me with concern. "Virginia, why not take an extended lunch hour? Look at you—you're shaking! Take some time to calm down. I'll keep looking for Chloe." He squeezed my arm discreetly. I began walking toward the diner while he went in the other direction along Queen Street.

He was right that I needed to calm down. I was still digesting the surreal scene I'd just witnessed. The distressing accusations had shocked me. Why had Taylor been so angry?

Why had Chloe accused Sally of hiding the porcelain? Had Sally actually done anything wrong? My head was whirling from all my questions and from the sheer drama of it all. I was deeply disturbed by the sight of Chloe, my very best friend at Gable & Co.—possibly my best friend period—fleeing the auction gallery in a rage.

The cataloguing room was quiet, and I assumed the others had gone out to lunch. That was fine with me, as I thought I'd cry if I bumped into anyone and was required to speak. Mechanically, I retrieved Constance's diary from the locked cabinet; I'd brought it to work to distract me during lunch anyway. But it wasn't simply a distraction. Ludicrous as it seemed, I was becoming more and more convinced that its contents would help me find meaning in the chaos that had engulfed me and everyone else at Gable & Co. Or perhaps I was just becoming more and more desperate for an end to this tumultuous time.

I entered A Step Back in Time, where Gable had spent his final fitful moments as a fully conscious human being. I went there now not because I was eager to return to the scene of his collapse, but because I knew no one I worked with would be there to bother me. No one would dare return just yet—not for a good long while. Being reminded of Gable's demise wasn't exactly pleasant for any of us.

No sooner had I sat down than Frank was hovering over my table. He looked at me with an expression of surprise that quickly turned to one of sympathy. "I heard," he said, his bushy moustache twitching restlessly.

I just nodded sadly.

"Jesus. I'm awfully sorry."

"The usual, please, Frank. Except I'll have tea instead of coffee today."

"Sure. Sure thing. And if there's anything I can do, just …"

His concern surprised me. I'd never considered the possibility that we were on the sort of terms where people say, "If there's anything I can do," to each other. Frank was just an acquaintance who'd never said much to me apart from asking what I wanted to eat. But sometimes people really don't know what to say after someone's died, so they trot out the standard meaningless platitudes.

"Thanks." I smiled as best I could, and Frank wandered away.

It was well past the lunch hour, and the diner was nearly empty. I noticed Alice Aberfoyle sitting alone in a booth at the back. Her pinched wee face and beady eyes made me think of a rat. Today she was decked out in a voluminous red velvet dress with white faux fur trim and lipstick that matched the red of the dress precisely. I figured this was her way of getting into the Christmas spirit early. We briefly made eye contact; she glanced at me in a haughty way that nearly made me laugh, and then I looked away.

After Frank returned with the grilled cheese sandwich, the little metal teapot that always spilled, a stale orange pekoe teabag, and a well-worn, stained mug, I opened Constance's diary and read the next entry.

July 12, 1928

I've been meaning to write for quite some time now, but really, what is there to say about my catastrophic life anymore? I've been devastated since that awful afternoon at the King Edward, and Freddy's just not the same toward me anymore. He's still pleasant enough most days and claims he cares for me more than ever, but he's ever so distracted. He can't seem to stop himself from staring at every pretty girl who walks by; it's a compulsion with him. Yes, we still go out on the town as we've always done, and I do try to be gay and cheerful to maintain his interest, but I can barely manage it most days. Even when I can, he must see right through me, for I'm surely the most unconvincing actress to ever walk the earth.

Ever since that day, I've been feeling as if my life has been unravelling like a moth-eaten old sweater. But perhaps I ought to hold out some hope for us yet; we're still together, and Freddy insists I'm very much "his girl." Furthermore—and I know this must seem unbelievable—we're now engaged to be married. Our engagement took place two weeks ago, and I suppose I ought to be over the moon. If the circumstances were different, I would be. But no wedding date has been set, and somehow I despair of ever walking down the aisle. And the engagement itself was hardly what I've always dreamed of—just about the furthest thing from it, in fact.

Freddy was acting most peculiar the day it happened. We'd arranged to meet that afternoon in Craigleigh Gardens, which isn't far from my home. For reasons I couldn't even begin to fathom at the time, he seemed jittery when we met at the lovely old wrought iron and stone gates of the park. We walked across the carefully manicured lawn, looking down at the densely wooded ravine below and watching passersby—families enjoying a leisurely Sunday outing and couples strolling arm in arm. Much to my delight, two fox terriers were running in circles and tumbling about playfully. Freddy was talking nineteen to the dozen and laughing nervously at both his own remarks and any I managed to squeeze in.

We sat down on a bench under the shade of a massive oak tree, hoping to find relief from the relentless sun. Behind us, pale pink roses trembled in a breeze that did little to cool us down. Freddy took my hand, sighed deeply, and looked into my eyes, his expression serious and his eyes a little moist. The afternoon sun lit his hair in a kind of halo. He at once became very quiet indeed.

Finally, he said, "I do hope we've gotten past our troubles now, dear girl. I'm willing to move on from that dreadful afternoon at the King Edward if you are. Let's forget what happened and make a new start." A smile spread across his face.

Against my better judgment, my heart began to swell with joy, and all the torment of the previous few weeks vanished in a mere moment. I clutched at his hand. "Oh, Freddy," I said, "you've no idea what this means to me. I want that too." Not a second later, tears were trickling down my face. I wanted to say more, to tell him how much I loved him, but I couldn't even find the words.

Freddy placed one hand on my cheek and carefully wiped away my tears with his thumb. He moved in close to kiss me, and with a jolt, there it was: that unforgettable floral, faintly spicy scent— indeed, the very one I'd smelled at the King Edward when Elsie had come up behind me.

I jerked away from Freddy violently.

Alarmed, he said, "Darling, what is it?"

"That smell!"

"What smell? You don't mean the roses?" He laughed. It was a short, humourless laugh. He began to shift himself around on the bench as if he'd only just noticed he was sitting on a hard, uncomfortable surface.

"You know very well what smell. It's that perfume your 'friend' Elsie wears."

He took my hand and let out another hollow laugh. "Good heavens, darling, what an active imagination you have! Of course it's not Elsie's perfume. I insist—it absolutely *must* be the roses. The scent is so powerful, it's confusing you. Or if it's not that, it must be your own perfume." He smiled in an ingratiating way.

The joyful swelling in my heart was already dwindling into nothingness, and I felt myself growing as cold as a stone. I withdrew my hand from Freddy's and edged away from him to the other end of the bench. I would not be convinced by this ridiculous sham. I would not be told I was confused, for I was as certain as I could possibly be that I'd smelled Elsie's fragrance. Even though I'd just dissolved into tears, my mind was sharp and clear, and I knew exactly what I wanted to say. I got up from the bench and stood in front of Freddy, looking down at him, my fists digging into my hip bones.

"Freddy, let me ask you this. How do you expect me to be happy with you when you insist on running around with this Elsie person?"

His eyes wide, he looked directly at me and said, "I am *not* running around with Elsie. Trust me on this." He didn't even flinch. Someone who didn't know him as well as I did would have been convinced.

For a moment, we just looked at each other. I watched him sitting there, lighting a cigarette and smoking in his white linen summer suit, the sun casting a warm glow over his sharp features. Although I'd always thought of him as tall, raw-boned, and devastatingly handsome, he now looked small and rumpled to me, his long limbs crossed and folded in tightly to his body, almost as if he were cold despite the oppressive summer heat. If I weren't careful, in another minute I'd be feeling sorry for him. As I felt myself soften toward him ever so slightly, I reminded myself he was a cad and held my more charitable feelings firmly in check.

"Freddy, this can't go on. I will not tolerate this." I spun around and started marching off.

He sprang to his feet and shouted, "Wait!"

Of the people who were meandering around Craigleigh Gardens, at least half a dozen turned to look at us now. Their curiosity piqued, they moved closer to us until they were hovering near the rose bushes and watching intently, wondering what might happen next. I had the unnerving sensation that they saw us as actors on a stage performing expressly for their entertainment. Some people looked alarmed by the commotion, while others seemed amused. All were silent.

A few gasps and murmurs of surprise came from the spectators when Freddy got down on his knees and said, "Constance—please!"

Was it sincerity I heard in his voice, or was I imagining it? I couldn't be sure until he caught at my hand, clutching it in both of his and pulling it to his cheek; that was when I saw the earnest expression in his eyes.

"Goodness, what is it, Freddy?" I twisted my arm in an attempt to wriggle free, but his grip was firm.

"*Will you marry me?*" I'd never heard his voice— or any voice, for that matter—fraught with such urgency. "I've got the ring and everything, dear girl. It's right here in my pocket." He removed a small green velvet box from his jacket pocket and held it tantalizingly before me. "Now you know why I was so insistent on meeting you here today."

Cheers and applause arose from the onlookers. I looked at their faces and was dismayed to see smiles and nods all around. Perhaps even more alarmingly, their number had increased. They'd gone from a mere cluster of people to a small crowd. Even the fox terriers had stopped playing and were gazing attentively at us.

"Go on," said one woman, beaming at me. "Answer the poor man." She was tall and striking and about my mother's age. When I'd first arrived to meet Freddy, I watched her floating through the park ever so elegantly in a chiffon and lace gown.

"If you don't want him, maybe I'll try my luck, dearie," said another, a rotund matron in a frock with a bold pattern of purple-and-yellow flowers all over it. She winked at Freddy, and titters and hoots swept through the crowd. He scarcely seemed to notice; he was still down on his knees and staring up at me imploringly.

In spite of the weather, I broke out into a cold sweat. I felt a sour taste in my mouth, a bitterness born of knowing that Freddy had flagrantly manipulated the circumstances to his advantage. How could I say no under such public pressure? No girl could possibly withstand it. The situation was not only ludicrous but unfair.

I knew I'd succumb, but I mounted a protest, ineffectual though it was. "But we have so much to discuss—"

"Which can certainly wait until we're married!" Freddy released an exasperated sigh. He stood up and turned to everyone and smiled in that charming way of his, as if to rally support for his position. That he was unabashedly playing the crowd made me seethe with anger, but I just stood there, silent.

"He's right," said a portly fellow wearing a straw boater. "It can wait."

An old woman with crooked teeth spoke next. "Why the hesitation, love? Just say yes. It's the sensible thing to do. He seems like a very nice young fellow, after all."

A middle-aged woman, resplendent in an expensive lilac-coloured silk dress, hat, and shoes dyed to match, coolly looked me up and down. With a note of disdain, she said, "Do you honestly expect to do better?"

I was dumbfounded. Why did these people think they had any right to comment? An outrageous thought occurred to me: perhaps Freddy had hired them especially to wear me down. No, it was simply impossible; he couldn't have planned this. Our raised voices had attracted their attention, and with nothing better to do on a dull Sunday afternoon, they'd naturally been drawn into our drama.

Freddy extracted the ring from the velvet box and held it up to me, turning it this way and that. It was an enormous European-cut diamond, terribly expensive, in a dainty filigree platinum setting. Catching the late-afternoon sun, the stone glittered like light dancing on choppy waters.

"Oh my!" said someone with a gasp.

"How extraordinary!" said the woman in the chiffon gown.

The ring held my attention, hypnotizing me with its sparkle. I didn't want to be another shallow creature charmed more by a superlative engagement ring than the man who proffered it, but I felt my resolve to refuse him weaken even more.

I glanced from the ring to Freddy's pleading face. "Very well, then. My answer is yes."

It was a very weak moment indeed.

Freddy leaped up and threw his arms around me, nearly knocking me off balance, and loud cheers erupted all around. He slipped the ring on my finger. While he smiled, his triumph complete, several of the men came up to him and slapped him on the back, and then they all lit cigarettes, while the women clustered around me to examine the ring closely and emit the customary oohs and ahs. I played the part of the ecstatic bride to be, smiling and thanking everyone for their effusive praise and congratulations. When the strangers finally lost interest in us and drifted away to the rest of their lives, the euphoric mask I'd been wearing rapidly slipped away. I sat quietly with Freddy on the bench, my hands folded in my lap. At first I could barely look at him.

"You won't regret this, Constance," he said. Gazing into his warm hazel eyes, I had no doubt he meant it; he really didn't intend to disappoint me. But I had sincere doubts he was right; surely I would regret it. How could I not when he didn't love me? He couldn't love anyone—of that I was convinced—but he'd keep expecting to find love right around the next corner, and if it wasn't Elsie, it would be someone else, and it would happen over and over again until the sharpness of my pain wore away, dulled to a dreary numbness. I'd made a terrible mistake by saying yes, and too exhausted to speak coherently, all I could do was weep in great heaving sobs on his shoulder—weep for his lack of real feeling for me, and for the loss of the innocent trust I'd placed in him.

"Oh, Constance. Are you really as happy as all that?"

I nodded. It went without saying that he was smart enough to see I wasn't happy at all, that in fact I was devastated. But his asking me that question and my pretending my tears were joyful ones started us off on playing a ridiculous game—one in which I'd pretend I wasn't wounded to my core and he'd pretend he loved me. Now we're willing and equal participants in this charade, and we both take a certain comfort in keeping up appearances. Sometimes I feel fleeting glimmers of hope—if Freddy happens to glance at me the way he used to in the beginning, for instance. In such moments I even believe it could still work out between us, and that's what makes me hang on. But I know extraordinary magic would be required for us to be truly happy together, and for reasons I fail to understand, magic seems in short supply.

And so we continue the sham. We're still seen at all the best parties, as smiling, poised, and glamorous as any other fashionable, well-to-do young couple. Sometimes, our photograph appears in the society column of the newspaper with lots of silly chatter about our engagement, including speculation about our wedding. WHEN WILL THEY SET A DATE? the headlines read. The society reporters must be desperate to whip up a bit of excitement on dull news days. Bernice and Lydia envy my so-called good fortune so much that they won't even speak to me. But neither of them knows what a farce our engagement truly is. Nor do they know how exhausting it is to keep pretending to be ecstatically happy when you're desperately sad. I'm hanging by a thread. Can nobody see it?

Frank slid the bill across the table just as I finished Constance's diary entry. This latest one reinforced my earlier thoughts about the source of her misery. It couldn't have been easy enduring

Freddy's two-timing ways, especially when she was just an inexperienced young thing. Yet he'd still wanted to marry her. What I couldn't comprehend was his insistence on doing so. He seemed like a standard-issue scoundrel and hardly the type to let himself get snared into marriage, let alone to insist on it. I wouldn't have been surprised if he'd been chasing anyone in a skirt. Learning he had been carrying on with another girl and didn't love her must have been bad enough for Constance, but knowing he wanted to marry her nonetheless and no doubt continue his womanizing ways must have driven her to the limits of her endurance. I was starting to see her in a new light; she wasn't so much crazy as heartbroken beyond repair, although the two often seemed indistinguishable. The foolish girl had allowed herself to fall in love with someone she barely knew, and she'd suffered greatly for the entanglement.

Just then, George appeared in my mind's eye. No—that wasn't it; Constance couldn't possibly be warning me about the perils of getting involved with him. Although I was only beginning to know him, my instincts told me he was as solid and sane as anyone I'd ever known. No, it had to be something else.

CHAPTER 18

That afternoon, the office was abuzz with gossip about Chloe's dramatic flight from the meeting, and no one got much work done for the rest of the day. Had Sally really been the culprit? It seemed too unbelievable. While the police searched the premises for evidence, I went to her office to see how she was taking Chloe's accusation. When I got there, she was calmly sorting through a messy stack of paintings in a storage bin.

"Hey Sally, how's it going?"

"Well, some nice policeman was just here interviewing me, but apart from that, it's been a pretty uneventful day." She winked. "He didn't come right out and say it, but I get the sense he's flummoxed about who killed Gable."

"So they're no further ahead than the rest of us, then. I wonder when they're planning to get around to interviewing me. Aren't I a key witness?"

Sally shrugged. "You'd think. Not the most efficient chaps, are they?"

"True. Say, have you seen either Chloe or Taylor? Neither seems to be around. I need to ask both of them what all that anger was about. And what did you make of Chloe accusing you of hiding the porcelain?"

But Sally was too busy clowning around to answer my question. She held up a cubist-style portrait of a woman howling; it was executed in violent shades of acid green and violet. The woman's expression reminded me of *The Scream*: her mouth was a huge O of alarm, and her hands were pressed against her cheeks. "So what do you think of this one? Looks a bit like our girl Chloe the other day, doesn't it?" She was right; the painting depicted exactly how Chloe had looked when Gable collapsed in the diner. "Do you suppose this sorry excuse for a painting could fetch ten dollars on a good day?"

Although I was still upset, it was hard not to laugh. "I see you're completely unfazed. I'm glad somebody is. I confess I'm feeling rattled about the whole mess."

"Of course I'm unfazed. Why wouldn't I be? Chloe, who you'll have to admit has been acting bloody weird lately, accuses me of hiding the porcelain? It's laughable. I know you really like the girl and consider her your bosom buddy, but she's not exactly Miss Credibility—or not lately. And what possible motivation would I have for sticking all that stuff in the basement, anyway? We're friends. I'm not about to try to make you look like an incompetent idiot who can't even keep track of things in her own department. Even if I did want you to look stupid, I'd find some other way of doing it than hauling porcelain all over the building. Who has the energy?"

I sighed. "I think Chloe's just a bit stressed out, that's all—like everyone else around here. She gets so stupid, she's apt to blurt out God knows what."

Sally snorted with laughter. "Stupid? That's an understatement, Virginia. She obviously felt Taylor was threatening her. Have you noticed that those two have detested each other since day one? What's it all about? There's something sinister going on there, I'm sure."

I waved her concerns away with a sweep of my hand. "Just a bad personality mix, I think. They may be about the same age, but they've got absolutely zero in common."

"Or perhaps they have much more in common than we realize, which is why they hate each other's guts," said Sally. "I've seen sisters like that—they're so much alike, they could be identical twins, but they scrap like cats and dogs and can't bear the sight of each other."

I nodded. "True enough. Well, I just wanted to check in with you." I turned to leave.

Sally swiftly reached out and grabbed my hand. Her eyes were shining with mischief, and she looked as if she was trying to hold back a grin. "Now you just wait one second, Blythe. You're not going anywhere until you tell me what's going on with you and George."

"My, you're blunt. And, um, I don't really know." It was true. I really didn't know, or not yet. Sally fixed me with an unwavering stare, and under her scrutiny, I felt increasingly flustered. I tried to leave, but she held fast to my hand.

"Now don't look at me all innocent like that. You know what I'm talking about. He adores you—that much is plain. And don't try to tell me the feeling isn't mutual, because it is. I'd stake my life on it."

Feeling Sally's eyes boring into me, I let loose an awkward little laugh. After I'd released it, I immediately felt better.

"See? I knew it!" Sally wrapped herself around me, smothering me in such an intense bear hug that I reeled with dizziness. When I recovered my senses, I decided to knock off early and head home. After all the commotion of the day, I craved nothing more than a hot bath and curling up on the couch for a quiet evening.

At home, the diary once again tempted me. A film of the ghostly Constance writhing in agony on the settee played over and over again in my mind, and I wondered if she'd ever managed to get over her disappointment in Freddy or if she was distraught for other reasons I didn't know of. I wanted to believe that Freddy had eventually realized what an absolute gem the girl was and they'd gotten married, had lots of babies, and lived happily ever after in the sort of unmitigated bliss that would have made Constance the envy of all her catty little friends. But of course it hadn't happened that way: my ghost was so young, so happily ever after wasn't even on the table. But how did it all play out? The only way I'd know was to read on.

September 21, 1928

It seems now it's all over. Or if not, it might as well be.

During the past couple of months, Freddy and I tried hard to make the best of everything. His efforts to please me were unquestionably sincere, and I couldn't help but love him for that. Despite everything, we had several blissful, languorous summer days when that oppressive black cloud of misery, which first appeared when Elsie did, floated away as if by magic, and we seemed once again as we were at the start—euphoric, carefree, and truly mad for each other. At such times I almost dared hope we had a future together.

Of course, we still stepped out to the finest soirees and other gatherings anyone saw fit to invite us to. But as the summer wore on, these became increasingly scarce. Until last Friday, I hadn't seen Bernice, Lydia, or Mildred in quite some time. Now it's become painfully clear that as I was drawn more and more into Freddy's world, those people I'd always thought of as my friends started dropping by the wayside.

Bernice used to be extremely keen on inviting us to her parties when Freddy and I first became an item. Perhaps she enjoyed the novelty of seeing "such a handsome couple" together, or perhaps she entertained thoughts that Freddy would soon discard me and she'd easily fill my shoes. Even if her motivation was unsavoury, she never betrayed it and was, in fact, very friendly toward me. We were beginning to enjoy what I thought of as genuine friendship and even spent several pleasant afternoons walking through Craigleigh Gardens. Have I appeared ungrateful to her? Is that why her invitations have dried up?

Lydia, whom I've always regarded as my very best friend, stopped inviting me for tea with her family. Of course, we did hit rather a rough patch. But even after she apologized for that time she eavesdropped on Freddy and me in Bernice's library and I accepted her apology, it was never the same. She failed to respond to any of my invitations to tea or to visit the Royal Ontario Museum with me. She just disappeared, and I heard nothing of her whereabouts for weeks. Many times I expressed my sadness to Freddy about losing her friendship, but he seemed unmoved by my loss. He said she wasn't worthy of me, and finally I'm starting to believe it.

Then there's Mildred, whom I've known since we were both five. We've been nothing if not as close as sisters. All throughout high school, we were inseparable—giggling our way through our classes and flirting outrageously with boys, as silly young things tend to do. It was no different after we graduated, really. Even though we didn't see each other daily anymore, we nonetheless maintained a close friendship, chatting several times a week by telephone and going to the pictures. Now, however, something's changed. All I get is a frosty reception from her each time I telephone her, so in the past couple of weeks, I've given up. She thinks nothing of ignoring me if we pass each other in the street; she doesn't bat an eye when I wave or call to her. She just gazes right past me with a hollow-eyed look; curiously, I seem not to exist for her now. I can't say why, but she seems intent on reducing me to nothing. I asked Freddy if he could explain his cousin's behaviour, but he claimed to be ignorant of her reasons for snubbing me.

Mildred's coldness was most apparent last Friday, a day I won't ever forget—or certainly not soon. That was the evening of Christopher Whitley's twenty-fifth birthday party. Christopher is a doctor who graduated from the University of Toronto and who also happens to be my next-door neighbour. Once Freddy entered the picture, Mama became very keen that Christopher and I should become acquainted and "develop an understanding," as she likes to say in that outmoded way of hers.

Throughout the summer, she and Papa continued to disdain Freddy and refuse to meet him in spite of our engagement. Papa was deeply insulted that Freddy didn't approach him to ask for my hand in marriage and has never forgiven him. But I suppose it's too late and none of that matters much anymore. Anyway, it's abundantly clear my parents relish the idea of adding another doctor to a family that's already full to bursting with them.

Though I adore Christopher as a friend—he's sweet, funny, and delightfully easygoing—I've never felt the head-over-heels romantic attraction to him that's so essential for marital bliss. Even after I'd explained all this to Mama, she said, "Poppycock!" and was still keen to play the matchmaker. She babbled on and on about what a tremendously good catch "that dashing Christopher" was. He received frequent invitations to afternoon tea at our house, during which, all too aware of Mama's intentions, he'd stammer and gallop his way through our conversations, often taking his leave early. Despite all this awkwardness, we came to like each other ever so much, but Christopher confessed to me he'd long had a secret engagement to Madeline Berry, a not-altogether-proper local actress, as least as far as his family's concerned. I wasn't to tell anyone, and I assured him I'd be the very soul of discretion.

I was delighted to receive an invitation to his birthday party, though it seemed Freddy wasn't wildly enthusiastic about the occasion. He and Christopher don't really get on; they're like chalk and cheese, altogether too different. When I first mentioned the invitation a week ago, Freddy was irritable, saying something along the lines of, "Well, if we absolutely *must* go." On the day of the party, when I asked him what his objections were, he shook his head and spent the next half hour moping on his parents' divan in the parlour. He was so morose, I didn't know what to say to him. One thing that's never worked with Freddy is making a concerted effort to bring him out of a foul frame of mind by making cheerful remarks. I've always had to allow him his moods, and then he gradually snaps out of them of his own accord and becomes more himself again. He spent the remainder of the afternoon reading the latest Fitzgerald novel, and by the time we were to go to the party, he was in a much sunnier mood and even started whistling "Blue Skies" as he put on his coat to leave.

Christopher greeted us at the door with his customary warmth. "Constance!" he said, and he shook my hand vigorously as I wished him happy birthday. I dare say he would have hugged me had Freddy not been there—he really is that sweet.

"Freddy!" Christopher grinned and clapped him on the back as if he were a brother. "Do make yourselves at home!"

I watched the two men—Freddy long and lean and dark and rather standoffish, Christopher of a much shorter stature, trim in his tuxedo, and fair-haired, his light blue eyes sparkling like champagne from behind horn-rimmed spectacles. He looked every inch the young doctor.

Freddy smiled. "Christopher—how nice to see you." His initial burst of enthusiasm fizzled noticeably toward the end of his remark. He looked around eagerly as if searching for someone. Then his eyes lit up. "Ah, there's Cousin Mildred. Why, it's been an age. Hold this, will you?"

Freddy removed his overcoat and hat and all but threw them into my outstretched arms. He dashed over to Mildred, who immediately got up from a sofa. She looked ravishing in a silk gown with narrow vertical stripes of vibrant peacock blue and cherry red. It complemented her short chestnut hair, which had been done in a permanent wave. She twisted a long jet necklace that hung around her neck as she waited for Freddy. I watched him plant a kiss on her indifferent cheek. Months ago, I would have waved across the room to her and received a brilliant smile for my trouble. She would have come over, embraced me, and chatted in her effusive way. Now I didn't bother to make the effort. Mildred looked from Freddy to me, and with one sweeping glance, her dark eyes took me in and she evaluated everything about me from my hairstyle to the shoes I wore. Her critical expression told me everything I needed to know, and she abruptly looked away. Meanwhile, I struggled under the weight of Freddy's things, which were piled up in my arms. Gallantly, Christopher came to my rescue.

"My goodness, Constance, do let me take those things!" He carefully hung up Freddy's coat, helped me off with my own, and then turned to study my face. "How are you, darling? You look a little peaky. You have been taking that tonic I recommended, haven't you?"

"I'm just fine, Christopher, and yes, I've been following your recommendations religiously. You'll be pleased to hear that Papa agrees with your tonic as well. He fully expects I'll recover my vitality in a matter of days." I smiled as brightly as I could. "Here, I've brought you a little something for your birthday." From my handbag I removed a small rectangular box tied up with a red ribbon.

Christopher flushed with pleasure. "Oh, how wonderful!" he said, before he even knew what it was. His enthusiasm was just one of the qualities that endeared him to me.

"Please open it. I do hope you'll find it to your liking."

"How could I not? The very thought of receiving a gift from you means the world to me." With nimble fingers, he undid the ribbon and removed a tortoiseshell fountain pen. He held it up to examine it. "This is magnificent! And precisely what I've been looking for. How did you know? Why, only last week I was at Eaton's shopping—quite unsuccessfully, I might add—for one. But this is just the thing. How can I ever thank you?"

He leaned across, squeezed both my hands, and gave me a light peck on each cheek. Something about the tenderness of his gesture and the great delight he took in my little gift suffused me with sadness, and my eyes welled up with tears. Christopher took one look at me and said, "Darling, what is it? Whatever's the matter?"

But my throat seemed to close up, and I couldn't speak. I'm always so maddeningly inarticulate when I get emotional. I just shook my head, waved my hand uselessly, and blinked away the tears.

"Now why don't you sit down here by the fire for a moment? There's a beastly chill out there for September, which is probably what's making you feel not quite yourself." Christopher steered me by the elbow to one of the crimson wing chairs beside the fireplace. "Would you care for a drink? A little something to revive you?"

"Oh, just water," I said, trying not to sound miserable. He smiled, squeezed my arm, and wandered away.

Lydia was hovering nearby, occasionally casting sidelong glances in my direction. She seemed to be watching Christopher, ensuring he was a good distance away before she sat down opposite me in the matching crimson chair. It was tempting to get up and just walk away, since I felt woefully ill-equipped for conversation at that precise moment. Locking myself in the bathroom for the rest of the evening was becoming an appealing option. But it was much too late for that; I had to pull myself together for the sake of appearances. Lydia, in another one of her drab frocks (I often wondered if she liked anything other than those dreary greys or browns) was peering at me like some sort of eager, inquisitive creature. Given her recent avoidance of me, her demeanour was most peculiar. I could tell I was expected to say something, though I couldn't possibly imagine what. Why didn't she just begin the conversation if she wished to speak?

"Hi, Lydia. How are you?" I regretted that my teary face and the quaver in my voice no doubt gave away my state of mind.

"The real question, I dare say, is how are *you*?" she said. "You do look pale!" The timorous quality I'd always associated with Lydia had disappeared, and in its place was something hard and brittle and most unpleasant. This person before me wasn't the dear friend I'd known but someone I scarcely recognized. I'd been sure we were past the eavesdropping matter, but was it possible she was still nursing a grudge against me for inventing an excuse (at Freddy's urging) not to have tea with her all those months ago? Long ago I'd made my apology to her, and she'd accepted it, apparently with no hard feelings. I assumed she was now well past caring about either incident, and before the party I'd even entertained the possibility (remote as it was) that I had a chance of being restored to her good books. However, the frosty look she directed at me now withered the meagre seed of hope I'd been cultivating.

Taking a deep breath and drawing myself up in my chair, I blinked away the traces of my tears and tried to muster what I could of my self-confidence. "I'm fine, Lydia, I assure you."

"Well, you could have fooled me. I think we all know that things aren't right with you." For the first time in our conversation, she smiled, but it was a hostile baring of the teeth, much as you'd see in an animal readying itself for an attack.

"Who is 'we all,' I should like to know?"

She shrugged and smiled—a most insipid sort of smile, I must say. Just then, Bernice, tall, slender, and exquisite in a burgundy gown, drifted into the room. I smiled at her, and the smirk she delivered as she looked me up and down felt like a slap in the face. She lingered beside Lydia, and her eyes glittered with amusement as she sipped her champagne and stared at me.

"I'll repeat my question. Who is 'we all'?"

"Why, just about everyone in this room," said Lydia, waving her arms around vaguely. "We all know that things aren't right."

"What things?"

"Ha!" said Bernice. "Isn't it obvious? I don't know why you keep pretending."

My anger simmered briefly before heating up into a burst of white-hot fury. "Just what are you saying?" I looked from Lydia to Bernice, tears once again forming in my eyes.

"You're pale, haggard, and drawn. Why, everyone's noticed how frightful you look, Constance. You've got a lot on your mind these days. Important decisions to make." Lydia's lips twisted into a tight smile.

"I haven't a clue what you're talking about," I said, fighting back my tears. "Furthermore, I don't care!"

Bernice let out a sharp laugh before she became distracted and decided that chasing after some dashing young rake was more worth her while than spending any more time listening to Lydia and me.

Infuriated, I stood up and marched across the room, arrested by the sight of Freddy and Mildred seated a few feet away on a red brocade sofa. They leaned closely toward each other, their heads inclined, as though they were involved in a most intimate type of discussion. Mildred giggled as Freddy touched her lightly on the arm several times. Oblivious to my presence at first, she looked up at me and immediately lowered her voice. They spoke in solemn whispers to each other, Freddy looking grim and Mildred glancing up and smiling at me periodically. But there was something cruel in that smile. Drawing much closer, I looked at the bevelled mirror above their heads and studied my reflection; the face that met my gaze was almost unrecognizable. Lydia was right about my appearance—I was a pale ghost of myself in a diaphanous light blue gown, and I'd dropped so much weight, my face looked pinched and drawn. Dark circles ringed my eyes. But I looked in the mirror every day. Why hadn't I seen the ghastly transformation in myself before?

Freddy took a long drag on his cigarette and looked uncomfortably from me to Mildred, who now fixed a politely inscrutable gaze on me.

"Hello, Constance." She got up to extend her hand to me. "Your Freddy and I were just having a little tête-à-tête—you know, as cousins often do. We rarely get the chance, you know. And there's so very much to talk about." She punctuated this last remark with the chilliest of smiles.

"Yes, I see. No doubt the subject was me— wasn't it, Mildred? Freddy, shall we go?"

"Go?" Freddy scrunched up his face as though he'd tasted something unpleasant. "But we only just got here. Besides, Cousin and I are far from finished. We're just getting started, in fact. Aren't we, Mildred?" His expression was hard to read as he glanced at her and she nodded her assent.

"Well, it's entirely too cold in here for me, so I believe I'll be going." I stood there awkwardly, unable to move as I hoped for a response that was at least remotely reassuring. But Freddy shrugged, and Mildred raised her eyebrows a little, looking faintly amused.

"Well, since you live next door, I won't need to accompany you," said Freddy.

I paused, waiting for something more. Anything. Freddy looked irritated. "Goodnight, Constance."

And as if I weren't even there, he turned his attention back to Mildred.

"Fine." Before I knew it, tears were flowing down my cheeks, right there in front of half of Rosedale. I felt several pairs of eyes fixed on me, but I dared not look back. I turned away, mortified, and started walking toward the front door, feeling a curious mix of anger, numbness, and for no reason I could understand, shame. I thought I heard someone murmur, "Poor thing." A sharp tug at my sleeve held me back.

"Where are you going, Constance? You just got here, darling." It was Christopher, looking aghast as he held a large tumbler of water.

Feeling weak, I clutched his elbow to steady myself. "I do apologize, Christopher. I'm not at all well."

Like the gentleman he was, he gently guided me toward the door and then helped me on with my coat. It seemed to require all the strength I had just to force my arms into the sleeves, and with thick, clumsy fingers, I struggled to button it.

"Now then, allow me to take you to your door and get you settled inside. You must rest immediately. Your parents are home, I'm assuming?" said Christopher, his voice edged with alarm. He supported me with one arm about my waist.

"You're very sweet, but that won't be necessary. I'll be just fine, I assure you. Probably all I need is a little night air." I tried to smile. Judging from his worried face, my efforts to downplay my misery were unconvincing.

He escorted me out the door, and the minute he'd closed it behind us, I collapsed weakly onto the verandah. The last thing I remember was Christopher carrying me inside my house and, amid gasps of shock from my parents, depositing me on the sofa.

CHAPTER 19

Poor Constance! I wondered how she'd ever recovered from the cruel treatment all those miscreants had heaped on her. Had the heroic Christopher Whitley, who seemed so fond of her, continued to come to her aid, proving himself the saint he appeared to be? My heart sank, and I tried not to think of what might have become of her. Abruptly, as I closed Constance's diary, the wind whipped itself into a frenzy and branches clattered against my windowpane. The howling reminded me of her forlorn wailing, and I passed a sleepless night in which I couldn't get her cries—or the sound of the violent gusts of wind—out of my head.

I dragged myself out of bed the next morning. It was Saturday, and I was scheduled to work the auction preview. This entailed long hours of standing behind a counter on a hardwood floor, repeatedly reaching up and bending down to collect various decorative objects, walking back and forth from one end of the counter to the other while carrying these objects, and plunking them down on the counter for clients to examine. It also entailed long hours of conversation and unfailing politeness—whether I felt like being nice to people or not. And after sleeping so badly, I definitely didn't feel like being nice. I felt even less like it once I arrived at work and learned we were short-staffed. Chloe hadn't shown up, and she wasn't answering my repeated calls to her apartment. The tone of my voice mail messages reflected my increasing exasperation with her.

Out on the gallery floor, I said good morning to Taylor, who was sharing counter duty with me. The second we opened our doors, throngs of people pushed up against the counters, and we were besieged by requests to examine items. During a quieter moment about an hour later, I leaned over and said, "No sign of Chloe anywhere."

"Yeah, I noticed."

"What's going on with you two? Why are you so angry at each other?"

Looking down, Taylor hesitated. When she looked up, it was with a mixture of emotions I couldn't pin down. Shame? Anger? "It's kind of a long story. Can we maybe talk about it after work? We could go for a drink or something. Now's not the time."

"You're right. Okay. But why don't we make it dinner?"

She nodded, and I thought I detected relief in her eyes.

Taylor took a lunch break, and for the next three hours after that, we breathlessly heaved the Snodgrass Royal Crown

Derby presentation urn onto the counter more times than we could count. It was poked, prodded, measured, scrutinized, and turned upside down and then right-side up again. The sharpest and most discerning eyes in the antiques business all looked it over hungrily. Our knowledge of the vase's provenance and condition was questioned and apparently not found wanting, for not one client grumbled at us or questioned our expertise. By 3:30 p.m., an hour and a half before the end of the preview, I was satisfied the urn would fetch the whopping great price it was slated to and perhaps even exceed our expectations.

Traffic was beginning to wane on the gallery floor, so I decided I'd take a break. But no sooner had the thought occurred to me than a commotion erupted a few feet away. I looked over to see Jared having words with Mr. Alabaster. The man was making the not unreasonable request that Jared climb up a ladder, fetch a painting hung high on the wall, and bring it down to him so he could examine it more closely. Although Alabaster's tone was pompous and imperious, it hardly excused Jared's rudeness.

"Climb up on the ladder and get it yourself, buddy. I'm not gettin' it for ya," said Jared.

"What? How dare you!" shouted Alabaster. His white complexion became increasingly rosy as the blood gathered in his cheeks. "You'll pay for this, young man. I've half a mind to tell Mr. Gable himself!"

Jared said, "Ha! Good luck with that," and started walking away.

I was flabbergasted when Alabaster released a rainbow-coloured stream of curses while shaking his fist vigorously at Jared's retreating form. I honestly didn't think the old guy had it in him.

Just then, George strolled into the room. He looked a bit tired, but he perked up the second he heard Alabaster swearing. Our eyes met, and I inclined my head toward Jared and mouthed his name. In response George nodded, smirked, and rolled his eyes.

Approaching the disgruntled client, he said, "My apologies, sir. Another member of our floor staff would be happy to assist you." One of the boys took the cue, hopping up on the ladder and climbing nimbly toward the painting. George spun around and levelled his unswerving gaze on Jared. "Follow me. Right now."

Jared followed sullenly behind him.

I turned to Taylor. "That Schmuttermayer's really a piece of work, isn't he?"

"No kidding."

"Listen," I said, "I'm run off my feet—we both are—but I'm also famished. I haven't had lunch yet. I think I'll take a break." I reached down to rub a sore spot on my foot.

"Fine by me."

Looking a little irritated, Taylor turned her attention to a hawk-faced elderly couple, the Buchanans. They were regulars who'd just arrived at the counter and were always too rude to voice their requests to see particular items; instead, they relied on vague gestures that left us guessing as to what it was they wanted to look it. Iris was wearing an outrageous plumed purple fascinator, while Hamish, a pipe dangling from his mouth, sported a tam-o'-shanter and matching bowtie in a bright plaid I assumed must be the Buchanan tartan.

"Girl!" said Hamish, apparently not realizing he already had Taylor's full attention. Both Buchanans waved at the shepherd and shepherdess figural group and turned critical eyes on Taylor.

"Okay, okay, just a second." Clearly, she'd need another break soon.

I eased my way out from behind the counter, smiled automatically at a few clients as I crossed the gallery floor, and slipped back into the cataloguing room. The lunchtime spread of sandwiches, raw vegetables, and dip had been decimated, and only a squashed egg salad sandwich and a few dried-up carrot sticks were to be had. The only thing left on the dessert tray was a minuscule brownie, which I snatched up greedily, eating it before anything else. I'd need the strongest possible coffee to get me through the rest of the preview—I was anticipating a last-minute rush of people looking at the Snodgrass urn—so I made my way down to the basement for a cup of Moroccan Mystique and hoped Constance wouldn't pick today for another meeting.

Everything was quiet, as the rest of the staff were working the gallery floor. Thankfully, there was no sign of my ghost. I listened to the satisfying sound of the liquid rushing into the cup, inhaled the warm, spicy aroma, and sat down to enjoy my coffee. It was a tremendous relief to get off my swollen feet, and I kicked off my shoes and rubbed all the sore spots, trying not to think about how much tighter the shoes would feel when I put them on again and how much more torture they'd inflict before the day was over. Settling in to leaf idly through a newspaper someone had left, I could hear soft, muffled footsteps, as if someone was wearing a pair of fuzzy slippers and approaching tentatively from a distance. Normally, I was very good at identifying people from the particular sound of their footsteps, but I wasn't sure who this was. And I didn't much care; I just wanted to rest my feet, so I kept staring at the newspaper and didn't think to turn around and look at the door.

When my eyelids became heavy, I closed my eyes and let my mind drift for a while. My head fell forward as I began slipping into a light, refreshing doze. I was awakened a little by the sound of a foot scuffing. Vaguely aware that someone was standing nearby, I was too tired to fully emerge from my drowsy state.

Without warning, I felt a searing pain as something sharp stabbed at my shoulders repeatedly, cutting me deeply. My hand went automatically to my shoulder, and pain shot through my knuckles. I jerked my hand away. My fingers were covered in blood. Shuddering and gasping, I cried out and collapsed to the floor.

I turned around on all fours to see my attacker fleeing, but all I could make out was a shadowy figure dashing up the stairs. Light, quick footsteps receded. On the floor I noticed a pair of small leather slippers. Beside them lay a metal object, probably a knife, gleaming dully in the light. It was dripping with blood—my blood.

The next thing I knew, George was holding one of my hands, staring into my eyes. The other hand sat in my lap, wrapped tightly in a white cloth. He looked wild-eyed and urgent, and he was talking in a very loud voice, but I wasn't taking in his words. They sounded like gobbledygook, as if he were speaking words I'd never heard before—an ancient language or possibly Martian. It took me a moment to realize I was sitting on a kitchen chair. A pool of spilled coffee had made its way to the edge of the table and was dripping on the floor.

"I've just called 911, Virginia. Someone should be here any moment." These were the first clear words I heard emerging from George's mouth.

"Oh, I'm sure I'm just … fine. Must get back … to the preview." I heard a voice, lifeless and disengaged, but it couldn't have been mine. Then I looked at the sleeve of my white silk blouse and noticed it was spattered with blood. "Oh God!"

"It's all right, sweetheart. Forget all about the preview." George was gently mopping up the blood from my shoulders with a towel. "Taylor, could you please fetch some more towels?"

I hadn't even realized she was there. She stood quietly, pale and transfixed, unable to look away from me, making me think I must have been quite a sight. "Okay," she said before moving off.

Rapidly, the room became crowded with people jabbering away—firemen, policemen, and ambulance attendants. I felt dizzy from the confusing din of voices, the glaring lights, and the whirl of motion around me. People were examining me, and I thought I heard words like *wounds* and *shock* being tossed around. Then there were the questions, endless questions, about what had happened. Amid the kerfuffle, I understood little of what anyone said to me, and I said even less. I couldn't seem to put two words together. A policeman picked up the metallic thing that looked like a knife and put it in a plastic bag.

CHAPTER 20

I could see Mom and Dad's faces so clearly. We were standing in the kitchen of the small bungalow I'd grown up in. Wintry grey light flowed in through the sheer curtains. I'd been crying, and Mom, her grey eyes serene and analytical, asked me what I thought we should do about the mess I was in. Overwrought and confused, I was capable only of shaking my head. She said, "We'll brainstorm and come up with a plan." Dad smiled in that toothy way he had, the crow's feet crinkling around his eyes, and without a word walked over to embrace me. My tears began to dry as I absorbed the message: with them behind me, I couldn't help but find a way out of this mess. I'd be all right.

Images of my parents flew from my brain as I woke up in my own bed. They occasionally visited me in dreams, but losing them again, and after such a short reunion, prompted a sharp pang of loss. After I shook this off, I realized I had no clear sense of how I'd got home or how long I'd been asleep. It might have been an hour or it might have been a week; everything was hazy. All I knew for sure was that it was morning. Autumn sunlight streamed in through the big gap in my curtains, revealing a patch of bright blue sky. I noticed one of my hands was bandaged and I was wearing oversized, very loud purple-and-yellow striped pyjamas. They definitely weren't mine.

I was startled to hear quiet footfalls in my kitchen. A picture of someone fleeing the kitchen of Gable & Co. flashed immediately through my mind, and my heart began racing. Swinging my feet too forcefully over the side of the bed, I fell with a muffled thud on the hardwood floor. In the process I'd dragged the duvet with me, somehow twisting it around myself. A sharp pain shot to my shoulders.

The footsteps were now running toward me. "Virginia! What's happening? Are you okay?" George burst through the door and rushed to my side with that same wild-eyed look I remembered from before.

"I guess so." But I just felt disoriented and sore.

"Well, you sure gave me a fright. Why don't you get back into bed, and I'll make you some coffee and toast. Or whatever else you'd like."

"Coffee and toast would be just fine." I reached out to him with my unbandaged hand, but he hoisted me up gently by the waist and returned me to the bed. He pulled the duvet from the floor, gave it a good shake, and tucked it around me. Then he yanked the curtains aside.

I squinted up at him, shielding my eyes from the light. "What day is it? How'd I get home? And whose clothes are these?" Looking down at those appalling striped pyjamas, I was getting vertigo.

George sat on the end of the bed and seemed slightly anxious. "It's Sunday. You were released from the hospital last night after they treated you for stab wounds, but you were in a stupor from the sedative they gave you, so Taylor and I drove you here. Luckily, she had the presence of mind to grab your purse from work, so we were able to get in with your keys. The doctor in ER recommended that someone stay with you overnight just to keep an eye on you, so I volunteered."

"And the pyjamas?"

"Taylor mentioned she wasn't sure if you had, er, suitable nightwear or not. She knew hers wouldn't fit, so I suggested we drop by my apartment and pick up a pair of my pyjamas. Just in case."

I laughed. "Seriously? Where would she get the idea I don't own a nightgown or pyjamas? I've never said anything of the sort."

George shrugged. "Who knows? You've got to admit, though, it was thoughtful of her."

"Surprisingly useful in a crisis, isn't she? Who would have thought? I'm starting to see her in a different light these days. Just one other thing, though, and then I'll stop pestering you with all these tedious questions." I was already wearying of asking him to fill in the blanks, as I could feel the stress of my ordeal in my aching shoulders.

George's eyes lit up, making me think he'd already anticipated my next question. "I know what you're thinking, but it was Taylor who put you into the pyjamas. I swear I had nothing to do with it. And then she sat right beside your bed until you were comfortably settled and finally fell asleep. She didn't want to leave your side, you know, but I insisted she go home and rest, seeing as she's working the preview again today. I gave her cab fare to get home."

A little lump made its way into my throat. If I weren't careful, I'd soon be bawling uncontrollably into George's shoulder, and it seemed much too early in our relationship, or whatever it was, to be doing that. "That's awfully touching. Her wanting to stay, I mean." I swallowed hard.

"Impressive, yes. She was really worried about you."

My voice sounded raw and strained as I said, "I was just wondering about something. What was she doing in your office the other day? I thought she'd gone home, but there she was, back again."

"Oh, she just wanted to be soothed a little, I think. And she seemed to want to tell me something, but every time I tried to probe her for details, she'd start crying again. She just couldn't seem to do it."

"Hmm, that's curious. Taylor and I were going to talk after yesterday's preview was over." Pondering for a moment, I realized I had no idea what she might have wanted to tell him—or me, for that matter.

"I don't know what it was about either," said George.

I hesitated before I said, "To be honest with you, I thought you looked awfully guilty when I found you with Taylor in your office, but of what, I couldn't say."

"I was just embarrassed because I knew you'd wonder why she'd come back. I was exhausted and didn't feel much like explaining." He looked down at the floor.

"And why were the blinds drawn?"

"I drew them before she arrived. I was preparing for a little snooze." He smiled. "Will you swear not to tell anyone I regularly sleep on the job?"

"Not to worry—I'm sworn to secrecy." I paused. "Do you know something, George? You have absolutely horrifying taste in pyjamas. I never would have thought."

He let out the most devilish-sounding, throaty laugh I'd ever heard, one that came deep from within his belly and shook his whole frame. He was grinning at me as he said, "Oh, I'm very mysterious, you know. There's so much you don't know about me, so much you'd never suspect, not even in your craziest dreams. Aren't you dying to find out more?"

I was laughing too as he leaned in for a long, lingering kiss. When it was over, I was tingling, so much so that for a moment I forgot my aching shoulders. We were back to exactly where we'd been when he discovered the porcelain in the basement. It hadn't been a dream, and maybe I wouldn't need to watch old movies by myself anymore. I allowed myself to bask in the euphoria of the moment.

"There was something else I wanted to ask you," I said, clasping his hand with my uninjured one.

"Really? I thought you were planning to stop pestering me with questions. Isn't that what you said?" He was grinning.

"Yes, but I really must know. Why did it take you practically a year to say more than a few words to me?"

George became pensive and took a moment to collect himself before he spoke. He gazed down at his hands. "When I first started working at Gable & Co., you'd just lost your parents. I could see you were grieving, but it was as if you were wearing a suit of armour and surrounding yourself with barricades. The only one who could get past all that was Chloe. I didn't feel I could talk to you—or not yet."

"I was that unapproachable?" I asked, my words tinged with regret.

George eyed me tentatively and nodded. "I bided my time, hoping that eventually you'd heal and everything you were protecting yourself with would fall away." He paused briefly. "Then your ghost Constance appeared, and that changed everything. Gable called that initial meeting—it was obvious you hadn't—and threw you to the lions. He did it again when the porcelain went missing. You started opening up. I saw a strong but vulnerable—and yes, beautiful—woman in need of a friend. I knew it was time to make my presence known."

I hardly knew what to say. I pressed his hand to my cheek. "I'm both astonished and overjoyed you were so patient."

"You were well worth the wait." His lips parted into a smile.

"I'll do everything I can to prove you're right," I said softly, a lump creeping into my throat.

"Sweetheart, relax. You have absolutely nothing to prove." George kissed me tenderly and then gradually pulled away. The moment he stood up, the spell was broken. "Breakfast?" he said brightly.

"Yes, thanks. If you don't mind, just one more thing. I remember now … someone came after me. What was I attacked with? After I fell, I was sure I saw a blood-covered knife on the floor."

He glanced at me before staring at the floor. "It was actually a Birks stainless steel meat skewer, the kind with a silver handle. It could have been so much worse for you. The skewer wasn't nearly as sharp as a knife, so your wounds aren't very deep. Your attacker must have been too dumb to know it wouldn't cause much damage. You were pretty fortunate he—or she— was such a dope."

"I wondered if a skewer had gone missing. And who was my attacker? Has anyone said?"

"No one knows, but I'm working on some possibilities," he said, again donning his Sherlock cap.

I reached out for his hand and held it in mine. "George, I just wanted to tell you how grateful I am for your kindness through all this and—"

"Please—think nothing of it," he said, smiling. "Did you really expect me to behave differently under the circumstances?"

He had a point. Based on everything I knew about him,

he'd behaved exactly as I would have expected. But I was still thankful.

"You just rest, and I'll be back shortly," said George.

"I was just going to read Constance's diary. I'll let you know the latest." I'd been giving him regular reports of her activities.

"Good." He got up abruptly and left the room. While he puttered around my kitchen, tunelessly whistling "Get Happy" and making me coffee and toast, I picked up Constance's diary once more. I was getting near the end of it; there were just a few more pages of writing before all those blank pages at the end. I didn't know to what extent she'd wrap things up or whether unanswered questions would linger. Knowing her, she'd leave me hanging; it wouldn't be the first time. All I knew for sure was that her tiny, neat handwriting had become larger and sloppier as the diary progressed, her slant veering this way and that. And the ink was smudged in places too—whether by her hand, tears, or later water damage I couldn't be sure.

November 18, 1928

Well, at least the thing has come to an end.

Freddy asked me to meet him last week in Craigleigh Gardens. I walked to the cold, windswept park, pulling my cloche tightly around my ears and wrapping my coat around me. But it was hopeless; the cold cut me to the bone. Dried leaves were swirling all around me in furious gusts of wind, and some crunched beneath my feet. Barely a tattered leaf clung to the trees, and the sky looked heavy, the low-hanging clouds black with rain. As I sat on a bench waiting for him, the bench where we always sat, all I could think of was that warm July day when he'd asked me to be his wife. I still remembered his desperate face, and how that ring had sparkled in the sunshine when he presented it to me.

Last week when he telephoned to arrange our meeting, I knew I'd be giving it back. We certainly couldn't have gone on much longer with our farce of an engagement.

I saw him coming across the park toward me, his stride full of purpose. When he reached me, I expected him to sit on the bench beside me as he'd always done, but he stood before me, his pale face a mask of indifference. "Constance, I can't marry you."

Without a word, I removed the ring from my finger and dropped it on the ground. He stooped automatically, sweeping aside dead leaves to retrieve it, and when he stood up we stared at each other for a few moments. I was watching for a sign—a glance, a gesture, anything—that he was unsure. Letting down his guard somewhat, he took in a shallow breath, and uncertainty flickered vividly in his eyes. Then it was gone.

I should have felt my release from him as a merciful act, as Freddy's done nothing but torture me with coldness these last couple of months. He's been acting as if I'm poison. Instead, I felt profoundly sad, confused, and sorry. I should pity him, really, for he's such a poor excuse for a man, and so utterly lacking in gumption; he couldn't even bring himself to tell me why he was releasing me. I had to beg.

"Freddy, I can accept that you've broken our engagement, but won't you tell me why you've taken against me so in the past couple of months? Why you've been cruel when you were once so tender? Don't I deserve an explanation? Can you not even grant me that?"

He opened his mouth as if to say something but then looked pensive for a moment. An eternity seemed to pass before he said, "I just wanted to let you know … I realize the rumours aren't true, so it's nothing to do with that. Goodbye, Constance."

"Rumours?" I'd known since before Christopher's birthday party that people were whispering about me, but maddeningly, I'd never discovered what they were saying. "Won't you tell me what they're about?"

Something in the sad look Freddy turned on me pulled at my heart. It was strange to feel a little tug of sympathy for him. I quickly pushed it away, for most likely his expression showed only how pitiful he found me. Or was there something more to it? I couldn't be sure.

He turned away. Standing there with his back to me, hesitating, he was cold and unreachable, more of a polished stone statue than a man. I no longer knew him; it was no longer possible. But had I ever really known him? He walked away, and the farther away he got, the more his movements appeared fluid. I watched him become smaller and smaller until he drifted through the stone and wrought iron gates as gracefully as a phantom and disappeared from view altogether. It then hit me with the force of a hammer's blow that I'd never see him again, that he was permanently lost to me.

And I haven't seen him, except when he comes to me in dreams, always the eager, loving Freddy I knew in the beginning, the one who so enthusiastically made plans for our future. When I wake up, I'm shattered by the stark contrast between dreams and reality. I think of him constantly. Papa looks at me kindly, asks me if I want to tell him anything, and offers me bitter-tasting tonics to soothe my nerves. Mama scarcely knows what to do with me, and I don't wonder that she's getting impatient with my behaviour—torrents of tears alternating with long periods of near-catatonic numbness, during which, despite the biting cold, I sit in the garden and smoke—a dreadful habit I picked up from Freddy—and stare into space like a madwoman. I'm sure she wants to shake me. If I were her, I wouldn't hesitate to do so.

I haven't seen any of the people in my former social circle. No Lydia, no Mildred, no Bernice. What few calls I made went unanswered, so I've stopped trying to call anyone now. I've stopped trying to do much of anything, frankly. I haven't a friend in the world except my lovely neighbour Christopher, who, when he isn't visiting me, is so thoroughly absorbed in his medical practice that he's out of touch with the social whirl I used to be a part of. Curiously, he seems no more enlightened than I am about the cause of my alarming tumble down the social ladder. He considers it his duty to gently urge me not to think of what I've lost but to look to the future; he informs me daily it will be very bright indeed. He even says he's broken off his engagement to that actress, not that it makes much difference to me. Dear Christopher—his glasses are surely of a rosy hue, but he does have the best of intentions. I don't know what I'd do without him looking out for me.

But I can't move on from this awful state of despair when I live in complete ignorance of

Freddy's reasons, and when people who used to call me a friend pass me by and pretend they don't see me. I don't know what to do anymore.

◈

It was the last diary entry. Blank pages taunted me, along with the photograph of Constance in happier times with the tall, dark, inscrutable man I presumed to be Freddy. Would I ever discover how she'd met her end? I didn't care much what had happened to Freddy—he'd probably done very well for himself, as scoundrels often do—but Constance was a different matter. I had, after all, come to know her; I needed to know her ultimate fate.

There was one possible way to find out. The other day, I'd finally had a chance to look into who'd brought in the velvet settee that the ghostly Constance had apparently claimed as her own, and into the diary I'd tucked a copy of the owner's contact information. The settee, along with several other pieces of furniture, carpets, and a few boxes of books, belonged to Mrs. Suzanne Winterdale. I picked up the phone and dialed her number, just as George brought in a breakfast tray and slipped quietly out of the room.

"Hello?" A vibrant, clear voice answered.

"May I speak to Suzanne Winterdale, please?"

"This is she."

"Mrs. Winterdale, this is Virginia Blythe of Gable & Co.

Auctioneers. I'm sorry to be bothering you on a Sunday like this, but I understand you recently consigned some furniture and other articles to us, and I wanted to bring something to your attention. I found an old diary near your settee belonging to someone named Constance Pendleton. Her name was inside it. Is she by any chance a relative of yours?"

She paused. "I had no idea I'd sent in anything like that."

"Well, diaries often sneak in with books." An uncomfortable silence ensued as I waited for her to answer my question. "Was Constance related to you?"

"Why yes, definitely. I'm a Pendleton by birth. She would have been … let's see now, my grandfather's youngest sister, if I'm not mistaken. My great-aunt. I heard her spoken of often when I was growing up."

"I wondered if you might like to have the diary back. These sorts of personal items often come in accidentally with consignments, and of course we can't sell them since they have no commercial value. And even if they did, we'd never dream of doing so, since they rightly belong with family members. I'd be more than happy to drop the diary off to you if you'd like."

A moment's hesitation followed as Suzanne Winterdale considered my offer. "Well, I'm not really sure what I'd do with it. I didn't even know her, of course. It was back in the twenties when she died."

"Think of it as an heirloom—an authentic piece of family history to pass along to future generations."

"Well, when you put it that way." But she didn't sound entirely convinced.

"I don't think you'll regret it. I'm afraid I've ... had an accident from which I'm still recovering, but I expect I'll be able to go out tomorrow. Would ten thirty suit you?"

"Let me look at my appointment book." I heard a brief shuffling of papers. "Why yes, it would."

"I'll see you tomorrow. I have your address as 127 Elm Avenue in Rosedale. Is that correct?" Why did the address seem familiar?

"Yes. I'll look forward to meeting you, then," she said, and added a cheery "Bye."

I hoped Suzanne Winterdale was the kind of sociable woman who'd put on a pot of tea for any visitor, regardless of the nature of the visit. We certainly had a good deal to discuss.

CHAPTER 21

From her address, I figured Mrs. Winterdale lived in one of those immense late Victorian houses in South Rosedale, the kind that have turrets with curved windows, roof tiles that look like scales, and even ghoulish faces carved into the stone. I knew that Constance, being an affluent young woman from a medical family, had lived somewhere in this neighbourhood as well, but I couldn't recall where. Suddenly, an image of her distinctive handwriting at the front of the diary flashed through my mind, and I realized she'd lived exactly where I was going, 127 Elm Avenue. The house had remained in the family. As I walked along the street that cold and damp November Monday, I imagined Constance strolling along the sidewalk exactly as I wanted to see her, her beautiful green eyes shining, a curtain of glossy black hair swinging across her face, and her silky, diaphanous dress fluttering in the summer breeze.

Plenty of grand mansions graced Elm Avenue, but Suzanne Winterdale's was the grandest of them all. It was an imposing three-storey red brick structure with a green-shingled roof. The house abounded with interesting details; foremost among them was a rusticated archway with Corinthian columns, above which floated a carved panel depicting foliate scrollwork surrounding a shield. The orderly front yard featured precisely trimmed square hedges surrounding young trees.

I walked up the steps and announced my presence using the brass lion door knocker. A slender middle-aged woman with a platinum blonde pageboy and green eyes greeted me at the door. She looked polished from head to toe in a cream-coloured suit with unobtrusive pale green stripes and a matching green silk blouse with a knotted tie. It was rather formal attire for our meeting, I thought. Though perhaps later she was going out to some occasion that called for formal dress, I somehow imagined she was one of those women who dressed to the nines every day of her life, and that nothing less would do.

"Hello, you must be Mrs. Winterdale," I said. "I'm Virginia Blythe."

We shook hands, and I saw her notice my bandages, but of course she was much too polite to say anything about them. Instead, she smiled warmly. "Virginia, it's nice to meet you. Please call me Suzanne. Do come in. May I help you with your coat?"

My shoulders aching, I eased out of my coat, and she hung it in the closet.

"Would you like some tea or coffee?"

"Thank you—I'd love a cup of tea." George had made me so much coffee over the last day or so that I needed a change.

I hovered in the foyer while Suzanne disappeared into the kitchen. A cheerful clatter of dishes and silverware could be heard. "Please make yourself at home and have a seat in the living room," she called.

I hovered near the kitchen and said, "What a lovely house, Suzanne. How old is it?"

"It was built in 1898. The architect, Frederick H. Herbert, built a number of the houses on this street. They call the style Richardsonian Romanesque."

"It's exquisite."

I drifted off into the living room. To my surprise and disappointment, it was done up in a cool, ultramodern way in the very same vanilla and pistachio ice cream colours Suzanne was wearing. An immense abstract expressionist canvas smeared with gloppy pastel paint hung over a cream-coloured sofa, dominating the room. The contemporary decor was a slight on the lovely old house, which was thirsty for the sort of antique carpets, old Chinese porcelain, and overstuffed, button-back furniture that would have been popular when it was built. The only items that belonged to the past were assorted paintings, presumably of family members. A large portrait of a formidable black-haired gentleman hung over a modern fireplace. It was impossible not to be drawn to the lively green eyes behind the wire-rimmed spectacles.

I turned around to see Suzanne standing behind me and holding a silverplate tray laden with tea paraphernalia. "Ah, I thought as an antiques specialist you'd be drawn to that portrait." She set the tray down on the coffee table.

"It's very impressive. You get a real sense of what sort of a person he must have been—a man of great character."

"That's my grandfather, Dr. William Richard Pendleton."

"Constance's brother?"

"That's right. How did you know?" She looked momentarily confused. "Oh, I did tell you on the phone that he was her brother, didn't I? Anyway, he was a prominent surgeon and art collector. The portrait was painted during the 1940s, when he was middle-aged."

I peered at the signature, a lively squiggle, but couldn't make it out. "Who's the artist?"

"I don't know. But down the hallway, I have a surprise for you."

Suzanne smiled, her eyes echoing those of the man in the portrait, and indeed of Constance herself. She led me down a narrow, dimly lit hallway. On the wall hung an Ashley and Crippen studio photograph of a beautiful dark-haired young woman in a pale drop-waist gown, her expression serene and confident.

"Constance?"

"Yes! Isn't she lovely? How I wish I'd known her."

"I saw a photograph of her. Here, it's in the diary." I pulled it out and handed it to her.

"Yes, that's definitely her, isn't it? And that dark fellow beside her must be the fiancé, I'd guess." The pitch of her voice dipped, and she raised an eyebrow.

"Freddy Alderdice?" I said, forgetting myself.

"Yes, I think that was the name." She looked at me guardedly. "Now how did you know that?"

I couldn't meet her gaze; I fidgeted like a naughty child, knowing I'd have to come clean. "I confess, Suzanne—I did take a peek at the diary." I paused. "Well, to be perfectly honest with you, I read the whole thing."

"You did?" she said, her eyes round with surprise. "Hmm. Well, I guess I might have done the same had I been in your shoes. It could be hard to resist the temptation, especially in your line of work." Her face relaxed into a smile again.

We returned to the living room and sat down on the leather sofa. She poured the tea from an Aesthetic movement silver teapot with twig handles. The 1880s pot was decidedly out of place in the bland modern room. Unbidden, a vivid image of Constance pouring tea from the very same pot came to me. Suzanne also offered me some bright pink rectangular wafers along with my mug. Nice as she was, I wondered if she'd be able to accept that I'd met Constance's ghost. It was much too early in our conversation to even consider springing that on her, and besides, there were questions I wanted to ask first.

"Do you know much about Constance? For some reason, the diary ends in late 1928—there aren't any more entries after that."

"My parents always said she'd died very young. She was just a girl, really. It was … suicide. That no-good, wretched fiancé had dumped her, and her friends wouldn't go near her, as if the poor thing were somehow tainted."

"Yes, she does talk about her sadness and loneliness in the last entry. I suppose it wasn't that much later that she took her life."

"My father told me it happened in 1928, during the Christmas holidays." Suzanne's gaze swept over me She stiffened, as though bracing herself for the inevitable question.

"I hate to be morbid, but … do you know how it happened?"

She sighed and looked at the floor. "The family was going to some sort of afternoon tea or what have you, and Constance complained of a headache and stayed home. When they returned, they found her on her bed, an empty bottle of pills beside her. They tried to revive her, calling in the young doctor who lived next door, since her father the doctor had gone abroad some weeks before to visit relatives in England. Anyway, it was this doctor, Christopher something-or-other—"

"Whitley," I said.

"Yes, I guess you'd know from the diary. Anyway, he was the one who'd prescribed the pills in the first place. For her nerves, apparently. But when he arrived, it was much too late—she'd already gone. Or so the story goes."

"And she did it because the rotten fiancé threw her over and her friends were ignoring her?"

Suzanne looked up again. "Tragic, isn't it? Especially when you consider she could have turned her life around. She was young, beautiful, and by all accounts, smart as a whip too. Wanted to be a novelist, I heard. And the young doctor was smitten with her and wanted to marry her. But she was still carrying a torch for that awful Freddy."

I broke off a piece of a dainty pink biscuit and dunked it in my tea. "Poor girl. And what hard luck for the doctor. The guilt must have pursued him for years."

"I'm sure it did. And guilt aside, he was heartbroken at losing her." She dropped a lump of sugar into her tea and stirred it with a tiny, gleaming spoon. "Oh, there was another thing I should mention." Her green eyes looked a little sly, as if she was about to impart a secret.

"Yes?"

"Her friends … it wasn't a simple case of snubbing. My father told me that after the suicide, the young doctor confessed something to Constance's parents. He said people had been spreading a terrible lie about her."

I thought back to the last diary entry, in which Constance had suggested Christopher didn't know why she had become a pariah. He must have claimed ignorance to protect her from the gossip.

"The rumour was probably what killed Freddy's enthusiasm for her and destroyed her standing in 'good' society," said Suzanne.

"What sort of a rumour? The diary doesn't say."

Suzanne sighed and looked at me grimly. "Oh, pretty much what you'd expect—that she was pregnant. It would have been utterly horrifying in those days—an unmarried girl of good family with child. It's really no wonder Freddy got as far away from her as possible. He wouldn't have wanted to be seen as the culprit."

Having read the diary, I thought I'd set her straight concerning Freddy. "But it wasn't the rumour that killed his interest. He'd stopped caring well before it started—before they were engaged, actually."

She looked incredulous. "Really?"

"Yes. Besides, he didn't believe it anyway."

She dunked her biscuit and said, "Yes, but if the rumour was widely believed, it could have been damaging to him. Even if he dismissed it, he still wouldn't have wanted it ruining his reputation. I heard he was already becoming prominent in the jazz scene, so he had his career to think of."

Suzanne was right, of course. What would have mattered to Freddy was what people perceived as being true, even if he knew it really wasn't.

"Was there any chance it was true?" I asked.

She was quick to react. "Oh, I doubt it. Her parents would have packed her off to some remote home for wayward girls to keep her out of sight until the baby had been born, and then it would have been put up for adoption. As far as I know, nothing like that ever happened."

"There was nothing about it in the diary. But I still wonder if there was any truth to it. Is it possible Constance's parents were in denial? After all, it wouldn't have been something they'd want to admit, even to themselves."

Suzanne sighed impatiently. "But her father was a doctor, so you'd think he would have known how to handle things. But who really knows anymore? It was an awfully long time ago, and I'm sure there are lots of things we'll never know. In a way, I'd rather not know."

Her reluctance to know all the details probably explained why she'd hesitated to accept the diary at first. Awkwardly, we paused to sip our tea, and I glanced at Suzanne's bookshelves. I noticed one volume amid her coffee-table books and interior decorating magazines that piqued my interest: a small paperback entitled *Toronto Ghost Stories*.

The book said a lot for Suzanne's open-mindedness, but this thought wasn't enough to distract me from the sadness I felt about Constance's demise. Once I'd reached the end of the diary, I suspected she'd taken her life, but it was sobering to have my suspicions confirmed by Suzanne. And that the girl hadn't found the wherewithal to ride out her troubles made me even sadder. Although she was too inexperienced in matters of the heart to have realized it, she would have eventually recovered from losing Freddy. And assuming Suzanne was right that she wasn't pregnant, her innocence soon would have come to light and the scandal would have blown over. The trouble with Constance was she'd been incapable of seeing an end to her misery. Thinking of all this, I remembered something that had struck me as curious when I read her diary.

"Do you know much about Freddy? One thing that didn't add up for me was how bent he was on marrying Constance despite not loving her. I mean, he was gaga over any pretty girl he saw and was carrying on with that Elsie and God only knows who else. His proposal was an absolute joke."

Suzanne blinked and looked at me curiously, as if she wanted an explanation. I told her about the fateful meeting with Elsie in the King Edward and recounted how Freddy had proposed to Constance in Craigleigh Gardens. When I finished, she squinted, as if she was trying to recall something.

"My grandfather said something about this when I was a teenager, something about Freddy being disinherited if he didn't marry Constance. He said Freddy's father took quite a shine to her and thought of her as his son's only salvation. He considered being a jazz musician to be the sure path to ruin and wanted someone to keep Freddy on the straight and narrow. He thought Constance was the one to do it. Maybe he didn't know about the rumours, or if he did he refused to believe them."

"If only she'd stayed away from that damn Freddy." The vehemence with which I spoke surprised me, and it seemed to startle Suzanne, who looked at me with wide eyes. "Don't mind me. I can't help but feel I know Constance, and it's not just because of the diary. The truth is, I've come to know her very well, but in a most surprising way."

"Oh?"

Remembering the book on her shelf, I couldn't help thinking she'd be genuinely receptive to what I had to say. I wasn't wrong. For the next hour, I regaled her with stories of Constance's ghost. When a shocked Suzanne regained her ability to speak, she said, "Extraordinary. I've never heard anything like it."

"Do you mean to say she never haunted this house?"

"Well, I thought *someone* did. I'd sometimes wake up in the morning to find that velvet settee, the one I sent into the auction, moved all the way over there"—she gestured toward the front door—"and I'd have to haul it back to its usual place. But I never heard or saw anyone."

"Amazing, isn't it?"

She just nodded, and then we smiled and said our goodbyes. As I walked down Elm Avenue, I turned around to take one last look at the massive house, a fortress so monumental it could easily provide a refuge from the vicissitudes of life—or so I would have thought. Somehow, though, it hadn't been enough to protect Constance.

CHAPTER 22

After leaving Suzanne Winterdale's house, I enjoyed a leisurely lunch of strawberry crepes and tea at Le Sourire, took a long afternoon nap, and then went to the office for the porcelain auction. It was with trepidation that I decided to go, as I knew my attacker could be lying in wait for me. But that wasn't going to deter me from watching the Royal Crown Derby presentation urn sell; Taylor and I had worked much too hard to catalogue and promote it. There was safety in numbers, and I told myself that if I avoided lonely places in the building, no one could harm me. Mark had been right to warn me not to venture into the basement alone; now I would heed his advice.

On the grounds that I had suffered a trauma, George had been opposed to my going to work at all—he hadn't even wanted me to leave my apartment—but now that I'd arrived he insisted I sit back and enjoy the evening's auction instead of working it, which for me always meant bidding by phone with buyers who couldn't attend the event in person. For once, I'd be a passive observer and sit in the audience, watching the show as item after item was projected on a screen and hammered down by the auctioneer.

When I arrived, Mark and Taylor were at their desks, frantically fielding last-minute calls about items to be sold that evening. Mark gave me a friendly grin and waved.

Taylor looked at me a little worriedly, and once she finished her call she said, "Hey, are you well enough to even be here?"

Her phone rang again, so I nodded, reassuring her with a smile that I was fit to be up and around and at the office.

Given Chloe's absence over the past couple of days, I was surprised to see her skulking around the office, making herself small in a corner and refusing to make eye contact with anyone. We all tried not to stare at her, but her face looked puffy; the gash had swollen up, and I wondered if it was infected. I sat down at the desk beside her.

"Good afternoon," I said in the perkiest tone I could muster.

She didn't say a word but cast a sidelong look at me. So this was how it was going to be. Having been stabbed by some skewer-wielding demon, I wasn't in the mood for her sullenness—even if she was still upset about the cut on her face.

"Really, Chloe, you might say hello, or even ask me how I am or something. You do know what happened to me, don't you? I'm assuming someone must have told you."

"Hello," she said, without looking up.

"By the way, where were you Saturday? You were scheduled to work, but you didn't show up. And George said you didn't even get back to him when he called to ask if you could come in yesterday. We really could have used your help, you know, especially after what happened to me. Taylor had to handle the counters alone yesterday, which you know is hectic."

"Yes, I know," she said, speaking just above a whisper.

Exasperated, I let a long sigh escape. "That's no kind of answer, Chloe. You still haven't said why you didn't come in."

"I don't owe you any explanation." She got up from her chair and angrily stalked out of the room.

"Jesus," said Mark. "What *is* that girl's problem? She's getting kookier by the day."

Taylor looked surly. "No kidding." Then she brightened and said, "Hey, guess what? I've had about fifteen phone calls about the Snodgrass presentation urn in as many minutes." For the first time in ages, she looked happy, as if she was proud of herself for the part she'd played in promoting the urn to prospective buyers.

I'd just said, "Super!" when Taylor's phone rang again.

I took the opportunity to wander out to the auction gallery, where several rustic but vibrant paintings—Canadian forest and lakeside vistas by the Group of Seven and their followers—decorated the walls. The room settings that had been created for the preview had been hastily disassembled, and in their place, rows upon rows of chairs had been set up for the audience. I sat near the back, trying to look inconspicuous, for the regulars would wonder why I wasn't at my customary post by the phones and would probably ask me about it. Over the next hour or so, clients started to file in slowly for the auction, and gradually the room filled with a conversational hum that rose to a din. The air crackled with an electric sense of anticipation. I heard a couple in front of me talking in subdued voices about the value of the Snodgrass urn. The question on everyone's lips was this: How much will it go for?

A hush swept over the room as 7:00 p.m. arrived. People began checking their watches, waiting for the auctioneer to ascend the podium. Only then did the question occur to me: Who would take on the role of lead auctioneer now that Brian Gable III was dead? Although Sally was also an auctioneer, she couldn't be expected to conduct an entire three-hour auction by herself. I expected George had seen to the problem, though I didn't know how he'd solved it.

I was astonished to see him sweeping into the room and down the aisle, dressed in a well-cut black suit and a conservative striped burgundy tie. He'd never auctioned off anything in his life—of that I was sure—but he appeared confident as he stepped up to the podium, gazed out over the audience, and smiled. He looked my way briefly, his eyes sparkling, and bestowed a mischievous smile on me.

Politely, he introduced himself. "Good evening, ladies and gentlemen, and welcome to Gable & Co. Auctioneers for our fall fine porcelain auction. My name is George Schlegel, and I'm the company's newest auctioneer. We'll now begin tonight's auction." And without further ado, he began selling the first lot of porcelain. The audience seemed captivated by his quiet, authoritative, direct manner, and I was struck by the remarkable ease with which he carried out his task, smoothly rhyming off the bids in his silken voice and never missing even the most subtle bidding efforts of the clients—a raise of an eyebrow or a flick of a finger. It was as if he'd auctioned a million times before, yet the freshness he brought to the process reflected how new it was to him. I was thrilled and confused simultaneously—thrilled to see yet another layer of George's personality but confused that he could be so strangely proficient at something he'd never done before, something that had always terrified an introvert like me.

I thought with a shudder back to Brian Gable III's attempts at auctioning. How tragicomic it had always seemed when, bloated and often unkempt in an old tweed jacket with corduroy elbow patches, he staggered toward the podium, wheezing like a sick old man as he ascended the steps. He'd begged for bids in his whiny voice, sweat beading on his forehead. And that was on a good night. On bad nights the smell of whisky on his breath assailed those seated in the first few rows, and he'd insult the audience, quivering and shaking his fist when the bids weren't forthcoming. If an item failed to sell, he'd swear under his breath. The spectacle was enough to make some of the stuffier patrons flee the room, muttering gruffly to themselves that they'd never, ever be back. But time after time, they returned because they couldn't find anything comparable to the items we offered at auction. For other clients this appalling freak show was the main attraction—far more riveting than any of the trinkets and baubles that were up for grabs. I couldn't deny that Gable had had his fair share of fans, but they were likely the same sort of people who subsisted on a steady diet of trashy reality TV and supermarket tabloids.

Trying to shake the image of Gable from my mind, I realized that George was moving at a brisk clip through the lots, and we were but a few minutes from auctioning off the Snodgrass Royal Crown Derby Floribunda pattern porcelain presentation urn. Its big moment had finally come. I twisted my hands nervously as my stomach executed backflips. I glanced over at the phone bidding desk, where several staff members were busy getting prospective buyers on the line.

When the slide showing the urn came up, George paused briefly and sipped from a glass of water. For the first time since he'd begun auctioning, he looked a little tense, and he pulled his handkerchief from his breast pocket and dabbed at his forehead. He then looked at me, smiling broadly. "Ladies and gentlemen," he said, "it's my great pleasure to present to you the highlight of tonight's auction, lot 1092, a magnificent Royal Crown Derby hand-painted porcelain presentation urn, signed by Lady Florence Twaddlebury and dated 1903. This item was originally purchased by eminent Toronto businessman Oswald P. Snodgrass of Toronto and has remained with the Snodgrass family until now. Let's start the bidding now at $9,000. Do I hear $9,000?"

Given the urn's estimated selling price of $12,000 to
$15,000, George was starting very conservatively indeed.
The audience was silent and perfectly still; everyone was on
tenterhooks awaiting the initial bid. George smiled with relief
when a man at the back of the room waved tentatively to open
the bidding. Immediately, a flurry of hands holding bidding
paddles flew up here, there, and everywhere across the room
in dizzying sucession, but George had little difficulty keeping
up. The hands flew up at the phone bidding table too as staff
cajoled reluctant phone bidders to hurry up and get in on the
action before it was too late.

When the low bidders had been weeded out, the pace
slowed but the tension grew. The battle was between two
bidders now. To my surprise, one of them was Iris Buchanan,
the matron with the purple fascinator I'd seen at the preview.
She was sitting in my row a few feet away from me. She'd
seemed much more interested in that shoddy shepherd and
shepherdess figural group than in the urn, which she never even
asked me about. Tonight she'd traded her purple fascinator for
a more elaborate plumed one in hunter green. Her headgear
jiggled up and down as she discreetly raised her paddle and
then lowered it. I watched her severe face as she turned now
and then to whisper in her husband's ear. Hamish was wearing
his customary tartan tam-o'-shanter and matching bowtie. I
was amused to see Mrs. Buchanan glaring at Mark, who was
on the phone with the one other bidder who remained. Because
he represented the competition, Mark had unquestionably

become an object of scorn to her, and I sensed that beneath her cool façade, she desperately wanted him to mess up.

"What's it going to be, sir? Yes or no?" I heard Mark saying to his bidder. He wiped the sweat from his brow. "Quick, quick, quick! You'd better make up your mind, or it'll be hammered down to the other bidder. Don't lose it!"

George looked at him, waiting.

Mark yelled out hoarsely, "Here!" and his hand shot up; the hesitant man on the phone was in after all.

Iris Buchanan sighed. She'd reached her limit.

George looked around the room one last time. "At $27,000 to the telephone bidder, then ... Do I have any other bids? Going once, going twice ... *sold* to bidder number 438 on the telephone for $27,000!"

Cheers and hearty applause broke out, and I swelled with pride; my baby had done well and would now go to its new home—likely England, where it had been manufactured in the first place. I saw the Buchanans get up to leave. As she made her way through the row past the other clients, Iris, probably recognizing me from the preview, looked at me in a disgruntled way. She probably believed I'd somehow thwarted her as well.

Anxious to feed my sugar craving, I got up as well to go to the cataloguing room, where inevitably cookies awaited me. I also grabbed a cup of watery lukewarm coffee from the urn in the front lobby. I was quick about it so as to avoid talking to the clients, as I was exhausted and didn't feel up to chit-chat. A few of the nice ones beamed and nodded at me, their way of congratulating me on the urn's success. I smiled back and waved, then walked briskly, pretending I had very important things to do. In reality, my shoulders were starting to ache a bit, and all I wanted to do was sit down.

Just as I was returning, George began selling the German porcelain, which meant the Dresden shepherd and shepherdess figural group would come up shortly. Of course, its price would be a joke in comparison to what the urn had just realized, but I was interested all the same. Although nothing about the piece warranted a decent price, I wanted the wretched thing to do well to compensate for all the aggravation its absence had caused me and Taylor.

The slide showing the figural group flashed up onto the screen, and I chuckled at the ridiculous expressions and costumes of the figures and the inept repair job. It took me a moment to notice something trailing down the shepherd's arm, and it wasn't glue. I squinted to get a better look. *Blood?* Mark's and Taylor's heads jerked in my direction simultaneously from the phone bidding table. Aghast, Taylor shook her head and raised her hands, her fingers splayed. How had blood managed to get on the figural group? And why hadn't Jared, who would have photographed the item shortly after we'd found it, had the good sense to wipe it off before taking the picture? A chorus of "eews" and a few anxious murmurs arose from several members of the audience. Others, presumably the myopic ones who'd forgotten their glasses, seemed completely oblivious. I was always surprised at how often auction attendees left their glasses at home and later tried to return items, complaining they couldn't see what they'd been bidding on.

George swivelled around to glance at the slide projected behind him. At first I wondered whether he'd somehow failed to notice the gore or if he simply thought it best to proceed as if nothing unusual were happening. Then he said, "Some of you have noticed a bonus with this lot," and calmly began to auction the figural group.

I was surprised by the number of bidders who were in on the lot. Perhaps the bloodstain added extra value for those of a macabre turn of mind. But based on some of the peculiar things I'd seen people buy at auction, a few clients were decidedly ghoulish. I could even imagine some who, if they purchased the figural group, would leave the bloodstain intact—either deliberately or neglectfully. The bids for the lot climbed to $1,500, well above the modest estimate, and George hammered it down to a grinning Mr. Alabaster. The audience burst into enthusiastic applause for the second time that evening.

I don't know why it took me so long to clue in to why the stain was there; perhaps with the shock of the recent attack, I just wasn't thinking that clearly. But soon the puzzle pieces dropped into place. The blood, Chloe's gash—it all made sense. My mouth fell open, and I looked up at Mark. I jerked my head to the back of the room as if to say, "Meet me in the cataloguing room." He nodded. God, how I needed George's backup. Mercifully, he'd soon be getting off the stand, and Sally would take over as auctioneer. Mark and Taylor would also be taking their breaks. I needed all three of them; I just didn't have it in me to approach Chloe alone. But where the hell was she? She'd deserted her phone bidding post, and she was the one I needed most of all.

I made my way through the throngs of clients clogging up the front foyer; they were paying for their purchases and wrapping them up. I needed a sugar boost, so I grabbed another cookie in the cataloguing room while I waited for Mark to arrive. I was disturbed to find Chloe quietly working at her desk; I'd been sure I'd have to scour the building to find her. I sat some distance away from her on the other side of the room. The vast table that was covered with antiques and collectibles separated us, making me feel somehow less vulnerable. She was scribbling something at her desk, and when she noticed me staring at her, she looked away.

My heart was banging away in my chest like a terrifyingly loud bongo drum being played by some out-of-control maniac. I got up and took a few cautious steps toward her. Not knowing how to begin, I said, "It sure is going well tonight, isn't it?" When she didn't react, I decided to ease into confronting her, thinking someone would probably show up soon if I needed backup. "Listen, there's something I need to—"

"Yes, it is. Going well, I mean." She shielded her face with her hand, turning slightly to peek out at me between splayed fingers.

"Can you turn around more and look at me, Chloe. I can't talk to you properly when you're hiding from me like that." I was surprised to hear an authoritative ring in my voice, and my heart swelled a little with newfound confidence; I could handle this.

"I can see you all right," she said.

"But the point is, I can't see *you*."

She turned around to face me and slowly dropped her hand from her face. The gash was nastier than ever. She looked at me with pitiful puppy-dog eyes; even though it was the last thing I wanted, I started feeling sorry for her again. "Please, Chloe, get that seen to. I swear it's infected."

She smirked as if she knew she'd manipulated my emotions. Then she shrugged and turned away to whatever it was she'd been scribbling.

It took me a second to find my voice again. "Don't turn away—I'm not finished yet. You saw the slide of the German porcelain figural group."

"I don't know what you're talking about." A brittle quality had taken the place of the pathetic demeanour. She watched me with an unwavering, flinty gaze.

Fury rose from somewhere deep within my gut, and I got up and strode toward her. Stopping a couple of feet away from her, I said, "Get up."

But she remained stubbornly seated.

I wanted to slap the smirk right off her face. "You saw the blood all over it. You couldn't have missed it. So why did Jared, that mindless idiot—"

She sprang up from her seat and stood before me, her face inches from mine. I could feel her breath on my face as she shouted, "It sure helped the price, so why are you complaining?" Abruptly, she sat down again.

Her words reverberated in my brain. Completely unnerved by this unexpected flare of anger, I struggled to regain my voice. "Why didn't he wipe it off before he took a picture of it? Hungover again? But what I need to know even more is"—I paused to inhale—"how did the blood get there in the first place? I think I already know, but I really need to hear it from you."

"Look," she said, "I don't have time for this. I've got to get out to the gallery again. I have more phone bids to do."

"Actually, you don't." It was Taylor's voice, which was quiet yet firm. She was just entering the cataloguing room with Mark following closely behind her. "I gave your bids to Helen to do, so no need to worry about them." She looked darkly at Chloe and edged closer to us.

His face creased with fatigue, Mark lingered in the door frame.

"Extortionist," said Taylor. She said the word quietly, but each syllable seemed wrenched from her. I'd never seen her look vicious before; her mouth was drawn back into a grimace, and anger sparked in her eyes. "Thief and murderer too, I'll bet."

We were all stunned into silence. Chloe shrugged. Mark perked up, moved away from the door, and shut it behind him. He flashed a grin at me, obviously relishing the prospect of a catfight. "Some pretty serious accusations, don't you think? Do you have proof of any of this, Taylor?" he said. The more things unravelled, the calmer he became.

But Taylor just stood there, her jaw working as she stared at Chloe. Rigid with barely contained rage, she couldn't speak or move.

"And what about the blood on the porcelain?" I wasn't about to let that go until I got a proper answer out of her.

"Yeah, what about *that*?" said Mark.

Chloe shrugged. "Jared must have cut himself while he was taking the picture of it."

My limited patience was withering away. "You're lying. And if you shrug dismissively at us one more time—"

Mark came up behind me and gripped my shoulders. "Easy," he said.

Demanding more and more answers, the three of us closed in around Chloe, who was starting to resemble a skittish gazelle surrounded by a ravenous pride of lions. Her eyes flitted restlessly around the room; she was looking for a way out and would bolt at the first opportunity. I whispered to Mark to stand by the door; he nodded and moved off.

At last I could now hear Sally's clear, ringing voice as she conducted the auction; George would have just stepped down from the podium. Stealthily, I shifted around until I could reach the phone, not taking my eyes from Chloe's face. I dialed his extension. When he picked up, I said, "There's some pretty major stuff going down in the department."

"Jesus. Are you all right?" he said. Although I was trying to rein in my escalating panic, he must have caught a note of it in my voice.

"Fine, darling. Just hurry."

"Darling. How very sweet," said Chloe.

Just as I was scowling at her, George entered the room. The second I glanced at him, Taylor flew at Chloe, who tumbled from her chair to the floor. I grabbed Taylor and she thrashed around, screaming, "Tell them! Tell them what you did!"

George clutched Taylor's shoulders, calmly steered her to a chair, and sat her down while a dazed-looking Chloe picked herself up off the floor and dusted herself off. In a fatherly way, he said, "Okay, we're all going to be very civilized about this. Taylor, I insist you tell us what's going on. What are you so upset about?"

"She just called Chloe an extortionist, thief, and a murderer—in that order too," said Mark helpfully. "Just thought you should know."

"Great." George nodded without looking at Mark. He was as unruffled as a person could possibly be under such circumstances. Intently, he watched Taylor, who was red-faced and panting. "I've known for ages you wanted to get something off your chest. Now's the time to say what it is."

"Yeah, spill it," said Mark.

Despite the tension swirling in the air, I couldn't help but giggle. "We're not in a detective movie, Mark."

"Could've fooled me."

Taylor looked helplessly from George to me, her eyes brimming with tears, and sniffled. Any resolve she'd had to come clean about what was bothering her died as she dissolved into a sobbing, heaving mass of inarticulateness. I knew the crying could go on for hours, so I put my arm around her shoulder and led her away to the basement. The way she collapsed on a sofa weeping reminded me of the overwrought Victorian heroines I'd read about or seen depicted in movies. I hoped she'd recover her equilibrium soon, but she was so distraught that I wondered if a dose of laudanum—had I been able to find such a thing—might not have calmed her, just as it had many a Victorian lady.

I returned to the cataloguing room to find everyone seated calmly and waiting for me. Now it was all up to Chloe. All eyes turned on her.

The first thing she did was sigh deeply. Then she told us everything.

CHAPTER 23

Chloe looked both exhausted and relieved, and I wondered if she'd wanted to confess for a while. Now she didn't have much choice, as there was no way we were letting her go anywhere.

"I've never been happy in the dolls and toys department," she began in a subdued way. "It's always been a nothing sort of department that's made me feel like a nobody—not much glory in it, not compared to silver, glass, and porcelain, which was the stuff I'd always been interested in. Now *that* was a department where I knew I could shine, if only certain people"—her eyes bored holes into me—"had given me half a chance. But there was no way of getting into the department, not with Taylor—Gable's precious little pet—in the way. And you, of course."

I sighed in exasperation. Although it was much too late to salvage our relationship, I said, "Chloe, why didn't you ever tell me you wanted to work in the department? Maybe we could have come to some arrangement. I was never opposed to your taking on more responsibility."

She looked at me blankly, as if she hadn't heard a word, and continued. "I decided to take matters into my own hands. I wanted to make your department look so incompetent that Gable would be compelled to fire someone—and I figured it would be you."

"Lovely," said Mark.

"What made you so sure it would be me?" I asked.

"Once you started talking about seeing flappers in the basement, I knew it was only a matter of time before you'd be gone. It was just the sort of hocus-pocus nonsense that would make Gable think you'd lost it, so I encouraged you in imagining you'd seen a ghost. But I was getting impatient, so I cooked up a plan to hide a few pieces of the porcelain that were supposed to be in the upcoming auction." Judging from the way her eyes started gleaming, she thought herself awfully clever. "Gable had never liked or respected you, so I knew he'd pin it on you. And he really put you through the wringer, even more than I expected him to."

"That's for damn sure," I said.

She smiled. "Ultimately, I didn't really care who took the blame. Hell, whoever he fired—you or Taylor—there'd finally be room for me in the department."

"So you put the missing pieces down by the furniture," said George.

"Yes, but not initially. At first I stashed them away in one of the kitchen cupboards, way up above the sink. But then I started getting worried, thinking someone might see them there, so I hid them behind the furniture. I knew it might take months before anyone ever found them."

She was right about this. We were so backlogged with furniture that it sometimes took months for certain pieces to come up for auction. Items could sit untouched in storage for ages.

"And I thought you"—she was grinning at me—"wouldn't look for them there because you were so afraid of your stupid spook."

My anger surged. "She's not stupid. And I'm not afraid of her."

Chloe's only response was a harsh, grating laugh that sounded like braying.

George looked at her, puzzled. "So you cut your face with the porcelain? That must have been tricky to accomplish."

"As if I was trying! It was completely unintentional. I was struggling to haul that huge hunk of porcelain around in the dark, trying to balance it, and suddenly it lurched toward me. The shepherd's arm was rough from the lousy repair and sliced open my face." She looked at us for sympathy but got none.

"Then what?" said Mark.

She looked at me contemptuously. "A couple of minutes after I'd set the bloody thing down and I was still trying to pick my way through the furniture maze, I heard you yelling at your damn ghost, so I crouched behind a sofa." She then turned her gaze on Mark. "And shortly after that, I heard you talking to Virginia. I started to panic that you guys would see me and wonder why I was stuck behind a sofa. And I still wasn't all that far from the porcelain and didn't want to draw attention to it. I tried to get away as fast as I could. What I didn't count on was colliding with a chandelier and giving myself away."

"Poor baby," said Mark. "Must've hurt, huh?"

Chloe ignored him.

"What I don't understand is why you didn't wipe the blood off the figural group before it was photographed," said George, shaking his head.

"Jared grabbed the piece from the floor and started snapping away without even noticing," said Chloe. "He was hungover. It wasn't until I brought the blood to his attention that he cleaned it off and did a reshoot. But somehow the wrong slide got shown."

George looked satisfied with her explanation. "I guess that could happen easily enough."

My mind was reeling from all of Chloe's revelations, and I hardly knew what to say anymore to this person who, until recently, I trusted and thought I knew intimately. "And ... and our friendship meant nothing to you."

She snorted and without missing a beat said, "What friendship? I never much liked *you*. But I pretended to in the hopes it might eventually get me somewhere."

She may as well have kicked me in the stomach. But after the initial stab of pain died down, I started to go numb. "But you were so kind after my parents died. I thought you were so caring, so ... compassionate."

"You thought wrong." She was enjoying this far too much; her eyes were twinkling.

It was staggering to me that I could have been such a lousy judge of character, that I hadn't seen through her. "And was it you who attacked me with the knife?" I said, dreading her answer.

She sighed. "It was a meat skewer, dummy."

I glared at her. "I stand corrected, then."

Mark was glaring at her too, as if he was thinking of how much pleasure he'd derive from wringing her neck.

"And it wasn't me!"

"What? Someone else was involved?" I gripped my chair, feeling I was going to be sick. I looked up, and the ceiling lights spun and whirled like a kaleidoscope. George steadied me by holding my arm tightly.

"No. It was Jared."

"Jared?" Slack-jawed, I stared at her. I couldn't believe she'd recruited that moronic scumbag to play a part in her scheme. "And he did it at your direction?"

"No. We did collaborate on the note, though—I dictated it, and he wrote it down so you wouldn't know the handwriting. As for the attack, he took it upon himself to do that. Seeing as Gable was dead and George wasn't about to fire you"— she looked from George to me—"he thought he'd better do something. After the preview, he phoned me to tell me what happened."

"Phoned you? And why would Jared even care?" asked Mark.

A smile crept across Chloe's face. "I'll let you figure that one out, shall I?"

"Chloe and Jared—resident thugs at Gable & Co. Have you two been robbing banks too? Maybe I should start calling you Bonnie and Clyde," said Mark.

I was floored that they'd gotten together. Even George, who was usually unflappable, looked disturbed by the thought of this unwholesome alliance.

Mark stared at Chloe. "Okay, so Gable didn't think much of Virginia. We all noticed that well before the meeting about the flapper in the basement. But he still could have blamed Taylor for the missing stuff. Why do you suppose he didn't? I mean, she's the type who always gets blamed for everything."

A spark enlivened George's eyes as he looked in my direction; I felt certain he knew the gist of what Chloe would say next.

"Well, Gable had a thing for Taylor—love, or more likely lust, at first sight. So no, he wasn't about to fire her. He liked having her around. I'm surprised you didn't notice, Mark."

He shrugged. "I wasn't paying much attention, I guess."

George had mentioned that Gable found Taylor attractive, and suddenly I remembered she was the one person who'd been permitted to call him by his first name. Maybe that little detail was significant. Was it possible they'd had a back-alley fling? The thought of my assistant and Gable embroiled in anything resembling an amorous relationship was alarming and repellent, and I felt horribly queasy. I gulped and said, "She didn't reciprocate, did she?"

Chloe burst out laughing. "Of course not! I'd known about his infatuation for a while. I caught him leering at her, but she seemed to take no notice. You know Taylor—she's always been oblivious, off in her own little world. A few weeks ago— you and Mark were out on an appraisal—Gable came into the cataloguing area, and I overheard him asking her out for a coffee, ostensibly to get her opinion on an 'important business idea,' as he put it. I think she was flattered that the boss would consider her opinion worthwhile, so she went. I was amazed she couldn't see what he was up to. I snuck out the side door and followed them. After walking a block or so, Gable wrapped his arm tightly around her waist, and she fought him off with everything she had. My timing was perfect: I snapped a photo of them just before she started struggling."

Mark and I exchanged puzzled glances. Only George looked as if he understood the significance of Chloe's last sentence.

"Blackmail," was all he said.

"If I was going to be cold in my grave before Gable ever doled out a raise, I needed to supplement my income, so I threatened to show the picture to Taylor's fiancé so I could extort money from her."

"Fiancé?" Mark squealed as though someone had touched him with a hot poker. "She has one of those?"

"It's news to me too." I was shell-shocked as one sordid secret after another, each more outlandish than the last, came to light. "But why would this fiancé even believe you that Gable and Taylor were having an affair?"

"Well, apart from the damning photographic evidence, there's the fact that he's my brother."

The silence fell awkwardly, like a stage curtain plummeting to the floor with a thunk. George and Mark and I all looked at each other before Mark finally spoke. "And your word carries more weight than Taylor's? Some fiancé he is!"

"Well, she knew he'd believe me," said Chloe, "and she was so desperate to keep him that she forked over the cash quite readily. Pathetic, isn't it?"

I felt weak, and my head began spinning; it was a bit like being drunk, but without the pleasant fringe benefit of euphoria.

George sighed and squirmed uncomfortably in his chair, bracing himself before he asked the inevitable question. "How much money are we talking about?"

"About $10,000 so far. I hit her up regularly for installments—every paycheque."

"Over what period of time?"

"Oh, I don't know … the last few months or so," said Chloe in a matter-of-fact way. She glanced at her nails.

Now my stomach roiled again, and I fought against it. When I recovered a little, my anger flared. "You've been draining the poor girl dry! How could you do such a thing?"

She just looked away from me, and we were all silent for a painful few seconds.

Mark glowered at her. "There won't be any more installments. That all ends right now."

Chloe harrumphed. "Well, obviously!" She looked sourly from one person to the next.

"And what about Gable?" asked George. "Tell us about him."

"What about Gable?" Chloe assumed a very convincing air of innocence, her eyes round and her expression mild. It was then I realized what a clever actress she'd become—or perhaps had always been—and exactly how much I'd been deceived by that sweet-looking face.

"Answer the question." George looked at her sternly. "It's already been a long day, and we have neither the time nor the patience for any more of your nonsense."

For the first time since our interrogation began, I saw fear flicker in her eyes. Then she said boldly, "Oh, that—well, that's quite a story."

CHAPTER 24

George, Mark, and I were sitting on office chairs, clustered tightly around Chloe. George sat ramrod straight on the edge of his chair, as if still expecting her to bolt from the room any second. Mark drummed his fingers impatiently on the adjacent desk. I stared at Chloe, hoping a steady gaze would intimidate her into spilling the rest of the story before the hour grew much later.

"We're waiting," said George.

"Damn right we are," said Mark.

"What did you do to him, Chloe?" I asked.

She looked back with limpid grey eyes, as if trying to gain some sympathy before she even opened her mouth. A slight sigh escaped her lips. "Everyone knows what a louse he was. It could have been any one of us. God knows, we all had our motives—every single person in this room, and a few others too."

Mark and I groaned in unison.

"That's your opinion," said George. "But the fact is, it was you, not anyone else. Now tell us what happened." He wouldn't take his eyes off her.

Chloe's ire rose, and the gash on her face appeared correspondingly redder. She stood up. "You, for instance." She leaned into George, jabbing her index finger into his chest. "Gable accused you of stealing from the company—right in front of everyone at a company Christmas party. Isn't that right? I wasn't there, but I heard the stories—and from a reputable source too. Gable was drunk and took a swing at you, and you were foolish enough to swing back. The whole episode embarrassed the hell out of you, didn't it?"

"Reputable source? Who would that be? Jared?" George laughed in a brittle, mirthless way. "Since I neither stole from the company nor took a swing at Gable, I wasn't embarrassed. He ended up looking like an idiot, not me."

"Yeah, but you hated him nevertheless." She nodded with smug satisfaction.

"Really, you'll have to do better than that." George started picking lint off his suit.

"Sit down, Chloe. All this deflection isn't accomplishing much," I said, feeling impossibly weary.

Still standing, she whirled around dramatically to face me, her fists planted on her hips. "And you. At that same Christmas party, Gable ripped your most expensive dress. Isn't that right?"

I burst out laughing. "Yes, but it was accidental. He stumbled into me, grabbing my sleeve as he tried to steady himself, and it ripped. It wasn't the worst of his offences, and not exactly a motive for murder. His recent threat to fire me would have been far more motivating to someone with murderous tendencies, which fortunately, I've never possessed."

Mark drummed his fingers on the desk again, and Chloe turned on him too. "Oh yeah, Mark, I almost forgot about you. Didn't Gable keep refusing you raises, year after year after year? Didn't I hear you say you wanted to kill him after one of your miserably unsuccessful meetings with him?"

Mark looked archly at George and me and said, "Yes, I probably did. With Gable at the helm, it was impossible for any of us to get ahead, including you. But you sure fixed him, didn't you? Don't be bashful—tell us how clever you were. Tell us all about your perfect crime. Then we can congratulate you on ridding the world of one of the most obnoxious bosses ever. You're right, we hated him as much as you did, and we're not exactly sorry he's dead."

George and I looked at each other and nodded vigorously; Mark had the right idea.

Chloe's anger ebbed away, and gradually the expression in her eyes softened. She sat down again and crossed her legs, clasping her hands over one knee. "Right after that meeting Gable called about the stolen porcelain, I went into his office. With you on your way out, Virginia, I knew the time was ripe to hit the old cheapskate up for a raise. I'd been working here for nearly two years at the same starvation wages. I told him in no uncertain terms that I was long overdue, and that I wanted a 20 percent raise or I'd quit. I was desperate, but I knew what to expect—he just laughed, as he'd done so many times before.

"'Do you have any idea how little revenue the toy department brings in? It's a joke,' he said. 'Quit if you feel like it. Just get the hell out of my office.'"

"Sounds typical," said Mark. "I think he said something comparable the last time I asked him for a raise."

"But before I got up to leave, I suggested there'd soon be a vacancy to fill in the glass, ceramics, and silver department. This infuriated him. He wrenched that stupid old dried-up stuffed pheasant from the wall and hurled it at me. Managed to hit me in the head too."

The image of Gable clipping her on the head with the pheasant made me giggle, and Mark hooted with laughter.

"At least the bird's good for something," said George.

Chloe's anger deepened. "I was furious. I'd had enough of being humiliated by him and wasn't going to take his crap anymore. I'd reached my limit. I even forgot that he needed to be alive to fire you, Virginia. First thing the next morning, before anyone else arrived, I popped into his office and 'apologized.' I said I shouldn't have had the nerve to expect so much and promised I'd whip the department into shape to justify any salary increase whatsoever. Gable seemed satisfied with this and sent me out for his breakfast: two large double-doubles and two Boston cream doughnuts from Tim Hortons. Little did he know he'd just handed me a perfect opportunity." Her eyes sparkled.

"Go on," said Mark.

But she needed no prompting. "When I brought the coffees and doughnuts back, I nipped down to the basement. I went through one of the storage cupboards, where I found all sorts of highly toxic-looking substances, like blue toilet bowl cleaner, abrasive cleanser for scouring a sink or bathtub, and rat poison. My head was swimming; I didn't know which one to choose, and I was terrified someone would see me studying what was in the cupboard and wonder what I was up to. I found an ancient bottle of antifreeze, and then I remembered what my brother had once told me."

She paused reflectively, looking from face to face. "Ethylene glycol—the sweet-tasting poison in antifreeze. Children and pets are attracted to the sweetness, and there have been many incidences of accidental poisoning. I figured I could slip some into Gable's double-doubles. Given his size, I guessed I'd need a lot to actually kill him. But with such a sweet tooth to begin with, he probably wouldn't even notice it. Fortunately, the clerk had been stingy with the coffee and left lots of room at the top of each cup. I didn't even have to pour anything out. I looked around to make sure I wasn't being watched, and I poured the stuff into both cups."

I felt queasy. George looked aghast. Mark went pale.

But Chloe was much too absorbed in telling her tale to take much notice of any of us. "I gave Gable the first double-double. He took a sip of it and smiled as he said how amazingly good it tasted today. I felt a tiny twinge of guilt, which I squelched by reminding myself that, even though he was drinking the last double-doubles he'd ever have, at least he was enjoying them. I watched him stuff himself full of the doughnuts, and I left.

"That morning, I was working right outside his office, unpacking a bunch of boxes full of teddy bears and writing out an inventory list for them. About two hours after I gave Gable the double-doubles, I knocked on his office door and got a muttered response. I peeked inside and noticed him swaying as he sat at his desk; he was moaning and talking gibberish to himself. He didn't seem to notice me. I stepped inside. Being careful not to touch his desk, I removed his empty coffee cups and the paper bag from the doughnuts and put them in my tote bag. Then I realized I'd better get rid of the antifreeze, which I'd shoved under the unpacking table—my fingerprints would be all over it. I grabbed the tote bag, put the bottle in, and covered it up with a sweater. I didn't dare throw anything away inside the building. Instead, I walked for about an hour and finally tossed everything in a Dumpster."

We all sat in silence as the full impact of Chloe's story sank in.

"Didn't anyone see you?" asked George.

"Astonishingly, no. No one was in front reception when I brought the coffee in. I didn't pass anyone on my way to Gable's office. No one was around when I went back to remove the coffee cup and the paper bag, and I didn't see anyone when I left the building with the garbage and the antifreeze. I never bumped into the few people who were in the building that morning. It was the perfect murder, almost as if it were *meant* to happen."

I shuddered at the unsavoury notion that anyone's murder could be fated as Chloe suggested. "But you must have been shocked to see Gable lumbering into the greasy spoon at lunch. Didn't it worry you that your plan was going awry?"

She looked pensive, and I glimpsed the old Chloe in the serious way she said, "Yes, I honestly did think the game was up. But then I realized he wasn't coherent enough to accuse me of anything. He just looked like a drunk who'd stumbled in off the street. So it was still the perfect murder. Oh, and by the way, I never went to the hospital with him. I took a couple of hours off and went shoe shopping."

Mark looked as if he'd had enough, and he abruptly stood up. "Yeah, just think, Chloe. There were no witnesses and, despite crime scene investigation and interrogation—such as it's been—no evidence you had anything to do with Gable's death. Maybe you could have gotten away with it—that is, if you hadn't opened your big mouth."

She stared at him as if she didn't comprehend.

"Don't tell me you're surprised I've been recording this entire conversation," said Mark. From his jacket pocket he pulled out a mini spy recorder and dangled it high above her head.

Chloe sprang from her chair and lunged repeatedly at the recorder, but her efforts were futile. Frustrated, she beat her fists against Mark's chest.

"Well, what did you expect me to do?" shouted Mark.

George pulled her off him and pinned her arms behind her back. He said, "Call the police, Virginia."

CHAPTER 25

J ust after the last clients had filed out of the building, Mark
apprehended Jared as he was trying to slip out the door.
Mark held him in a vise-like grip until the police arrived.
Similarly, George continued to grip Chloe's arms, and she
struggled against him. What made the scene particularly
ugly was how she directed the lion's share of her rage at me,
screaming and cursing while I stood there, numbly taking her
abuse. Sally came out and gamely tried to steer me away from
Chloe, but mesmerized, I was unable to move.

An exhausted-looking Taylor had just emerged from the
basement when the police burst through the front door. Taylor,
Sally, and I watched the arrest from behind the safety of the
reception desk. Sneering all the while, Jared went quietly, but
Chloe flailed and kicked out at the officers with all her might.
She howled too, a gut-wrenching sound like that of a wounded
animal; I could still hear it even after she'd been taken outside.
You almost would have thought the police were horribly

mistaken and she was innocent, and I wondered if some part of her believed she was. Maybe she'd always felt like a victim and I'd just never realized it. George and Mark followed the police out the front door.

Sally smiled at Taylor and me. "You're all right," she said, holding me in a bear hug for a few moments. "Or soon will be. Shall I stick around?"

"Thanks, but it's okay. You must be tired, so go home. I need to talk to Taylor for a moment."

Just then, a red-faced, panting, and perspiring Mark staggered up the stairs. His suit looked rumpled, and his hair had been rearranged and was flopping over his face. "Wow, that kid can really throw a punch." When he saw the three of us staring at him in wonder, his big frame started shaking with laughter and he said, "I need a drink!" Off he went to the cataloguing room.

"So I guess Jared didn't go that quietly after all." Sally smiled and then drifted away.

I turned to Taylor. "Why didn't you tell me she was taking all your money?"

Embarrassed, she hung her head before she finally worked up the nerve to look at me. "I didn't think I could tell you much of anything. I barely felt I could talk to you at all."

The words were painful to hear, and I couldn't help cringing. "It won't be like that anymore, Taylor. You know that … right?"

She nodded sadly.

"You better get some rest, all right?" I smiled at her. "And great job with the Snodgrass urn, by the way. I'm proud of you. We'll have dinner this week to celebrate—it's on me."

She perked up a little, smiling sheepishly. Then she turned around and started heading out the door, lifting her hand in a brief wave before she exited.

Badly shaken by Chloe's confession and arrest, I headed downstairs for a cup of Moroccan Mystique. Athough it was well past midnight, I knew the caffeine wouldn't keep me awake. I searched in the cupboard for a mug, the arrest playing over and over again in my head. Even when they were taking Chloe away, I still wanted to believe she hadn't done the devastating things she had and that she'd never hated me. Now I had to wrap my mind around the fact that, as head of the department, I'd been the biggest obstacle to her dreams. I wondered what she thought awaited her in my department. Wealth? Glamour? Power? The only person in the company who'd ever had that was Errol Thrasher, and he'd been born into a life of privilege. Maybe getting me out of the way was just the first rung on the company ladder and she aspired to ultimately rule Gable & Co. Whatever her plans, they obviously mattered much more to her than our friendship—or what I'd perceived as such. Worse, her ascent to what she saw as her rightful place mattered more to her than Brian Gable III's life. Who knew that mild-mannered, seemingly benign Chloe was actually filled with raging resentment and violent impulses she could no longer restrain? I still wondered why I hadn't seen behind her pleasant and unassuming facade much earlier. Was she really that clever an actress? Or was I just easily duped?

As the coffee machine hissed and gurgled, I was reminded of that late night in October when I'd first heard the wailing in the basement. Constance had died so tragically, her youth and beauty gone in the blink of an eye, and thinking of this now filled me with sorrow. But somehow I felt I hadn't seen the last of her. I'd finished the diary, but did she have anything more to tell me?

No sooner did I wonder than I heard squeaking coming from the back of the basement. I hesitated, cocking my ear toward the source of the sound. Then I heard it again, this time slightly louder. It was the sound of someone gently settling down on an old sofa with noisy springs.

"Constance?" I picked my way through the dining room chairs, tables, settees, cabinets, and heaps of carpets. "Is that you?"

There she was, sitting in the same place I'd always seen her—the old midnight-blue velvet settee. She wasn't crying or hysterical but clear-eyed and calm. A look of expectation enlivened her face, and it occurred to me that maybe she wanted her old diary back. I hadn't taken this possibility into account.

"Sorry, Constance, old girl, but I gave the diary to your …" I searched my brain for the correct term to describe how she was related to Suzanne but drew a blank. "She's a relative of yours, your brother's granddaughter. Her name's Suzanne Winterdale. I think you'd like her; she has your eyes. I hope you don't mind that I gave it away. It seemed right to keep it in your family."

I expected her to approve or disapprove in some way, but she didn't react. I didn't know what to do other than just blather on.

"Was that wrong of me? I mean, it did contain all your intimate thoughts—things you wouldn't necessarily want to share with everyone. It was very well written, I might add."

I hoped that my smile and compliment would lighten the mood, but Constance kept gazing steadily at me with those stunning green eyes. Then her mood changed abruptly; cranky impatience flitted across her face, and she thrust out her hand and waved a piece of paper at me. She released it, and I watched it sail through the air and settle softly on the floor. I bent over to retrieve it, and when I looked up Constance was already fading from view, a soft veil of pale blue covering her entire form.

"Hey!" I called.

Not even her customary grey trail hung in the air. She was gone to wherever it was she went.

I unfolded the piece of paper, smoothing the creases. The handwriting was small and cramped, and I had to squint to read it. It was dated November 27, 1928.

Dear Constance,

We were once the very best of friends. As you must know, you were the sister I never had, and I imagined you regarded me as a sister too. I deluded myself into thinking you needed me. Although nothing in life is constant or predictable, I somehow assumed we'd remain close.

When you became enraptured with Freddy Alderdice, I was left behind. Forgive me, but I can't conceive of what it's like to have a new love. We both know I'll be exceedingly lucky if love ever brightens my life, since I don't have the good looks and easy charm you're favoured with. Like many in your position, you've taken these gifts for granted.

You can't deny that your affair with Freddy was all-consuming. You thought of few others, least of all me, your intimate and steadfast friend of many years. I felt I was of little consequence to you, or worse, that I'd become a nuisance—someone to be gotten rid of because I distracted you from dear, darling Freddy.

Can you blame me for being angry, Constance? I have few friends and am the object of either contemptuous or pitiable glances, but at least I had the comfort of your friendship to sustain me. But with Freddy's arrival you changed. You know it's true, but there's something you don't know.

I wasn't envious just because you were in love; I was envious that you had Freddy. That's what hurt the most. I know you're laughing as you read this, thinking that I represented no competition. And you're right. With you in the way, I didn't stand a chance, though I thought I might if you stepped aside.

Of course, you wouldn't go willingly. To your credit, your love for Freddy was sincere and deeply felt—any fool could see that. But you're hopelessly naive, so you didn't realize he was a common rogue, and that his feelings for you didn't and would never run deep. He was much too busy watching every pretty girl who passed by. Whatever shallow feelings he managed to work up for you would soon taper off into indifference, and he'd become captivated by another face and figure. Maybe once I'd spruced myself up, I'd be worthy of his attention, if only briefly; I would have settled for a brief affair over nothing at all. I know I'm not completely unattractive when I trouble to work at it.

But I didn't want to wait. Just four little words would change everything. I blurted them out to Mildred at a party. She'd been wondering aloud if you were coming to her next soiree; that was back when she still retained a high regard for you.

I replied, "Not in her condition," which understood to mean just one thing.

I didn't exactly whisper the words, so any number of people might have heard. But even if

Mildred had been the only one to hear them, they still would have been damaging. Despite supposedly being your dear friend, she was quite capable of leaving your reputation in tatters; she never could resist the urge to talk. Predictably, Freddy soon withdrew his affection and Mildred her friendship.

You could argue that I did you a favour. Freddy would eventually have rid himself of you without my intervention—I merely accelerated the inevitable. I've saved you from a future sorrow more intensely felt than the sadness you presently feel; in time, you would have become even more attached to him, and your pain would have been correspondingly harder to bear. Still, I do see why you're not grateful; my four little words ruined you socially, and now you have only that wearisome Christopher for comfort.

You might pity me somewhat, as in the end I failed. Freddy, who'd been agreeable enough to me before, loathed me after hearing what I'd told Mildred. We're in the same boat, as they say. And somehow it seems destined to sink lower.

Yours sincerely,

Lydia

As I folded the letter up, I felt someone come up behind me. I was so on edge that I jumped. But it was only George, standing behind me and placing his hands lightly on my shoulders.

I turned to face him. "How'd you get to be such a crack auctioneer?" I said, trying to distract myself from my emotions.

He looked modest. "Really, it was nothing to get all that excited about. I've watched and listened to so many auctions, I think I must have absorbed the patter by osmosis."

I laughed, but my hand was shaking.

"What have you got there, Virginia?"

I passed him the letter, and he said, "So she's been back? I knew she'd return." I turned around to watch him frowning as he read the letter. "Poor Constance. I had no idea."

"It's all finished now. She won't be coming back anymore." My voice grew strained as sadness swelled my heart.

George peered at me and wiped a tear away from the corner of my eye. "Why so blue?"

"You know—and you'll think I've gone mad—I'm going to miss her. Sure, she could be a bloody nuisance with all her wailing, but once I understood her, I really began to care about her. And what … what … a tragic end." I began choking up and paused to swallow the lump in my throat. "Her diary—it was the most incredible thing. I almost wish I still had it. She was so much smarter than I gave her credit for. She knew it all along: I had my own Lydia to contend with. She was trying to warn me—me, a complete stranger from a world she'd never know— the only way she knew how." A sob caught in my throat, and tears began pouring down my cheeks.

George passed me his handkerchief, and I dabbed at my eyes.

Composing myself, I said, "You know, it's absolutely mind-blowing when you stop to think about it." A chill rippled through me.

George, looking tired and pale, said, "Why you? She made special trips from wherever it is she goes just to see you."

"That's the part I'll never understand. But maybe there's not much point wondering why she chose me. I don't wonder why *you* chose me, after all."

He grinned. "I might not have chosen you at all if she hadn't lured me to the back of the basement."

"What?"

"Remember I told you I heard someone coughing right before I discovered the missing porcelain?"

"Yes ..." Eventually, it dawned on me. "Do you really suppose ... Constance?"

"She wanted you to come down here and talk to me. You see, she already knew something about us we were only beginning to realize."

George laughed his deep, throaty laugh and leaned down to hug me close to him. I closed my eyes and let the warmth of his embrace drive away the chill that had seized me during these last few terrible days.

When I opened my eyes, I could have sworn that, just for a second, a hazy Constance emerged from the shadows and hovered before me, the beginning of a smile on her lips.

ACKNOWLEDGEMENTS

The seed for *Virginia's Ghost* was planted while I was still working at an auction house much like the one described in the book. I left that career behind in 2007 and it's 2014 as I write, so the book has been a long time coming. For years I didn't show it to a soul, and it probably wouldn't have been published at all without the contributions of a number of people.

As a freelance editor myself, I know that editors are hardly immune to errors both big and small, and of course I'm no exception. I enlisted the help of two talented editorial colleagues in B.C. who also happen to be my friends, Irene Kavanagh and Arlene Prunkl. Irene has been a *Virginia's Ghost* enthusiast since our very first conversation about the book. She took first crack at it through a manuscript evaluation, and I was delighted that she "got" the book from the get-go, saw the touches of humour in it, and offered so many helpful suggestions about both the broad strokes of plot and character and the fine points of wording. Arlene carefully line edited the book and was particularly astute at identifying aspects of it that didn't quite add up or needed further development. She saw what I couldn't and pushed me further than I realized I needed to go. She also offered much helpful advice as I navigated the self-publishing process for the first time. I owe both Irene and Arlene a huge thank you for helping me write a much better book than I would have without them.

I had a third editor in Wilf Gladstone, my significant other. Though Wilf isn't trained as an editor, he is a psychotherapist and was particularly interested in questions of character development and whether Virginia and company were acting in character. We had numerous conversations about the book that helped clarify my thinking when I felt stuck or uncertain. Wilf was there for me completely throughout the writing and production of the book. As well, I got quite ill during the later phases of the book's production and will always be grateful for his love and support during a challenging time.

As I hope you'll agree, my designer Scarlett Rugers, who lives in Australia, has done an exquisite job of cover and page design, evoking precisely the spirit (no pun intended) of *Virginia's Ghost* through the dazzling combination of a dramatic cover image, carefully chosen fonts, and artful flourishes and borders. She seems to have read my mind and has portrayed Constance the ghost exactly as I envisioned her. Scarlett is a true professional who is incredibly talented, passionate about design, and a delight to work with.

As well, my good friend of thirty years, artist Louise Kiner, has provided a deliciously eerie photograph of one of Rosedale's Victorian mansions for the back cover. Louise and I were walking through this Toronto neighbourhood one sunny Saturday when she snapped the photo. Thank you, Louise, for this spooky contribution to my book.

Finally, I wish to thank two women who are no longer with me—my grandmothers Florence and Rose. As a nod to their influence, I have included both of their names in *Virginia's Ghost*. My memories of them have grown hazy, since I was a little girl when they passed away, but they were both young women during the 1920s, and somehow I know that their spirits have informed the character of Constance the ghost. I dedicate this book to them and everyone else who has helped in some way to bring it out of the shadows and into the light.

ABOUT THE AUTHOR

Photo by Holly Sisson

Caroline Kaiser worked for nearly fourteen years as an antiques cataloguer and appraiser at a busy auction house, where she headed the glass, ceramics, silver, and toy departments. She has enjoyed a lifelong love affair with both old things and old Hollywood movies. She now earns her living as a freelance fiction editor. A native of Toronto, she hasn't yet decided to live somewhere else. *Virginia's Ghost* is her first novel.

Made in the USA
Charleston, SC
13 October 2014